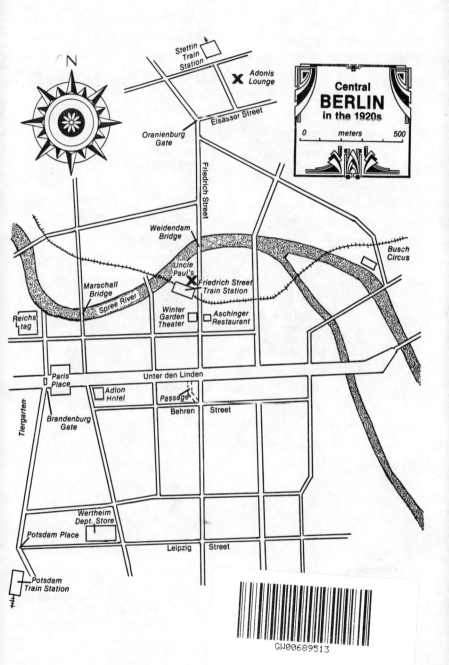

N

Stettin
Train
Station

X Adonis
Lounge

Elsässer Street

Oranienburg
Gate

Friedrich Street

Central
BERLIN
in the 1920s

0   meters   500

Weidendam
Bridge

Busch
Circus

Marschall
Bridge

Uncle
Paul's

X Friedrich Street
Train Station

Spree River

Reichs-
tag

Winter
Garden
Theater

Aschinger
Restaurant

Paris
Place

Unter den Linden

Tiergarten

Adlon
Hotel

Passage

Behren   Street

Brandenburg
Gate

Wertheim
Dept. Store

Potsdam Place

Leipzig   Street

Potsdam
Train Station

GW00689513

John Henry Mackay

John Henry Mackay

THE
HUSTLER

The story of a nameless love from Friedrich Street
Translated from the German by Hubert Kennedy

Boston : Alyson Publications, Inc.

This is the first English translation of *Der Puppenjunge*, which was first published in 1926 in Germany. This edition is a paperback original from Alyson Publications, Inc., PO Box 2783, Boston, MA 02208. Distributed in England by Gay Men's Press, PO Box 247, London, N15 6RW.

First edition, February 1985   5   4   3   2   1

ISBN 0 932870 58 9

The capital letters that begin each chapter of this book are 'Fan,' designed by Marcia Loeb and taken from the book *New Art Deco Alphabets* by Marcia Loeb, Dover Publications, 1984. Reprinted with permission from Dover Publications.

"If one of them would once fall in love with me, I would really take him for a ride!"

> *—Remark of the hustler and pimp Arthur Klemke, called 'the refined Atze,' from Friedrich Street in Berlin*

"Walk, walk... always walk!"

> *—Sigh of the 'Petit Jésus' André Devie from the great boulevards of Paris.*

Introduction

When they mangled his name, he would cry:
"If you please just pronounce it Mackay!"

he man who thus insisted on the correct pronunciation of his name — note the rhyme — was in his sixties and had been living in Berlin for over thirty years when he wrote the novel *Der Puppenjunge*. He knew his Berlin, and he knew the love he wrote about: the love of a man for a boy, the love of a boy for a man. He called it "the nameless love" because, as he explained, he found all the names then in use derogatory. He was perhaps also influenced by Oscar Wilde's expression, "the love that dare not speak its name."

When *Der Puppenjunge* was first published in 1926, Walter Hauer wrote (as quoted by J.S. Hohmann in *Entstellte Engel*, Fischer: Frankfurt am Main, 1983, pp. 297-298):

> This story of a young, serious person, who comes from the provinces to Berlin, with no idea of the homosexual circles and the prostitution of the metropolis, and is gripped here by this liking for a boy, who has likewise just come from the provinces and fallen into the arms of prostitution, is, in its masterly composed, so to speak, strictly symphonic presentation, the only novel on a grand scale that homosexual literature has to exhibit. Gunther is the hustler with whom Hermann Graff, the true hero of the book, falls in love. The chaos of Berlin opens up before us with its queer bars, its hidden prostitution, its police roundups.

Because of its subject matter, however, and the fact that it was published under a pseudonym (Sagitta) and sold privately, the novel had little success. In a review in 1931, Kyrill (identified by J.S. Hohmann as Christian von Kleist, born in Quebec on April 6, 1893) could write in the homosexual magazine *Der Eigene:* "Until now his circle of readers has regrettably been only limited" (vol. 13, no. 2, p. 61). But Kyrill, too, noted that this novel "belongs to the few books in the literature on 'our subject' that may raise a claim to art."

Two years later Hitler had assumed power and all literature on "our subject" was forbidden — art or not. Kyrill fled to America, to disappear from sight; Mackay died that year (1933) — of illness, or perhaps suicide — but would not have survived in Germany at any rate, for his over forty years' dedication to the cause of individualist anarchism had made him anathema to the Nazis.

John Henry Mackay was born on February 6, 1864, in Greenock, Scotland, but his father died when he was two years old and his mother returned with her son to her native Germany, where he grew up. After studying philosophy and the history of art and literature at the universities of Kiel, Leipzig, and Berlin, he went to London in 1887, for a year, where he became acquainted with the "social movement" at first hand. Several years were spent in Switzerland and traveling; then he returned to Berlin in 1892 to complete the research begun in 1889 into the life of Max Stirner, the philosopher of egoism, and he was resident there until his death on May 16, 1933.

Mackay began publishing in 1885, but instant fame came in 1891 with his description of his London year in the non-novel *Die Anarchisten* (The Anarchists). It was also published in English in the United States that same year and was quickly translated into six other foreign languages. This was followed by poetry, short stories, novellas, the biography of Stirner and, in 1901, *Der Schwimmer* (The Swimmer), one of the first sports novels. Mackay was at the height of his fame. Then for nearly a decade nothing further appeared under his name. "People thought my artistic power had died out," he later wrote. In fact, they were the years of his literary campaign as "Sagitta" for the recognition of same-sex love, particularly man/boy love. Mackay himself was primarily attracted to boys fourteen to seventeen years old.

This campaign had little success because of the lack of support by other boy-lovers, and antagonism on the part of the mainstream homosexual liberation movement, which (then as now) often attempted to gain respectability by joining in the condemnation of man/boy love, and finally because of the intervention of the state in a legal process that ended by declaring his writings "obscene" and fining his publisher, who refused to identify "Sagitta," an amount equal to about $30,000 in today's money. (In fact, the total amount was paid by Mackay.) The Sagitta project, however, was completed and published in a one-volume edition in Paris in 1913 — and sold under the counter in Germany.

During the First World War Mackay wrote the book he considered his most important, *Der Freiheitsucher* (The Freedom-seeker), which was published in 1920. This work contains the mature development of the individualist anarchist views he had expressed in *Die Anarchisten* in 1891, but it did not have the recognition that the earlier work enjoyed. Indeed, that was not a good year for anarchists of any variety: Mackay's friend Erich Mühsam was in prison for his part in the Bavarian Soviet Republic and Emma Goldman, with whom Mackay had lunch in New York in 1893 on the first day of her trial for "inciting to riot," had been deported from the United States to the Soviet Union, where she was likewise unappreciated.

Mackay's own situation rapidly worsened, for the runaway inflation in Germany wiped out the value of the lifetime annuity he had purchased in 1900 with money received from his mother. Thereafter his life was a struggle with poverty, although he managed to survive by exercising the double profession of author and publisher. His major project as publisher was a one-volume edition of his earlier works. As author, he wrote two more novellas, some short stories, a one-act play, several poems, a volume of memoirs and — as his major project — *Der Puppenjunge*.

This novel is of undeniable literary merit. Because of its subject matter — and the dead silence over Mackay altogether —

it has been ignored by the literary critics. As one of the central characters in the novel says, describing his unrequited love: "If it had been a woman for whom he suffered — how they would have understood him!... But since it was only a boy...." It is, in fact, a beautifully crafted story of the eternal joys and sufferings of love. For anyone willing to see this love as *love*, Mackay's masterful treatment of it is universally compelling. At the same time, the action of the story takes place in a determined time and location that are described with historical exactness, making it a valuable document of a Berlin that will never be again. Set in the milieu of the male prostitute in the 1920s, *Der Puppenjunge* tells of a year in the life of one of the boys and of the young man who falls in love with him. Along the way Mackay describes various homosexual scenes in Berlin with unsparing realism. One is amused by Christopher Isherwood's depiction of a Berlin gay bar and perhaps muses over a description by Klaus Mann; one is convinced by Mackay.

The personalities of the story come alive for us in the sure sketches of Mackay. The brief chapter describing the gathering of a dozen boys around the hustler table of one bar is a masterpiece of characterization. But Mackay does not romanticize these boys. He sees them as limited by the hypocritical, bourgeois morality of the society, on the fringes of which they must lead their empty, often sordid lives.

Unlike Mackay's earlier "Books of Freedom" (*Die Anarchisten* and *Der Freiheitsucher*), *Der Puppenjunge* is a novel and not propaganda. It would be remarkable, however, if Mackay's anarchist views did not somehow come through, and indeed they do: in his description of the force of the state being used to crush a young personality and the development of a man into an individual determined to go his own way and prove to himself who is the stronger. And — this is, after all, a novel of "Sagitta" — there are passages which give Mackay's views on man/boy love: propaganda, if one will, but integrated into the story and necessary when treating a subject on which the majority (now as then) have ideas which are as false as they are deeply rooted.

Thanks to the Mackay-Gesellschaft, re-established in Freiburg, Germany, in 1974, many of Mackay's works are again in print (including a complete, two-volume edition of the Books of the Nameless Love of Sagitta). The current reawakening of interest, indeed rediscovery, of the unique personality of John Henry Mackay can only benefit a world that for too long has seen a virtue in conformity and submission to authority. *The Hustler* may contribute to the understanding that variety — also in sexual matters — does not lend vice, but rather richness, to life. Its availability in English may help to fulfill the hope expressed in 1931 by Kyrill, that it would "last beyond the day and gain the literary recognition it deserves."

Hubert Kennedy

View from Paris Place to Brandenburg Gate, (ca. 1910).

Friedrich Street, with train station (entrance to Aschinger Restaurant on right), (ca. 1910).

Friedrich Street, corner of Unter den Linden (looking south down Friedrich Street), (ca. 1910).

Unter den Linden, entrance to Passage in center of photograph

THE HUSTLER

PART

1

1

Punctually the four o'clock afternoon train from the north rolled into the Stettin train station. The travelers streamed out, crowding and jamming the gates, then dispersing — to be met or not — into the large room, finally to be drawn out the various exits, and to submerge and disappear in the life outside.

The building was again empty, as it had been a half hour earlier. Only in its middle did there still stand, as if lost, a boy about fifteen or sixteen years old, looking around indecisively. Wearing a grey, wrinkled, ill-fitting suit, heavy boots, and a yellow sport cap, he carried a simple cardboard box wrapped around many times with string.

Eventually he found what he was looking for. He resolutely walked up to the hand luggage checkroom, handed over the check piece, and, ready to pay right away, was abruptly — for he was now in Berlin — rebuked: "When you pick it up!" A minute later he was standing at the entrance to the train station, the great city and its boisterous life before him.

He paused, hesitant and still expectant. For what he saw, the flood of human activity, the confusion of vehicles of all kinds, the noise and bluster, all immersed in a haze of smoke and the humidity of the spring afternoon, was completely new to him and stunned him. But not for long.

Once more, he pulled himself together, turned instinctively

to the right, and resolutely set foot on the pavement of Berlin, which from that moment, for the duration of the coming year, was to be his true home.

Letting himself be pressed and shoved, he reached a street so long that it seemed never to end and turned into it, stopping in front of each fourth shop. Driven and pushed along again, he eventually halted spellbound before the show-window of a men's clothing store. There, among an enormous quantity of splendid things, were straw hats. He must have something like that, he felt. But which? — the one with the thick ribbing, or the one with the colorful band? The price written by each was the same — three marks. He could not decide: he liked both. The colorful one won out.

He gathered up what courage still remained to him since fleeing home and rolled his yellow cap into the side pocket of his jacket. Without speaking he pointed out the desired article to the young salesman. The hat was put on, fit, and became his.

Happy again outside, he looked at himself for a long time in the mirror window of the shop. Finding himself handsome, he contentedly walked on.

Those streets really did seem to have no end. He walked and walked — stopped and walked on. Coming to a wide bridge under construction, he saw black water under it, and a huge train station stretching above the street. The street grew narrower and narrower, but then, quite suddenly, spread to the right and left, becoming very broad and open, with trees in the middle and tall buildings on either side. He was on Unter den Linden — under the linden trees.

It was still early in the evening, hardly six, and still quite light. The wide street was busy, especially on the south side, and all the benches among the trees were filled with people on this splendid spring afternoon.

The boy was able to find a place on the edge of a bench. He was tired from the long train trip, the trek through the strange streets, and from all the new and unfamiliar things.

Between the cabs, stopping just in front of him in a driveway, he could peer through the incessant flood of automobiles, jamming up, when the passage into Friedrich Street became closed for a moment. The cabs stopped and pulled on again, sliding through and disappearing, their horns sounding awful. Buses, heavily loaded with people, stopped and rocked around the corner like monstrous animals. Motorcycles and bicycles darted through the crowd, and the boy stared in amazement, marveling that the riders, plus the people who so carelessly walked through it all, were not crushed under thick wheels of iron and rubber.

Tired of watching the traffic, he looked up at an immense yellow building precisely opposite. As his eyes slid down it, he read over its entrance — an entrance to a high passage, it appeared — on a semi-arc, in black letters, the word: PASSAGE.

Passage! He had heard that word once; and it could have been none other than Max, Max Friedrichsen who had named it for him on that memorable afternoon. Max had repeatedly talked about Friedrich Street and the Passage, and had smiled so peculiarly...

He leaned over to see better. Yes, it was obviously the entrance to another street. People were streaming in and out of it in masses, and some were just standing around. He wanted to see where it led to if you went inside.

He got up, waited for the traffic to allow him to cross, and entered the hall. For it was a hall, as he saw, very high and covered with a roof of glass. On two sides were shops which he began to examine. The first ones he saw did not interest him. But then, to the right, where some people were gathered in a knot, he saw a splendor unknown to him. There, behind high panes, were hanging and standing some wonderful pictures. Their brilliancy of color blinded his eyes — pictures of beautiful women in sumptuous gowns, of proud men in colorful uniforms, of sweet children and lovely girls. Plus, far in the background — he had pushed his way through, to see everything — there towered, magically lit, entirely in white and larger than life, the grand figure of a woman with blond hair, a crown on her head, shield and sword in her hands, gazing victoriously into the distance. He did not know what the picture was supposed to represent. But he did know that it was the most beautiful thing he had seen, today or ever, and he could barely part from the enchanting sight.

Finally, he tore himself away and walked on. After what he had just seen, the other shops didn't attract him as much. Only at one with odd tools, small machines, wires and coils, with strange and unintelligible names on their tags did he again stand for a long time, perplexed about the instruments' purposes.

Why were the people here pushing and shoving so? he wondered. It was even worse than it had been in the street. And just what did that guy want from him, the one who kept standing beside him, who seemed to be talking to himself? Again and again when he moved off, the stranger placed himself beside him and nudged him — intentionally or not? — with his elbow, leering sideways as he did so. He was a repulsive man with hollow eyes and protruding cheekbones.

The boy left the window with the incomprehensible objects and crossed to the other side. There he saw a case containing tools of magic equipment — dice-boxes, decks of mysterious cards, a skull — things such as a traveling magician and illusionist had used to delight an audience in his home village once. He recalled that time as he looked at the paraphernalia in front of him.

But he was nudged here too. Again a man was standing close beside him. Not the same one as before, but a taller, fatter man, who said nothing, but smiled at him familiarly. What did this man want from him? He felt uneasy inside.

He walked on into the middle of the hurrying, driving human flood. The hall made a sharp bend and opened above to a high dome, with a café with a porch beneath it. Music sounded from the café. He stopped to listen.

And again it felt as if someone were standing beside, or behind him, looking at him. He dared not look up, for fear of meeting another strange gaze. Just what did all these men want from him? Surely no one knew him! Was he being pursued? But that could not be possible — who knew that he was here?

With a feeling of uneasiness and fear, his only thought was to get away from this throughway as quickly as possible. He started for the other exit, visible in the distance, but he could not proceed very quickly in the crowd.

Finally he reached the exit, and the streets opened out before him. He stood still, removed his new hat and wiped his forehead with a dirty handkerchief. He felt safe now, on the outside. But as he glanced about he felt a gaze on his face, the gaze of a young man who was standing close, in front of him, looking neither malicious nor obtrusive, not smiling nor questioning, but obviously aroused as if about to speak to him. Fear gripped him anew; hat and handkerchief still in hand, he began to run. He ran across the street, between the automobiles, by the entrance of a subway, over the avenue, and down a street on the other side. On and on, without looking up or around, as if being pursued, he ran. Through a sidestreet, he continued on further, until he arrived in a large square, in front of a tall building and beside a low, isolated church.

There he finally halted and looked around. No one appeared to be following. There were benches all around but he did not sit down. He walked on and on, down new streets until he found himself on a street that was quiet and empty of people. He looked around. No one was following him. He was entirely alone.

More slowly and calmly, he strode on further. He passed over a large square and across a bridge, going always into new streets, but narrower and poorer ones. Suddenly he felt hungry, but he dared not go into a pub. They all looked sinister, and through their open doors he saw noisy, drinking men standing around at the bars by the entrances. In a nearby bakery he bought a couple of rolls and ate them as he wandered along.

He decided he should look up Max, but it already was almost too late in the day for that. Besides, how was he to find the street where Max lived? It was probably far away, perhaps hours away. He could no longer roam today with his feet so tired.

He wanted to sleep. Should he return to the train station? He had seen hotels there. But there must be hotels in other regions of Berlin, he thought, so he began to watch the signs on buildings. It was not long before he read, over the door of an old and narrow building, "Guest House." In the doorway stood a man in shirt-sleeves and an apron. The boy approached hesitantly, asking, "Could I perhaps sleep here?"

"Sleep? Well, why not? You have money then, little one?" the man replied.

"Yes, I have money," he informed the man.

"How much?"

Then, as he gave no answer, the man, said, "Can you pay five marks?"

It startled him at first — five marks! But then he nodded yes.

"Well, just come along then . . ." the man beckoned him to enter.

He walked two flights up to a tiny hole of a room where, except for a wobbly bed and chair, there was only a washbasin made of sheet metal. He put a five-mark bill in the landlord's red, dirty fist, and was left alone. Dead tired from the long and exciting day, he stripped off his jacket, pants and boots, and fell immediately asleep in the unclean bed before reflecting clearly about the unconscionable fleecing he had just taken from the brute of an innkeeper.

2

That same day — as chance would have it — and almost at the same hour, there arrived at another train station in Berlin — the Potsdam station — a traveler coming from far in the south of Germany. The traveler was a young man, perhaps twenty-two or twenty-three years old. He, too, was coming to Berlin for the first time. But he had become familiar with the major streets and squares of the capital from books and maps, so he quickly and surely found his way around. He washed and changed clothes in the Fürstenhof, where he had taken a small room on the top floor. Almost everything seemed to him, as he slowly walked along, to be recognizable, even familiar — the busy square, the unique construction of the department store on Leipzig Street (in front of which he stood for a long time), the Tiergarten, and of course, the splendid gate with the row of trees and buildings — Unter den Linden...

He was in no hurry to enter Unter den Linden. He sat for a while, not wearily, though the trip had indeed been long, but comfortably, on one of the chairs at the nearby lake, enjoying the afternoon hour on this warm spring day. The first, tender green of the trees, the mild sweetness of the air, the happy feeling of at last being in the great city — for which he had secretly yearned for so long without being able to say exactly why — all of this filled him with a cheerfulness that was usually foreign to his serious nature.

After an hour he rose, strode through the gate, and gazed down the broad street. Unter den Linden lay before him in its entire length. It charmed him with its new fresh garment of trees, even though he had imagined the trees and the buildings would be taller and more majestic. Joyful at the sight of something so lovely, he strode down the broad street.

The human and vehicular traffic was lively, but not overpowering. One flower shop looked magnificent with its profuse splendor of blooms, and another tiny one next to it exuded one single kind of perfume.

He stood in front of the shops a bit, but preferred to keep to the middle of the street where there was more elbow room and he could better survey the lovely street on both sides, all the way to its far end.

After a stroll that seemed short to him, he came to a long, narrow street that cut across the width of the Linden, and he knew immediately that he had reached Friedrich Street. He felt no desire to plunge into its thick and loud traffic. Instead he sat down, somewhat apart, on a folding rental chair and let the traffic just pass by him.

He wanted to remain seated for a while but the behavior of some youths sitting nearby drove him off. Young boys and girls were laughing loudly and shrieking, with words and gestures so frankly vulgar that he soon got up again, disgusted. As he did so, his glance fell on a space between the buildings opposite, and he realized that it must be the Passage.

He too had read about the Passage. It was the notorious Passage, the meeting place of a certain segment of the Berlin population at all times of day and night. He knew he could not find there what he was seeking — and he would seek until he found it. Yet he was curious, and he walked over to it and was not surprised to find the entrance populated by young chaps in age from seventeen to twenty. With a cursory glance he scanned their faces, which seemed to him partly worn-out and greedy, partly crude and common. He noticed that his glance was immediately and provocatively returned by some youths. He walked into the hall, without further concerning himself with their invitations or with the mass of humanity flowing round him.

The hall appeared to him, though high, neither beautiful nor light. The window goods were mostly shabby compared with those he had just seen. These windows were full of cheap trifles and had no elegance. The public here also had no elegance. In front of one shop a mass of people was shoving and crowding.

He threw his glance over the crowd to the brightly lit window and drew back immediately, wanting to laugh out loud. For what he saw were paintings of such mesmerizing richness of color and intoxicating beauty they froze the eye. One depicted a young, supernaturally handsome officer on whose breast snuggled his bride, sobbing with the grief of parting, while she fastened violets on his uniform that was already so very blue. Another showed an old man in a slouch hat and full beard, with fiery eyes in a foolish sheep face. Then there was, in the backgroud, a Germania — a grand woman with sword and shield. It was overpowering! And the crowd was held entranced. *Holy smokes!* he thought as he walked on, and an amused smile passed over his usually so serious face. *If that is the taste of the Berliners!* . . .

He already had had enough of this famous Passage but what he yet saw only made him leave all the faster. All around the sides, figures were standing, suspicious-looking and not very likeable. There were bums and idlers, hard-up or shabby-elegant, who killed time there or attended to their dirty transactions. And everywhere, many remarkably young faces lurked, as if waiting, yet squeezed into corners and shopfronts as if they did not wish to be seen. He wanted out, and pressed faster through the stream of humanity.

And then it happened.

In front of him, walking as hastily as he, obviously driven by the same wish to quickly get out, was a boy of fifteen or sixteen years. His clothing was a crude, ill-fitting suit and heavy boots, which did not agree with his light walk and his tender, still undeveloped figure. From his slender shoulders rose a thin neck with brown hair at the back. Oddly drawn against his will and suddenly at a loss, the young man was unable to take his gaze from the boy's neck; he did not want to lose the boy from sight. To see the face those shoulders bore, he shoved himself more quickly through the crowd.

They vanished, the shoulders — disappeared. He walked faster still, and saw them again ahead of him just where the exit opened up. He saw the boy pause indecisively and take off his new straw hat. He watched the boy dry his hot forehead with a handkerchief, balled into a dirty lump, which he removed from his pocket.

He must, he *must* see this face! Three steps further and he was standing close in front of him.

The boy looked up. A pained expression of fright came over his features. Then abruptly the boy turned and, running more than walking, went out to the sidewalk, crossed the street, now running as if pursued, and vanished across the way into the swarm of pedestrians.

The young man stood transfixed. The spot where the boy had just stood was empty. The people around pushed and crowded, and shoved him away.

Another face popped up close in front of him, a young, impudent face with an importunate grin, challenging and boldly questioning him. Was this one of the rude fellows from the entrance, who had followed him here? . . . *Disgusting!* he thought, and scared the fellow away with an angry gesture. His first feeling had been to follow the strange boy. His second: impossible! — the boy was gone now. Vanished there on the other side! . . .

There was nothing left to do but walk on. Hesitantly, he turned to the right into a quiet street and walked slowly along. His heart was beating hard and he was trembling, like after a sudden scare. But why and from what? What had just happened? He visualized quite clearly the small, pale face, which for a fraction of a minute, for a second, had just appeared in front of him. He could still see the gray-blue eyes which had looked up at him with an expression — of terror? — no, not exactly of terror, but with visible alarm and obvious fright. He could see the full, red lips, the upper one had twitched so oddly, and the blond, almost brown, disheveled hair across the hot forehead — a small, shy face, scared by something!...

He stopped and laid his hands over his eyes, as though to enable himself to recall the boy's face more clearly. But in vain — he could remember no more. The encounter had been too fleeting. He felt a sudden pain, but it passed as he walked on. He held his head down, lost in thought as he walked along the street. What was it — why had the boy run away so suddenly? Why had the boy run away from *him?*

And what was in the expression the boy had given him? Fright, no doubt, but he had read something else in the look. Something plaintive, begging, as if the boy were saying, "Leave me in peace! What do you want from me?"

He could not make head nor tail of the episode. Only one thing remained certain — the boy had obviously been a decent sort. A boy, strange to the area, who had strayed into the Passage, noticed where he was, and had wanted to escape as quickly as possible! That seemed quite clear. He smiled bitterly. From *him*, especially from him, the boy would have no need to run. He would have done nothing to the boy. Again he felt a momentary slight pain, knowing not where it came from. He walked on, not thinking about time nor place.

Finding his way back to Potsdam Place and his hotel, he had a meal in the neighborhood. Over and over he kept recalling that small, pale face before him and how it had looked up at him. He was unable to drive the vision away. He saw it as he undressed, and took it into his dreams on his first night in this strange metropolis.

3

hat boy of his dreams was awakened toward noon the next day by a rough knocking and a raw voice that roared through the door, suggesting he finally get up. He stared around at first at his strange surroundings, drunk with sleep. Then he reached under his pillow, where he had put his money yesterday evening before going to sleep — it was still there.

He washed himself and dressed. Later, standing on the street with no idea of what region he was in, his first feeling was intense hunger. Since his train trip yesterday he had only eaten a couple of rolls. After wandering some streets, he ventured into an empty bar. There he thought about his situation. The main thing now was to find Max.

He pulled out a dirtied, bent calling card and read for the hundredth time what he knew by heart: — Skalitz Street 37, c/o Hampel. "Where is Skalitz Street?" he inquired of the proprietor when leaving. Near the Silesian train station, he was told. He was instructed to take a 48 and then ask a green. He knew neither what the number 48 meant, nor what a "green" was. He decided to inquire along the way.

This he did, at first hesitantly and timidly, then with increasing courage. After a walk of almost two hours he arrived, not in the vicinity of the train station — from where, he was told, it "should not be far away" — but in a large square, with a brown church and a water basin formed by a canal. Finally, also on the square, he found Skalitz Street.

He stood for a long while in front of the number 37. Perhaps Max would come out? But Max did not appear, so he went through the courtyard to the back of the house. An old woman directed him to Max's flat — upstairs, to the right. Above was a door with the name Hampel on a metal plate. He shyly rang the bell. The door was promptly thrown open by a slovenly, untidy woman holding an infant at her half-naked breast.

When he announced he wanted Max Friedrichsen, a flood of verbal abuse poured over the disconcerted boy, from which he gathered that Max had lived there. The woman said Max "hauled those guys up here," and that, if Max hadn't got out, she would have called the police to arrest him, for Max was certainly one of the "queer boys" and "looked it, too"!

The crying of other children in the background ended her tirade and she slammed the door. The boy was glad to get down the stairs again and away from that dreadful woman. Compared with her, the farmer women who shopped in the store in his village, raising beastly outcries when they thought they were being cheated of a penny, were the purest angels!

He trembled with the thought that he did not know where to find Max. He became discouraged, and almost started to cry. What was he to do here — without Max!

The best thing was to go back home. To do that, he had to go back to the train station where he had arrived yesterday. With tired feet he set out to retrace his path. He now had experience in asking his way. Dead tired, he finally arrived in late afternoon at the Stettin train station. He was about to go up the stairs when the thought came to him to eat his fill first. He still had enough money for that.

He found a decent pub and a seat in a corner, where no one paid attention to him. After eating several sandwiches and a glass of beer his situation no longer seemed quite so desperate. While paying, he saw that he still had a good deal of money, more than twenty marks. He immediately ordered another glass of beer and remained seated.

He thought the situation over. He had enough for another couple of days. If forced to return home after all, then he at least wanted first to see more of Berlin. And maybe he would find Max yet. Berlin was big, but not so big that you might not find someone you were looking for in two days.

For today, he had to sleep again, tired as he was from the long walk plus unaccustomed drinks of beer. He climbed to the train station, picked up his box, and then searched the side streets for a hotel. One stood beside another. He only had to choose.

He found a room, a small and narrow one. It contained not much more than a bed, but it cost only one mark fifty for the night. An old waiter in a black, greasy tailcoat took payment immediately. Again the boy sank at once into the deep and dreamless sleep of healthy youth.

Why had he come to Berlin from his village? For he had come into the world in a village: He was the child of a mother who had made off soon after his birth to roam the world. No one knew if she was still alive. His father, who had been one of many guests on the estate where his mother was employed, had taken her, then thrown her aside. His father was said to have been a distinguished gentleman.

Grandparents had to keep him. He grew, attended the village school, and became an apprentice to a merchant. The whole day he emptied sacks, filled bags, weighed, and worked for four years' apprenticeship, then presumably the rest of his life .

He never left the village, and his life passed uneventfully up to the day of Max Friedrichsen's return. Max was another village boy with whom he sat on the same schoolbench, with whom he was later confirmed. One day, all of a sudden, Max vanished. Then, just as unexpectedly, Max reappeared and by his appearance set the village boys into a state of astonishment, wonder, and fascination.

For the Max who returned was entirely different from the Max who had run away a year before. He was an *entirely* different Max, wearing new duds — a tight-fitting jacket, pants with cuffs, yellow gloves, a ring on his finger, a wristwatch, and a walking stick in hands that were carefully groomed. Moreover, Max had money, so much money that he invited the boys, on a Sunday afternoon, to go to the neighboring village. There he got them all drunk, not only from beer and schnapps and grog, but also from his tales of Berlin.

He told of Berlin with its theaters and lounges; its cinemas, where there always were seats for five thousand people; its circus, which played every day; its cafés and fine restaurants without number — this Berlin, where money nearly lay in the street, so that you only had to pick it up.

The boys sat around him, with open ears and jaws, elbows propped on the table, listening, and when someone tried to question or object he cut them off with a grand wave of his hand: "None of you have any idea of it!"

In the evening, staggering home arm in arm with Max, he asked if it were all true and if you could really make so much money there and how. Max stopped, looked him up and down, and said:

"Such a good-looking boy like you! If you don't believe it, just come there!" Then he reached into his pocket and drew out his billfold — a real billfold, with monogram, and corners covered with silver. From the billfold he drew a calling card with his name in printed letters. Under the name, in pencil, was his address. "Just come there! You'll soon see..." Max pressed the card into his hand and promised, "I'll help you..."

On the next day Max, who had so unexpectedly popped up, vanished again; the village became too hot for him. Max's card had been kept and preserved like a sacred possession, its promise burning in his breast. He felt transformed. Again and again he secretly repeated to himself the words he had heard, and each time a decision was growing in him — he, too, must go to Berlin! To Berlin and to Max! He knew going would not be easy. He would never receive permission to go, neither from his grandparents, nor from his guardian. So, like Max, he would also run away.

Thus, when spring arrived, lovely and careless spring which arouses so many wishes — some of which come true — he could no longer be held.

One evening, while the household slept, he donned his Sunday suit, packed some underwear and personal possessions into a box, emptied his savings bank, and crept out of the humble house. He left a note saying not to worry about him. He promised to write when he found work and to return once things were going well for him.

He walked half the night, all the way to a train station other than the one in his village. He bought a ticket there to another station so as not to give away where he meant to go. From the second station he would go directly to Berlin. Everything went well. No one spoke to him or stopped him. The trip had lasted that whole night and into the next afternoon. Now he had already spent his second day in the city of his longing.

When he awoke on the third day, earlier than the day before, he thought less than he had the evening before about returning. As long as his money lasted, he was staying. He counted the money again, carefully, confirming that it would last for at least two or three days. He decided to pay for the room for the next two nights in advance. The old waiter acknowledged his payment with the indifferent words, "All right, it's paid until early Thursday!"

To be sure, he was bored being so alone with no one to talk to. But there was a lot to see!

The buildings and streets soon did begin to bore him. Some buildings were narrow, long, and level, while others were high and grand. The buildings, like the streets, seemed endless. But the shops! What marvels there were to see and buy! He could not get his fill of looking at the merchandise and he would have liked to own everything — this stylish suit and those colorful ties; that wristwatch and this cigarette case of silver, no, that other case there, the flat, gold one. And this here! And that there! Thus he stared in wonder, and could stand before the same shop window an hour without stirring.

He was also no longer as shy as on the first day. When he felt hungry and thirsty, he went into the first beer hall he came to and ordered, thinking every time, *you've still got money.*

He gradually came to know the part of the city where he usually roamed. The long street that started up and seemed to never end was Friedrich Street. The broad one with trees and benches in the middle and a gate at the beginning — or at the end? — was the Linden. He even rode on streetcars and buses, up on the top. Once, just for the pleasure of it, he rode through the Tiergarten. Another time he went down to Kreuzberg and back.

If he became too bored all alone, there was always the cinema. The cinema seemed much lovelier, more colorful and mysterious in its darkness than the bright life outside. There were some cinemas open in the early afternoon. He could sit for hours looking at the flickering screen, mostly without comprehending the films, but held by the quivering and ever-changing spell of the pictures. One day, he no longer knew which it was, he counted his money on awakening, then counted once more and realized it was not even enough for the return trip. He was terribly frightened, especially when he counted back and realized that the day was Thursday, the day to which he had paid for the room.

He had to go home now. What was he to do here without money? He would a thousand times have preferred to stay, but he had to go home.

He thought it over. His things in the box were worth nothing. But he still had his watch, his confirmation watch.

He crept out of the hotel, luckily without being seen. Somewhere near the train station he remembered having seen the sign of a pawnbroker. He found it again.

"Silver? Nonsense, nickel," the pawnbroker said, and announced he would give one mark on it. One mark! No, then he'd rather not. But in the end, the boy took the mark anyway.

Now he had two marks and seventy pennies altogether. What was he to do? He still had to eat and spend the day in the city.

So he purchased a cup of coffee and a couple of dry rolls, then sat hungry almost the whole day in one corner of an all-day cinema. His loitering was ferreted out by an usher and he was made to pay an additional fare. He saw his money shrink to a bit over one mark.

For today, a meal was out of the question, or what would he live on tomorrow? He crept around his hotel, going inside in an unobserved moment, and reached his room unhindered. He fell uneasily asleep.

Early the next morning the old waiter came to his room, exclaiming angrily.

"What is this? The room is not yet paid for the night. You sleep and not pay? What, leave your old box of rags here as security? Naturally it is staying here. You will get it again when you bring money. Now you are to get out of here, quick as possible."

The boy begged: "Just a couple days more . . . I'll pay then, by all means."

"Nothing doing!"

The old man remained standing beside him until he finished dressing, reminding him that when he had money, he might return and pick up his things. "Not before, understood?"

Standing outside, in the street, he could have howled with rage. Couldn't the old guy let him stay at least this night, when he already had slept there four nights, and paid for them on time, in advance even! What now?

If only he could find work. But where and how? He had no idea how. The day had to continue, however, and he did have to eat, especially since he had gone to bed hungry yesterday. So, cutting into his last mark, he bought a couple of rolls and some garlic sausages, eating them in a corner of the train station.

He spent the morning loitering near the Friedrich Street train station until sent away by one of the porters. He spent the afternoon on the benches of the Tiergarten, going from bench to bench, sitting on each a while. Finally, he fell asleep in the evening on a bench in a less lively part of the park.

In the night he awoke and felt something moist and warm on his hand. He sprang up, to the curse of a watchman, and ran away as fast as he could. The guard, with stick in hand and a dog on a leash, was after him for a while, but didn't catch him.

At the Reichstag building he crouched in a dark niche and slowly dozed off again in the mild spring night.

He woke in the early morning feeling a painful hunger. He still had twenty pennies — enough for four rolls and a couple of cigarettes. When he smoked, he noticed, he felt less hunger, for a while. He had to smoke.

Again, he loitered through the morning on the benches of the park. From time to time he nodded off, but rose quickly when he felt the gaze of a passerby on him.

Once, when he looked up, sitting close to him was a small, well-dressed but ugly man, looking at him through a pince-nez, attentively, with no malice but still so oddly that the boy got up. What did the man want from him? Certainly not to help.

On the next bench he was startled by the laughter of two youngsters, who suddenly were in front of him asking what his watch said. He did have one? When they saw his dull face, they walked on laughing. From a third bench he heard a coachman shout an insult to him from his coach-box, which he did not understand.

He was now too tired to become angry, too dull to be startled, and too hungry to reflect on what all these people wanted from him. He sat longer, undisturbed on an out-of-the-way bench until noon. A boundless rage, such as at times had gripped him as a child, came over him. He felt rage at Max, at the old waiter in the hotel, at the whole world. He stamped on the ground with the heels of his shoes and bit a blade of grass into tiny pieces.

His rage passed and he broke out bawling. Great pity for himself, his misery, and his desolation came over him. What was he to do?

He wanted to speak to the first passerby that came along and tell him everything. But hardly anyone was coming just then, and he realized that it would help nothing. In Berlin, he had seen, you had to have money or you went to the dogs.

When he had cried himself out, an angry defiance gripped him and he got up, furious, and crept behind the nearest bushes. There he threw himself down at full length and soon fell asleep.

After hours of a deep sleep he woke. He no longer felt tired and his hunger no longer pained him. He washed his face and hands at a nearby fountain, then he walked slowly into the city, to Unter den Linden. It had become afternoon.

Over and over again, as he had since yesterday, he thought about what Max had said to him. He tried to recall every word, so as to finally understand its meaning.

What was it he said? — that you could make money in Berlin, much money. But with what? With what kind of work? And where was work to be found? And why did good-looking boys — of which he was supposed to be one — find work easier than others?

He did not understand. No, he did not understand.

Yet, he remembered, his former friend always talked about Friedrich Street, and one afternoon, when they were alone, about the Passage.

The Passage — surely that was the large throughway he had been in on the first afternoon, right after his arrival. The place people had looked at him so oddly, where he had become frightened, and run away? So frightened that ever since he had always made a wide detour around it.

Young guys had been standing around there, but they had not seemed to him good-looking, but ugly and common. Were they gathered there looking for some kind of work?

He wanted to go there again and take a closer look at the situation — maybe ask somebody. No one could do more than chase him away, or laugh at him.

But suddenly hunger gripped him again. At the same time his heavy boots pained him; he had not taken them off since yesterday. He sat down on the nearest bench and pressed his hands against his stomach. He was unable to think clearly any longer. In his burning head everything was all mixed up. A complete lethargy to everything seized him. If he fell down, someone would pick him up. Or let him lie.

He sat for almost an hour, dully staring straight ahead, when he felt a coin pressed into his hand. He saw an old, simply dressed woman, who walked away before he could thank her. He stared at the money. Ten pennies! *Bread!* he thought first. Then immediately — *cigarettes!* Ten pennies' worth of bread could not ease his hunger anyway. Better to smoke once more.

Across the way he bought four cigarettes for two pennies each from a peddler. He smoked them hurriedly, lighting one from the other.

They made him feel clumsy, knocked out. Avoiding the middle walkway of the Linden, he walked beside the buildings on the north side. Then, crossing over, he looked for a seat on one of the benches opposite the Passage. Gloomy and irresolute, he stared through the confusion of carriages at the entrance. Only the hunger that continued to make itself felt kept him alert. He was on the same bench, the same corner of the bench, where he had sat that first afternoon a week ago. It was the same hour, and he had looked across then, strange and shy, but oh! — with what other feelings.

4

he other young man, who had arrived in the capital at almost the same time as he, spent his first day in the most cheerless and tiring of all activites — the search for a room.

Disgusted by almost all available lodgings, the triviality of their furniture, the impossible manner of their landladies, he arrived, half dead and despairing, at a dead-end street. He was reluctant to enter at first, but then was drawn by its obvious peace and quiet. The street had houses on one side only, the other side being taken up by the high firewall of a large warehouse followed by another lower wall that apparently led into a neighboring courtyard or garden. Only one door, the last one of the ten houses on the street, showed a room-for-rent sign. The house seemed quiet and clean, and the rental room seemed to be on the first floor up on the left side. He rang.

A woman dressed entirely in black, with scrawny features and strikingly dark, sharp eyes, opened the door, scrutinized him, and let him enter.

The door to the available room was close beside the house entrance. The room was large and faced the street with two windows. It was fitted out with large, old-fashioned, comfortable furniture — a two-person sofa, an armchair with wings, a desk and bookcase. A smaller room joined it, serving as a bedroom. Altogether it made a cold but clean impression.

Bath and toilet were opposite and the landlady's own rooms were at the dark end of the hall. Therefore, a tenant would be independent of her, the young man thought with satisfaction. The lodgings were altogether not bad.

But the wall? Was it possible to stand the sight of that bare wall across the way for long, without going crazy? Then he considered that he would mainly be in only evenings, when it was beginning to be dark, or was dark. At worst, he would have to endure the bleak view on Sundays. The quiet and peacefulness of the street decided the matter. Carriages almost never would come by, and seldom pedestrians. With a few more questions asked, he decided to rent the room.

The price was fair and he paid a month in advance. With clear, firm handwriting he signed his name, Hermann Graff, on a registration card, and a couple of hours later moved into his new quarters.

The following day, after a long sleep, he started his new job in a large publishing house. He was assigned his place in the office, seated by a window that faced a courtyard where there was constant life and activity. He read manuscripts and proof sheets, he copied letters and bills. He began to familiarize himself with the work, and his co-workers, strangers all. The employees were the usual types: the smart and the stupid; the aspiring and the indifferent; the friendly and the grumbling; the old, grown gray in service, and the young, still to grow gray. And all of them working among books, books, books... He had to be in at nine o'clock, and remain until five o'clock — with an hour break at noon — then his eight-hour workday was at an end.

During the first days of working, he was so tired at day's end that he only went out in the evenings to eat. Only toward the end of the first week did his thoughts turn to his new life. What form would life take for him? He was a very serious person, very solitary and introverted, who experienced difficulty joining others.

He had never felt a mother's love, since he lost her quite early. He had had one friend, of his own age, but lost him too. His father had never loved him. After his father died several months ago, he decided to come to Berlin. He applied to the publishers for a position and was accepted. Now he was here.

He felt that he must change his life. He must win someone to love, and knew that his love could only be for another boy. He knew that he could not search for love; rather he had to find love as one finds one's fortune.

He had read much and thought much, about love and about himself. He knew that his love was directed toward boys by virtue of the law of his nature. His emotions always were directed toward few people, so he knew that among many boys there were probably a very few, singular individuals whom he would be able to love. Perhaps only one. Could he hope to meet him? He must hope, nevertheless — because life without hope is meaningless.

Perhaps he had already met him, right on the first day? he asked himself, only to see at once how foolish this question was. He was not a person of quick decisions, not a person who gave in to strange impressions. Yet he knew that he had never experienced such a feeling as in the moment when that strange boy at the Passage had walked in front of him and looked into his face for a second. But that had all been much too fleeting to be taken seriously. He had almost forgotten that meeting over these recent days.

Yet he had not totally forgotten it. For now, during his quiet moments in the long, lonely hours of the evening before going to sleep, that small, pale face popped up again before him. He saw again the gray-blue eyes as they had looked into his, startled and fearful, and he tormented himself again with the question that had disturbed him on that first evening, all the way into his sleep. The answer he had given himself then no longer satisfied him.

Where was that boy now? Submerged amidst the millions of people of this huge city. Perhaps gone to another city far away, out of reach, lost to him forever... If, as he believed, the boy was a decent boy, he would never meet him again at the only place where he could look for him — the Passage. And, if the boy was not a decent boy, should he still hope and wish to see him again?

An inner unrest gripped him so strongly during the last days of the week that it drove him out, for the first time again, to the

Linden. He wanted at least to try, just once. If chance and luck were favorable? If he met him again — what then? He did not believe in chance, nor in good luck, he just wanted to see again the place where he had met the boy.

He walked this time directly to the entrance of the Passage, strode through the hall without looking around, and stood at its southern exit. Everything was like before. The people shoved and crowded, shouting and laughing. He was where he had stood. There was where the boy had run across. He recalled him again before him, as he had run... Naturally the boy was not there — and why should he be there!

He turned and walked back through the Passage and out. He did not look around, never guessing that the boy he sought was sitting on a bench not twenty steps away — sitting tired, hungry, and completely in despair.

Unaware of the boy's presence so near, he strode down the Linden, head low, away from that place so abhorrent to him.

5

he boy was still sitting on the outer edge of the bench, staring across to the entrance. A whole troop of young guys stood there, he could see, entirely indifferent to the fact that they were blocking traffic. They were laughing and talking, all at once. He still did not venture over.

Then, as the pain in his stomach again became especially strong, he slowly got up and walked, eyes lowered, across the road up to the Passage entrance. At the corner, near a mailbox, a boy was standing alone. He was bare-headed, looked down and out, and under his dirty jacket showed a lean, shirtless chest. He stood there as if waiting for someone.

The boy positioned himself beside the shirtless youth. His legs trembled. Hunger? Fear? Of what? he told himself. No one looked concerned about him. Yet it did seem that the passersby and people coming out the Passage — and mostly the older men — looked at him peculiarly before walking on. He became aware also of being watched by a group of young people in the middle of the entrance. They turned toward him and laughed disdainfully, then went on talking among themselves. Were they talking about him, he wondered. He did not dare go ask them if anyone knew where he could find work. He would sooner ask the one standing next to him, though even he looked as if he had not had work for a long time.

Thus thinking, he suddenly heard a hissing, angry voice close to his ear. It was the shirtless boy beside him.

"Stupid lout! Ain't ya got eyes in ya head? Can't ya see that the john there is keen on ya? What ya standing here for, messing up my chance?" He paused and then said, still more furiously, almost threateningly, "Go after him!"

He became terribly frightened by the youth's angry tone. What had the boy said? Whom was he talking about? What did he want? He could not stay there any longer.

He walked rapidly away from the Passage, down the Linden, laughter echoing after him. Were they laughing at him again? He walked past the buildings with their shops, then across the middle promenade, and again, to another bench. He could not go on.

Why had the shirtless boy been so angry? What had he wanted from him? His head was spinning. He understood not a word of it all.

Sitting on the bench, trembling from the scare and from hunger, it suddenly occurred to him that he was being watched. A gentleman on the bench next to his leaned forward and looked over at him. Then the man got up and came to sit close beside him.

The boy rose and walked away. He felt a sudden rage. What did these strangers want? Would he nowhere be left in peace? Was he not allowed to sit quietly on a bench like anybody else? He wanted to get away — no matter where — just away.

He crossed to the other side and turned into a quiet side street. He crept along close to the buildings, tired enough to drop. *I would like to just drop*, he thought, *drop and stay there. Then it would at least be at an end.*

He did not know how long or where he had walked when he heard a voice beside him, a friendly and encouraging voice.

"Well, little one, also out for a walk? Don't you want to come along with me?"

He looked up. Was this the gentleman on the bench, or another? He could not say, but he thought he recognized the man. Was it someone from earlier, who had looked at him so?

The gentleman wore a light summer coat. He carried a briefcase under his arm and had a beardless face. He was smiling and flushed, as if from walking fast.

When the man saw the astonishment on the boy's face, he changed his tone and said pleasantly, "You really don't need to be afraid. Nothing will happen to you. And you get ten marks."

He still received no answer and asked once more, "Well, are you coming with me or not?"

In his head the boy's thoughts were racing like crazy as he stood before the stranger and looked up at him.

"Ten marks — what for then? — Come with you — where to?" he stammered.

The gentleman seemed to have missed the question entirely.

"Just come on. It's not far. Right over there..." He was already walking on. Turning back to the still hesitant boy, he spoke again: "But only if you want to. I won't talk you into it."

For fear of losing the ten marks, the boy pulled himself together and stepped along beside the gentleman. By now he was entirely without willpower. It mattered not where he was led ... Only the money — he needed the ten marks. They talked no more.

A couple hundred paces further the gentleman entered a house, waved him in, and they climbed up some stairs. At a door on the second floor the man rang short and loud.

The boy stood on the top step of the stairway, full of fear. He could still turn back and run away, he knew. But he followed the man through the door that opened just at that moment.

Standing on the street again a half hour later, ten marks in his pocket, he felt like laughing out loud from joy. If it was nothing more than that! The pastor in his village had done that with him, only he had not been friendly, but clumsy and rough, and had only given him a couple of apples from the garden.

So *that's* how one could make money! And he had thought for a moment on the stairs he was to be murdered!

The hundreds of thoughts that were ready to storm over him were for the present drowned by a single one — eat, now, just eat! Eat as soon as possible, and as much as possible! Eat! Eat and drink!

He dashed to Aschinger's on Friedrich Street. He sat in the farthest room back, in a remote corner, where he was alone at this early afternoon hour. He shoved the ten-mark bill at the waiter.

The waiter laughed: "You've got time! What will it be, then?"

"Sausages. And bread. Right away. And then a glass of dark beer, a large—"

The waiter laughed again and first set a basket of bread in front of him. He soon came back with the rest.

The first pair of sausages the boy devoured and then he studied the menu. There were many unfamiliar things listed so he stayed with sausages — a second and then a third pair — with lots of potato salad and much more bread. Eagerly, the first glass of beer was followed by a second, then a small cognac. Next he bought cigarettes, ten all at once. And everything was paid for immediately. A half hour later he felt ready to calmly think over the unprecedented experience he had just had.

So that's how one could make money... he mused.

He felt well and relaxed, as never before in his life. Also, he was no longer tired. He had not a trace of fatigue — it had all been only hunger.

He did not want to leave the café. It was so cozy in the corner, alone, with beer and cigarettes in front of him, as many as he wanted.

So that's *how one could make money here in Berlin!* he thought again.

Now he knew how Max had acquired the stack of money, the ring, the watch, the cane and everything! Finally he saw what was behind Max's talk about good-looking boys, Friedrich Street, and the Passage! Max had not plainly spelled it out, the deceitful dog! Did Max think he would have betrayed the secret! How well he knew that you just did not tell something like that — to no one!

He was unable, though, to become really angry at Max. His good feeling of being filled up was too great, and he felt relieved, released from the puzzle which had racked his brains so much these past days!

Now he knew why so many boys stood around in the Passage. He realized why the gentlemen nudged him, looked at him, and whispered to him. He understood the reason the shirtless boy had been so angry with him. It was clear why the other guys had laughed at him, and why the nice gentleman just earlier guessed that he was new to Berlin.

Now it amused him that he had been afraid! Even if the encounter had not been any great fun, there had indeed been nothing frightening about it. *God, how stupid I have been!* he thought. But now he would no longer be so stupid.

The thought came to him — *what if I went to the Passage now? And looked the affair over again, but now with entirely different eyes? Right away, today?*

He had enough money, more than enough for today and tomorrow. He counted. He still had seven marks and twenty pennies. Aschinger's was cheap. With the remaining money he could go to his hotel, pay his room for the night, and redeem his things. Yet it would also be nice if he got some more money, maybe ten marks again... He wanted to go back to the Passage once more. Right now. But something else occurred to him.

While he was loitering around the train station, across the way he had noticed that besides the toilet there were also washrooms, in which travelers could clean themselves and change clothes. He had nothing to change into, but after these last two days he really needed to wash. He felt ashamed that everything about him was so dirty.

He walked to the station, found an empty washroom, and after generously adding another fifty to the fifty-penny fee, received soap, a second towel, brush, and comb. He put himself in order, as well as he could. His dirty shirt he tucked under his jacket, leaving his chest bare; his pants he smoothed over his boots. He viewed himself in the mirror, and found, as Max had suggested, that he was a good-looking boy, and felt confident to show himself. Now he would learn whether the two of them — Max and he — were right.

Refreshed, cheered, with no trace of fear now, he strode to the Linden and sat, not on one of the benches, but instead on one of the chairs for rent. He sat directly across from the Passage, yet near enough to keep an eye on it and to see what took place. To begin with, he lit another cigarette. He would soon see how things were done.

He had no suspicion of the acquaintance he was to make this very day, within the next half hour.

People streamed by, including some individual gentlemen. He observed them now, carefully, but none paid attention to him, sitting with one leg carelessly crossed over the other, comfortably smoking and digesting his meal.

He began to be bored and decided to walk over to the Passage, when three young men came by, talking loudly and laughing. He could not understand what they were saying, but all three were finely dressed, it seemed to him. Then one of the three, after a quick, brief glance at him, stopped, shouted something to the others — to indicate to the group to go on without him — and then came directly over and sat down on the chair beside him. To his amazement, he heard himself addressed and a hand was extended to him.

"Hello, Chick! Well, how's it going with ya? Have ya not got a cigarette for me?"

He thought at first he had not heard correctly, and stared disconcertedly at the hand extended to him.

This stranger was a slender boy, somewhat older than he — maybe seventeen or eighteen — with brown hair smoothly combed back over his forehead. He had cheerful brown eyes, a strikingly red, as if painted, mouth, and white teeth which, as he laughingly returned the boy's look, he showed as much as possible.

The boy was still so taken aback at being spoken to that he could only bring out the words, "Do we know one another then?"

The stranger laughed out loud. Then, withdrawing his hand, he said in an almost reproachful tone, "Are you really not going to give me a cigarette?"

The boy brought out the package of cigarettes and handed it over to him.

"Thanks! One's enough. For the moment." He handed the package back. "Light?" *What a fresh guy!* the boy said to himself.

Then he noted how he was being examined from head to foot, critically at first, then more approvingly, and he heard the stranger say, "Now tell me, Chick, how long have you been here in Berlin now? And just what is your name? First name only, of course!"

The boy answered, "My name is Gunther...:" and he found the courage to add, "And what is your name, sir?"

"'Sir' is good," the stranger replied, grinning. "What *my* name is? Mine? Mine? Man, where do you come from, that you don't know me? I'm Atze, the refined Atze!"

Now Gunther had to laugh. Atze! He had never before heard such a funny name. The ice was broken.

"What does it stand for, 'Atze'?"

"Atze — well, it just stands for Atze. Or Arthur..."

Leaning over in his chair in the tone of a world-wise Berliner, Atze continued. "Man, you don't know from nothing! I'll just have to take the Chick under my wing as quickly as possible, or else he'll fly wrong. Well, let's see to that — all right, who am I?"

"Atze. The refined Atze" said Gunther, laughing and taken with a sudden liking for the other boy.

Arm in arm they walked along the promenade to Friedrich Street. His new friend said scornfully, "Passage? A boy who thinks highly of himself just doesn't go to the Passage!"

Gunther was astonished. He was not to come out of his astonishment the whole evening.

First they went to a café, not one of the best, because of Gunther's clothes, but still a decent one, where they ate pastry and drank a couple of fine liqueurs. Then to a cinema, and after that a cellar restaurant in a side street, where the food was simple but good, and the portions were large. Everywhere, the refined Atze was recognized. He met acquaintances, and was greeted by name. And everywhere, when Gunther made an attempt to pay, Atze rejected it. "Just never mind, it will be all right," and Atze would cover the whole check.

In the cellar restaurant, at a scrubbed white table, when they were alone, sated and smoking, Gunther told Atze everything — everything that he had to tell — and Atze listened quietly and attentively, without interrupting him. Gunther told of his earlier life in the village, of Max's visit, of his flight to Berlin and the misery of these last days. Finally he told of his encounter with the man who had just given him the ten marks.

Atze pricked up his ears at this. He inquired about details, made Gunther describe the exact appearance of the gentleman, and finally asked what he had received. When Gunther told the amount Atze gave his opinion thoughtfully, again as a Berliner:

"Ten marks is not exactly plenty. But in those duds..."

When Gunther indicated, about midnight, that he must go to his hotel to sleep, Atze said curtly:

"Sleep? You can sleep at my place..." and he packed Gunther into a real automobile. The trip in the auto was the high point of the evening. Gunther was blissful.

Atze was a friend! Gunther had no fear of him. With Atze he would go to the end of the world! Atze listened, and he held nothing back like underhanded Max, the ape! Gunther wanted to learn much more from Atze — everything he did not know. Everything.

At Atze's dwelling, in a respectable-appearing house far up in the north, they did not even have to ring. Standing at the door was an enormously fat woman, with a rosy, good-natured face, wearing a dazzling white nightgown covering huge breasts. She held a burning lamp in her hand, as if expecting the late guests, and she greeted them with the words, "Well, Atze, what kind of a shady little bird have you brought with you again, you shameless rascal, you!"

But Atze, already in her room, took the lamp from her hand, grasped her around the hips, and whirled the reluctant woman around a couple of times.

"Little Mama," he cried, "Little Mama, just think, he lost his virginity only today!"

During this night, as they lay side by side in Atze's bed in his room, with Little Mama audibly snoring, Gunther learned much more. He learned what a hustler was, and what a john was. He learned which gentlemen one should go with, and which not; what one should do, and what not, and what price to ask for. Also, he learned what a cop was, and what an auntie was. An auntie — well, that was just, "oooh nooo! an auntie — like girls when they're young and then like old maids..." Cops however — the police were called that — were the criminal officers who were always after the boys, and against whom you really had to be on your guard. Then there also were the boys over twenty — smart guys, hot heads, toughs — precisely those who were so dangerous to every auntie.

Gunther, awake and entirely spellbound by everything he heard, listened with both ears as if to a revelation. He drank it in. His respect for his new friend knew no bounds. Atze knew everything. There was nothing that Atze did not know.

Atze, however, as much as he enjoyed hearing himself talk, finally grew tired of his own wisdom, and since at the bottom of his black soul he "loved 'em young," he threw himself on Gunther.

PART

2

1

There now followed a splendid time for the young Gunther ... at least it seemed so to him.

He and Atze were together the whole day and Atze took care of everything. First, another suit. In Atze's clothes closet were remarkably many things which did not fit Atze. Most were youthful. Atze had either grown out of them, or they had belonged to other boys. Gunther asked him about it.

"That's not really your suit, is it?"

But he received only a short answer. "It must have been left by someone..."

There were shoes, too, low ones with wide heels, somewhat too large, but still quite wearable. There was underwear, too. And a fine cravat. Atze was big on neckties.

Thus Gunther was newly dressed, from head to foot. Only his straw hat was still suitable, despite the strain it had suffered.

Above all, Atze saw to Gunther's identification papers.

"What," Atze said, "ya don't have any papers! Man, how can ya hit the pavement then? They could arrest ya at any minute."

While Little Mama made coffee, Atze disappeared and stayed away half the morning. When he returned he had identification papers. False ones, of course, but they suited Gunther well.

"So: Your name is Michael Koslowsky, you're fifteen and a half and from Kattowitz. Understood?"

"Kattowitz? Where's that?" replied Gunther.

Atze cut him short. "By the Polacks back there," he said with a wide wave of his hand.

Atze had Gunther repeat everything before carefully tucking the papers into Gunther's inside breast pocket. He gave no hint of where the papers came from.

The two knocked about during the day, but not in the hustler areas of the Linden or the Tauentzien. For these areas Atze had only scorn, speaking with downright rage of the Brandenburg Gate. "The only ones who go there are those who don't have anything more to eat and don't have any place left to stay . . . and they always get arrested there. . . "

Instead, they went into the lounges, especially when evening fell, and then in the lounges of the west. There, everything was outwardly quite decent. At mostly small tables sat more or less well-dressed, often over-elegant young men, many with affected manners, wearing make-up. But others still were quite vigorous and manly, waiting until customers came and sat at their table, or called them to theirs, while light music accompanied the usually softspoken conversations. No one was allowed in without a necktie. Nor, or course, was any female admitted.

Only toward evening, after nine, did it become really full. Many couples showed up, composed of an older man and a younger boy. They sat together and no one approached them.

Then the dancing began, and people swayed to the sound of the violin.

Atze knew everything and everyone. He went from table to table, greeting and being greeted, being invited to join some. Gunther sat alone then.

On the very first evening, in the second lounge, at a still early hour, Gunther made the acquaintance of a gentleman, who sat with him, treated him, and asked few questions. The man did not leave Gunther's side until he finally took Gunther home with him, to a house like Gunther had never seen before. In the morning, Gunther received twenty marks, took a taxi, and rode back to Atze. The evening before, when they separated, Atze had left without even saying goodbye. As a matter of course Gunther handed over to Atze his money, which Atze calmly pocketed as an installment.

And so it went, day by day. Sometimes, when no suitor who found favor in their eyes approached, they came home together, to Little Mama, who was always awake. But most of the time Gunther was taken away — to a hotel, to a strange house, to a quiet corner of another lounge. Neither one ever returned without money, even if it was only what Atze called "table money," money a gentleman shoved into Atze's pocket, while paying the bill for their carousing, for having had Atze's company. There was enough to eat and drink every evening. More than enough. Especially to drink. On the third evening the "Chick" — that became and remained Gunther's name — who was not yet used to all this drinking, became so drunk that he had to be driven home.

Atze paid careful attention to the men with whom his protégé went. If Atze approved the acquaintance, he left Gunther alone with the man, and disappeared. If Atze was opposed, he did not budge from the table or Gunther's side. Once it could have come to an argument, since the john absolutely did not want to let Gunther go — if an argument were at all possible with Atze. Later, asked why he had not let Gunther go, Atze said, "He's got lice!"

When Gunther stared as if Atze had gone crazy, Atze added, "Of course he hasn't got them. But he spanks. Do ya want to get spanked?"

No, Gunther certainly did not want that. Gunther learned about those who spanked, just as he learned, little by little, everything else that he wanted to know — to the extent Atze thought it good for him.

Thus he quickly became used to his new loud and colorful life, as well as to his nickname. He soon lost all bashfulness, and above all, every fear. He learned to answer when he was questioned; never to tell the truth (which was neither expected nor wanted); and to look the gentlemen over, to see if they had "dough" and how much.

He was flattered to be the sought-after new face. He felt no disgust, but he felt no pleasure — he simply went along. In the end, the main thing was the money.

Atze saw to it that Gunther did not receive too little money, nor throw himself away, nor fall into bad hands. Usually, before Gunther went out with a new gentleman, Atze and the man would stop together a moment, whispering and squinting over at Gunther. Sometimes it appeared that something was slipped to Atze before he let Gunther go, or suddenly left himself. But Atze never mentioned anything about it.

Those were splendid days, those early ones. Everything lay behind him — his village and his escape. Behind him, those last days of need, of loneliness and of hunger were all forgotten, along with the cardboard box of belongings in the hotel, up by the Stettin train station, where he no longer went. He had Atze now. Atze was his sworn friend, and Gunther was happy each time he could show Atze his gratitude by handing over what he made. Little Mama, too, seemed satisfied.

Whenever the two boys wanted to eat at home, there was always something good there. However late they returned, Little Mama was always standing above, in her snow-white nightgown, lamp in hand. They grasped her around the waist, while she boxed their ears painlessly. She gossiped and laughed with them, often until morning.

Atze himself was priceless. His good humor and even temper in all situations were astonishing. For him, life had no problems. His motto was: Take what you can, no matter where it comes from! However, as open as he otherwise was, he stubbornly kept silent about this "where."

Once, there appeared at the table of the café where they often sat in the afternoons — drinking and playing dice to kill the long afternoon hours — a young girl who sat down with them. "My fiancée," was Atze's only explanation and he soon left with her, after quickly arranging an appointment with Gunther, who stayed behind. Another time Atze left the lounge late in the evening — which almost never happened — with a gentleman whom he obviously must have known very well, and he laughed strangely when Gunther asked him the next day who that had been. The man had looked like a real criminal. A third time Gunther surprised Atze in Little Mama's lap, in a not exactly motherly embrace. They all three laughed over it. They were generally always laughing over everything. It was a merry time.

It lasted exactly two and a half weeks, during which money was always available in abundance. Then, one day, Atze suddenly vanished.

This was one of Atze's traits — suddenly to stay away for half, or even a whole day, without saying where he was going. Then he would return, as if nothing had happened, without a word of explanation or excuse. Atze did not like to be questioned. Gunther had learned that and had adjusted accordingly.

But this time, Atze stayed away and did not return. When Gunther, who was beginning to be bored, pressured Little Mama, she only said, "What can you do! That's just the way he is. But I know that rascal . . . He'll come back!"

Gunther gave her an uneasy look.

"You can still come here, Chick, if you've got money, and sleep in his bed. I get four marks a night." Until then they had always slept together in Atze's bed, or Gunther had slept on the old sofa in the corner.

Now, Gunther had no money, since he always handed over everything to Atze, but he now knew where to get it. The couple of days until Atze returned would go by all right without him.

Early in the afternoon, when the lounge opened, Gunther went in, but was stoped by the proprietor.

"Not under eighteen! Strict police regulation!"

"But I've been here already so often—" Gunther stammered.

"Yes, but not alone. Where is your friend?"

So Gunther went into another lounge where he was allowed to sit, but he was not served. Besides Gunther, another boy, even younger, sat there. As the lounge began to fill up, the waiter drove them out.

What was he to do now?

He was not supposed to be a streetwalker, but what else remained for him? He went to do Tauentzien Street.

It was toward evening, and a huge mass of people crowded one side of the street. An elegant but very mixed public — West Berlin. Many young girls, many young gentlemen. He had not gone twenty steps before he was signaled into the side street. Then he had five marks, though that too had been forbidden him — "Never under ten!"

He slept again in their bed and at noon, after enough sleep, he got coffee from Little Mama. But the next days were bad.

He no longer ventured into the lounges. Of the gentlemen he had met there, he knew none closely. He had hardly heard their names, had forgotten their houses.

But even if by chance one gentleman had remained in his memory, Gunther would never have ventured there. Even if he had by chance met one of the gentlemen, the man would hardly have picked him up again. Never had he been picked up a second time. Gunther was for them too indifferent to the one thing they wanted. When they saw him again in the lounges, they hardly knew him, but instead went with others.

What was left for him, as long as Atze was away, but to walk the streets — Tauentzien Street, or even the Passage? This he did but, to his astonishment, without particular success.

There in the west, nothing happened the whole evening. At the Passage, which he entered and walked through without excitement but with a feeling of discomfort, he was driven out by hateful looks from young guys loitering about, and by the threatening looks of several men who were quite certainly criminal officers.

He had been spoken to by a repulsive old guy who had muttered something about three marks. Gunther would have liked to spit in his face. With effort, he caught a traveler later in the Friedrich Street station, and in the man's hotel nearby Gunther received six marks.

It was now too late and he was too tired to go to Little Mama's. Besides, he could not give her four of the six marks — what would remain then to eat with tomorrow?

He remembered the hotel in which he had slept earlier. A room for the night there had cost one mark fifty. He found the hotel. The old waiter wearing his stained tailcoat was still there, and recognized the boy again when he asked for his things.

"What? Those old rags?" A peddler had taken them and had

not given him as much for them as the boy still owed him. Could he pay today? Yes? Well then, just hand it over right now!

Gunther paid and went to his old, small room. But he did not find again the peaceful sleep of the first nights. *If only Atze were here* was his recurring thought. Things just did not go along without Atze. The next days were no better. They were worse.

He walked his feet sore. First, a long hour in the Passage, until that became uncomfortable. Then, in Friedrich Street, all the way down to the Halle Gate.

He made enough that he did not have to go hungry, and could sit half the day in a movie house, and pay for his hotel in the evening. But he did not like his life now, at all.

A constant rage boiled in him. He, who in these weeks had not known money worries, who had sat in club chairs, at finely covered tables, with coffee and liqueurs before him, eating fancy cakes with whipped cream, waiting until men came to *him*, who had pocketed mostly twenty marks, once even fifty, another time thirty — he now walked the streets until he almost dropped, to finally go with the first comer! No, that did not suit him. But what was he to do?

The fifth day was really bad. It was jinxed — not a john far or wide, where they were usually stepping on your heels!

There was still enough money for a couple of sausages, but no more for cigarettes, which had become indispensable. He finally decided to inquire at Little Mama's, despite her strict prohibition not to come without four marks. But he had to know if Atze was there again, or if she had heard from or knew about him.

Little Mama was at home — she never went out — and she received him most ungraciously, not even letting him in at first.

"I'm a poor woman and Atze exploits me enough as it is. Atze? No, he's not been here again. For the present he probably won't come back at all. It's probably become too hot for him. That's why he skipped out. I'll tell ya, Chick, you can come anytime, but only when you've got money. You can surely make out, such a good-looking boy like you!" and she slammed the door in his face.

If he had not run into another boy on Unter den Linden — he had come back the whole long way by foot — an acquaintance of

Atze whom he touched for two marks after much begging ("But only because you know Atze"), he would have had to sleep that night in the Tiergarten. He woke up hungry and spent the new day hungry.

Finally, late in the afternoon, he found a pick-up. But what a disgusting little bandy-legged guy it was, with head sitting between hunchback shoulders, eyes lurking behind glasses — and how unclean, how old!

"Coming with me? A quickie. Three marks..."

Again only three marks! But what was Gunther to do?

"Where to then?" he asked.

"Just come along!" They walked into a sidestreet, entered a house, climbed up empty, dead-silent, carpeted stairs.

Here? But if someone came?

No one is coming.

And no one came.

Below again, after the short stay, his stomach turned from disgust. Gunther wanted his money. The old man, in the nearest doorway, brought out a wallet whose thickness aroused confidence.

"Wait here a moment. I just have to make change," and the old man slipped around the corner.

Gunther waited. He waited five, ten minutes. He waited a quarter of an hour. Meanwhile he was thinking about where he would go now, and what he would eat. He waited a half hour. Finally he realized — he had been gypped!

What a scoundrel! What a swindler! Taking away a poor boy's hard-earned money! And the man had money, he had seen it! But if he saw him again, he would have the man arrested! Fix him for good, and on the spot! Tears came to his eyes.

He crept back to the Linden and sat down to brood.

It served him right, he thought. Why had he not obeyed Atze! Atze had said to him more than once, "If you go for a quickie, get your money first!" Now he was empty-handed. He had no more will, none at all. First to go with such a skunk, and then to be cheated besides!

He was brooding and rummaging through his pockets. Not a

nickel, not one penny left. Only a broken matchbox and a squashed cigarette butt. He smoked it up.

He *had* to have money — this very day — no matter where it came from. Where did it usually come from? From now on he would look those guys over! No one was to come to *him* again for the sake of "come along and pay later"! Not to *him* again!

He looked up and glanced around. No one was even looking at him. But over there on the bench? That young man? Was he not looking over at Gunther? Was he one? He did not seem so. But he was looking over. At Gunther?

No matter. It must be tried. He got up.

2

oung Hermann Graff had adjusted himself, one might say, to the city and to his work.

His days had a purpose. He gave the evenings purpose by reading at home, or attending a theater and a good concert. Yet mostly during these magical spring days — each one better than the other in the purity of the air and the gentle luster of the first sun — he made trips in the countryside. Out to Treptow, or to Wannsee. And on Sundays, out to Potsdam, which he loved above all others.

He also spent many an evening under the trees of the Tiergarten, where he soon knew every turn of the paths. When tired of wandering around, he sat in one of the outdoor cafés on the Spree, near the pavilion. In one café was a table in a corner, far from the other guests. There he sat many an evening, the Spree below, and above him the branches of old trees.

This spring was so lovely that it seemed impossible not to be happy. Alone with himself and the magical charm around him, why was he not happy?

Something was missing. He knew well what it was.

He lacked a friend to share this joy with him. A friend, to be beside him in his walks and trips, to be with him after the long day's work.

He wanted a young friend, a quite young friend, still impressionable, before whom the world lay as a closed book full of suspense and mystery, whose first pages he wanted to turn and read with him, making clear to him what he did not yet understand.

A young friend whom he would love, who would love him in return. Such a friend — did destiny have him in store for him? Where was he?

Was it possible to hunt for him? No. And again no. One day, this friend simply had to stand before him, and smile at him. "Here I am!" Yet these first weeks had come and gone without having brought Hermann's dream.

The boy must, of course, be a boy who was not his friend just because Hermann gave him presents. The same interests must bind them together — although he did not really know what kind of interests they would have to be! The two must be able to talk together, about anything and everything, just as friends do — although he was not really clear about what they would talk about!

Such a friend could not be found in the street. But where else? That was the big question.

However, it was probably only in the street that chance could bring them together. He himself knew no one in Berlin. He sought no acquaintances. To make visits; to be invited into families — possibly with still marriageable daughters — to join a club in order to talk shop ... such thoughts filled him with secret dread. Only chance could bring this good luck to him.

Such a fateful chance as on his first afternoon, when so much came together? That sudden secret attraction, that indescribable feeling — "was this he?" — and then that entirely incomprehensible disappearance, at that very moment, and forever and ever!

He still sometimes thought of that strange boy from the Passage, who had run away from him. At first, he would see him again — the disheveled, dark blond hair, the light walk, the odd blue-gray eyes. And that peculiar twitch of the upper lip...

But he no longer could see him so clearly. It escaped him, this strange face; it grew pale, disappeared. The moment had been too brief.

Hermann was not thinking of him at all today. Almost four weeks had already gone since his arrival. He was coming from the Tiergarten, and wanted to go to the library to consult a book he needed for his work. Walking down the middle promenade of the Linden, he smiled over the contrasting colors of the first, new green leaves on the trees, and of the golden yellow, freshly raked gravel.

In the gravel walkway his foot stopped still.

On one bench a boy was sitting, his arms propped on his knees, and his face buried in his hands so that only his bare head and the back of his neck showed. But that neck — where had he seen that neck before?

The blood streamed to his heart. He walked on. He turned back. He had to turn back. The boy was sitting there as if asleep. Was it really he? *Could* it be? It was not possible!

Hermann felt he could not walk further. He walked a few steps back and sat down — as his legs gave way under him — on a bench opposite. It would have been quite impossible for him to go closer to make sure. What if it really was he? — and he ran away again?

He looked across as if spellbound. It really was he. The boy was wearing a different suit than on that day; but a straw hat, like he had been holding that day, lay on the bench beside him. In place of the heavy boots, the boy had on worn-out and obviously too large oxfords. The suit appeared to be thrown together, as if it had not been purchased or selected for him. The coat was too big, the pants too short. But it was he. It must be. That neck! That hair!

He could still recognize nothing of the face buried in the boy's hands. His thoughts raced. Should he walk over, sit beside him, remain still and wait until the boy looked up? Should he speak to the boy, ask him if he recognized him? Ask him why he ran away so quickly that time?

He could not do it. A growing uneasiness, a secret fear welled up in him, holding him in his place. He could only watch steadily, waiting for the first signs of life to return to the small, bent-over figure. Minutes passed — five, ten? — but he did not know how many.

Finally the boy moved. His hands dropped. He stretched himself, looking around. Then the boy seemed to look over at Hermann. The boy's expression appeared angry and cross, as if awakened from sleep.

Hermann now saw the boy's face. Because of the distance, it was not entirely clear — but he recognized that face. It *was* he!

At the same time, it appeared to Hermann that the boy was inspecting him too. He was not mistaken, was he? Was it possible that the boy recognized him? Would the boy jump up and run away again, as if hunted?

The boy rose slowly, as if tired, and walked, without glancing back, slowly toward the gate.

What should I do? Should I follow? The fear of losing him again made Hermann totally indecisive. Then the same fear drove him on. Hermann rose and slowly followed.

The boy had stopped, but without looking around, as if he were waiting. Now Hermann was beside him, and with a terrible effort, searched for the first words. The boy looked up at him and and Hermann spoke with difficulty.

"Excuse me, sir, if I speak to you. But haven't we seen one another before?"

The boy's odd eyes looked at him, not with fear or anxiety, not startled or curious, but with complete indifference.

"Where then?" he heard the boy ask in return. The young voice was bright and clear.

"In — the Passage. About four weeks ago..."

Four weeks ago, Gunther thought, *I've not even been here that long. Or have I?* Gunther had stopped counting the days and weeks. Then it must be one of those men from the early time. Gunther looked at Hermann. He had no recollection. He had not gone with this man, had he? If so, he would probably have recognized him. But those had been mostly older men, not a young one, like this man. Perhaps the man had just spoken to him, and nothing had come of it. So many had done that. Besides, it was really all the same. Best to act as if he remembered, he decided. Gunther looked at Hermann again, and thought, *He appears decently dressed. Does he have money? Young people usually do not have much. And how excited he is! He probably can hardly wait! For sure he can hardly speak. And the way he looks at me!*

They could not remain standing where they were. People were looking at them. The both felt it, so they walked on further beside one another.

Hermann thought and thought. what should he say so as not to lose the boy again? He finally spoke. "Do you have time for a bit of a walk? In the Tiergarten perhaps, if it's all right with you. . ." He was thinking of his garden café in the pavilion. There they would be able to talk undisturbed.

Rage welled up again in Gunther. *In the Tiergarten, naturally, again in the Tiergarten! So he does not have money for a room in a hotel, or he wants to save it. So probably not much will come from this. And why did he say "sir" to me?* No one before had addressed Gunther with "sir." "All right, then, to the Tiergarten, for all I care."

Gunther resolved that he would no longer let himself be caught with fine words, as this had the appearance of being to him. If he let himself be taken into the Tiergarten, tired and hungry as he was, he wanted to see money, beforehand. Letting himself be gypped a second time, on the same day, was not going to happen!

Hermann was thinking meanwhile, *Of course he recognized me again! Even if he doesn't say so. Otherwise, he would not have stopped, and waited until I spoke to him. But why is he so sullen? Perhaps he is tired. It appears it isn't going well for him. Does he have an occupation? Probably not, for otherwise how could he be free at this hour of the day? Perhaps he has no work at all. But I must not just ask him about it. That would be obtrusive. He seems tired, with no desire to go for a walk.* They had reached Paris Place. Cautiously, Hermann asked, "Perhaps you're tired and would rather not walk further? Should we sit in a café and enjoy something?"

The boy nodded *yes* for an answer.

They left the Linden and turned into the sidestreets on the north. Hermann spoke, fearful that it could all suddenly come to an end, and he would no longer have the boy beside him.

"We could go to a restaurant, if you would rather?"

The boy finally opened his mouth. "It's all the same to me..." He sounded almost angry, at any rate not friendly. He was thinking to himself, *food, just food, and as soon as possible.*

They were now near the Spree, and at the sign of a simple, decent beer house they entered, finding the pub almost empty. They found a table in one of the niches in the back room.

They sat opposite one another. Gunther immediately reached for the menu that was lying before him.

"What will you have? Please, select whatever you like," said Hermann.

Again the answer sounded unfriendly: "Doesn't matter. A cutlet..."

The waitress arrived at their table and asked what she should bring.

"Two cutlets. And beer? Yes, beer. Light. Two glasses," Hermann told her.

After the waitress left, Hermann felt he must finally give an explanation.

"You seem angry with me, sir, that I spoke to you. But we have seen one another before. I wanted—"

He went no further. He felt it was stupid, what he was saying. Gunther looked at him. He was much too hungry to follow Hermann's words, or even to just listen to them. He said, "Why do you always say 'sir' to me?"

Hermann did not know what to say. However, since the beer was now before him, he responded, "Well then, without formalities..." and he raised his glass.

Gunther paid no attention to Hermann's answer, and drank hastily. Then the food arrived, and he set himself to it without a word.

It was a relief for Hermann. He did not need to say anything more now, and just gazed into the face before him. At the same time, he felt impolite just to watch the boy eat. *How hungry he must be! How fast, almost greedily, he is eating!* Hermann occupied himself with his own plate, but he was unable to swallow a bite, he was so nervous inside. He reached for a newspaper. But he only looked at it, without reading.

Finally the boy finished and shoved his plate away. Hermann, too, shoved away his untouched plate, and the newspaper, and looked into the face opposite him. In the dimness of the narrow room the boy appeared strange to him, but of an enchanting beauty, so that he could now no longer take his gaze from him. He felt that he had to speak, but he did not know what he should say. He would have liked to remain sitting here for hours, all the time looking into that face.

Gunther, too, kept silent. He, too, did not know what to say. He recalled what Atze said — "Always wait! You get the most that way." A man like this, however, had never come along before. Gunther sat there, staring at Hermann, and made not a sound, thinking. "He is looking at me in a friendly way, and seems certainly a decent man, with his clean-shaven face and his regular, young features. What would he be likely to give me?"

Gunther decided something must be said. He asked, "Do you perhaps have a cigarette?"

Hermann hastily reached into his pocket. A smoke, of course; how could he have forgotten?

"Yes. Here, you're welcome. I hope they're good enough!"

As the two smoked, they became somewhat more comfortable, and questions came.

They asked each other's names and gradually began a conversation. It dragged a bit, since Hermann worried whether he was questioning too much, while Gunther wondered more and more about this john, sitting here, ordering beer again, making no move to finally come to the goal. Yet it did not matter to him — it was nice sitting there.

What questions, however, were being asked! "It's an interrogation," Gunther thought, and he began coolly to lie with each new question.

Work? No, he had none now. Lost his position. Friends? Sure, he had friends, but they don't help. You only have friends when you have money. Relatives? No, no relatives. Where does he live then? Together with another boy, but he couldn't stay there longer, for he was already a week behind in his rent and couldn't pay. Last night? Well, in the Tiergarten.

Hermann Graff's heart contracted. *It is going badly for him! Therefore his hunger!* Hermann felt he had, therefore, come at just the right time. Pity welled up in him, that most dangerous of all matchmakers of love, and made him ask whether he might help. Help him as a friend — for that's what he would like to be to him, a true friend!

Now Gunther was dumbfounded. *Is this man serious or is he making fun of me? Help? For nothing? As a friend?*

Then it occurred to him, "a steady relationship!" That's what this man wants. Gunther, however, did not want it. Atze had always said, "Just no relationship!" But why shouldn't he let himself be helped, if the man absolutely wanted to?

Hermann, however, abruptly stopped questioning, and kept silent, thinking.

Then he laid his hand lightly and tenderly over the slim and dirty hand of the boy. How beautiful it was, this small and tender hand with its unclean but well-grown nails! How warm and beautiful it was, this hand, which he was touching for the first time! He said, as if entreating, softly and urgently, "Let me help you, Gunther! I would like to help you! You should suffer no more need!"

Gunther did not answer. Hermann's hand was not withdrawn. The boy looked straight ahead, crumpled up the remaining bread, and reached for a new cigarette. Hermann spoke further. "We'll see one another again. As soon as can be — even tomorrow. I just have to think it over. I will see if I can find a position for you. I can't promise it to you today, but I will help you, as well as I can. Where will you sleep today? Do you know a decent hotel that will take you for tonight? We'll see, then, tomorrow where we can find a room for you — with good and decent people. Can you manage with this?" Hermann reached into his breast pocket and drew out his wallet. How difficult it was to offer money! "Can you get along with this until tomorrow?" A blue bill was furtively pressed into the boy's hand.

With a quick glance Gunther had seen that the bill was five marks. Not much! However, he was getting it for nothing — the meal besides, and cigarettes. He quickly shoved the money into his pants pocket.

Gunther assumed they could go now. He finally grasped that Hermann wanted nothing more today. They left, after the bill had been taken care of.

Outside, near the bridge, they stopped. Hermann again held Gunther's warm hand in his.

"Will you be here on this bridge tomorrow afternoon at a quarter past five, Gunther, and wait for me? I'll come from work at five. I can't any earlier. But about a quarter past five I'll be here. And you will be too, won't you?"

The gray eyes — they appeared now more gray than blue — looked up at him. It sounded quite earnest, what he said, "If I've promised to come, I will come."

They shook hands, and parted. Gunther walked away with quick and light steps, and without looking around, but Hermann immediately stopped and looked after the small figure which disappeared around the corner. How beautifully he walked! It seemed to him he should rush after the boy. Call him back. Say something more to him. Something important. Something forgotten. Much more. But he did not.

He looked at his watch: It was not yet eight. They had been together hardly longer than an hour. What an hour! Or had it all been only a dream?

He felt unable to return to his room. The evening was so lovely after the hot day — now came the cool of evening. He walked slowly to the pavilion. He found his old place, unoccupied. He had seen *him* again!

What he had no longer hoped for, what he had almost buried and forgotten, had become reality — incomprehensible, but undeniable reality! He had found him again. He had sat opposite him. He had held his hand in his own, just a moment before. The fleeing shadows of a fleeting moment had taken on tangible form. Did that picture-become-life hold what its appearance promised?

His senses, caught in the spell of those eyes, in the sound of that voice — which he had heard for the first time — in each movement of those shoulders and hands, his senses affirmed the question. His reason understood nothing yet and tried to resist.

Now if he tried to visualize that face again, he had to succeed. For it had not been one minute, not just one second, in which the boy had shown up and disappeared again — no, he had seen that face before him a full hour, close enough to touch. With a single movement of his hand he could have reached out to it, held it, caressed it.

He wanted to call it back before him. He tried laying his hand over his eyes.

He saw it. Those eyes, whose color he was unable to name, appeared to him unfathomable — were they gray, were they blue, were they both? Did not a green-gold gleam sometimes glimmer in the pupils of those eyes, with their strikingly long lashes and the light lines under them? The soft, smooth cheeks — did they show dimples when he smiled? The light brown hair was thick and uncombed over the narrow forehead. The full mouth with its no longer quite so red and fresh lips as before, the not quite regular, but white, rows of teeth.

He saw the face before him again, and recalled what had especially struck him. Often, usually when questioned, before answering, the upper right corner of the boy's mouth raised a bit, with a light twitching, so that a tooth became visible. So curious, but so attractive, too. . .

He saw the face before him, and now knew that he had never in his life seen anything more charming and infatuating than the face of this boy named Gunther!

Then he tried to visualize Gunther's figure. It was a boyishly slim, undeveloped and tender figure, which had nothing girlish about it, with a thin neck, slender shoulders, and extraordinarily beautiful hands with slim fingers. Finally, he recalled his walk, that light, careless, but tired walk. . . And he knew at once that he would have given his life's salvation to enclose that figure in his arms!

No doubt, he reasoned, Gunther must be from a good family. How different he was from these other guys, with their uncouth, fresh, and loud conduct, their crudeness and insolence! Gunther was neither crude, nor loud nor fresh.

But friendly, no, Gunther had not been friendly. Rather, just the opposite — almost unfriendly, unapproachable, rejecting — taciturn and sulky. How was that to be explained? With each answer he gave himself, he sought to excuse Gunther (as we who love do, and have always done, so as not to lose — even in our own eyes — what we love).

"Gunther had followed me. No, had waited for me. Of course, because Gunther had recognized me, from seeing me that first time. But why, then had Gunther not admitted it? Because he was ashamed of having run away that time, so irrationally? Today, he had been unfriendly, grouchy even. Yet how could one be friendly and cheerful, if one had slept outside, and had eaten nothing for twenty-four hours? But, even after the meal, he had still remained so quiet and withdrawn — it was probably shyness with a new acquaintance, his uneasiness under my many intrusive (even if so well-meant) questions. Would Gunther have preferred to be left to bare his own heart to me, a stranger, to me, who am myself so scrupulously withdrawn in regard to others?

"No, it was me who had behaved so falsely, and quite unreasonably!" he felt now. To be sure, there was also an excuse for him. He had never really had contact with boys of Gunther's age, had never spoken much with such boys. With the few to whom he was irresistibly drawn, the secret fear of being misunderstood, and the shyness of not finding the right word, had always closed his mouth.

He felt he should have begun quite differently. He should not have talked about the first meeting at all. He should have realized that he had before him a poor, half-starved, young chap, a lonely little chap obviously abandoned by all the world.

Hermann felt he himself had been too awkward. If he had presented himself as cheerful and unaffected, the boy would have come out of himself and everything would have been different in that first hour, so often the decisive one.

He tormented himself further in his thoughts: "My questions had bored him. Was he really full from the one portion of food? I should have ordered another course. Did I give him enough money?" Indeed it seemed enough to Hermann. He, under such circumstances, would have managed with five marks until the day after tomorrow. He could have given him still more — ten, or even twenty marks. But then Gunther, whom he wanted to help further, would have received a false idea of Hermann Graff's circumstances.

Everything had been wrong. Wrong, also, that hasty parting. Now Hermann did not even know where to find him again, if Gunther were prevented from coming tomorrow. No power on earth would prevent Hermann from being on the bridge at a quarter past five.

He felt he should not have allowed Gunther to go away like that. He should have accompanied him to a hotel, paid for him, entrusted the manager and clerk with taking good care of him, and then tomorrow picked him up there himself. That would have been the right thing! But now it was too late.

Poor little chap! Life has certainly treated him harshly. He probably had never known real love — no friend by his side to help him. No one to care for him in this monstrously big, strange, hostile city.

How needy he seemed! That suit — not at all the right kind of suit for him, so randomly bought, piece for piece. By what second-hand dealer did he hunt that up! And how tired he had been! And above all, how hungry!

He had been serious — much too serious for his young years! Could he also be cheerful, like other boys his age, heartily cheerful and carefree? He had smiled once, and that smile had been almost the most beautiful thing about him. That was when Hermann promised to procure work for him.

Gunther was not to be disappointed in him, Hermann resolved. He would spare no trouble or effort in procuring Gunther a new position, and until he was able to take care of himself, Hermann would stand by his side. Hermann Graff was determined his boy should not suffer hunger anymore, and should always have a roof over his head. Hermann was there now for that.

Right away, tomorrow, he would ask in his office if there was a position available for Gunther. Then he thought it perhaps better to wait one more day, and hear tomorrow what kind of work Gunther would prefer. Perhaps he would prefer an apprenticeship, with a businessman, or in a bank office. For that, Hermann must know what Gunther's previous schooling was, know much more about him.

Tomorrow! How long yet until then! A whole night, and half a day away! An eternity! And if Gunther does not return?

Fear rose in him. Gunther would be lost to him again and what new chance would ever bring them together again?

No, no foolish fear. Why should he not come? He had no one here, perhaps no one in the whole world to help him! He would come. Surely he would come.

What was it, then, that still tormented him? What kept him from being entirely happy, now, when joy and jubilation should be in his heart? He did not know.

The pavilion emptied out. It was late. Night came — the summer night, cooler than the hot day, but not cool for him. From the water sounded the last voices of the passing rowers — lovers.

Then it came, the longing. It came on silver wings, clung to him, took possession of him, more and more, stronger and stronger, as if to smother him. And all his thoughts were lost on Gunther: "Oh, if he were here! If he were sitting here opposite me! No, here by my side! If I could see his sweet face again, hear again his bright voice, if I might lay my hand on his, hold it, forever, forever!... Why is he not here? Why not with me? Why did I let him go? Why? Why!...

Meanwhile Gunther, overjoyed that all the foolish talk was over, had strolled down the Linden. He no longer had any desire to go into the Passage again, but five marks were a bit too few. He decided to go through once, and if he did not find anyone, then before looking up his old hotel, he would spend the evening in the movie at the Stettin train station. A film with Harry Piel was running, which he just *had* to see — Harry Piel sprang from a burning airplane onto a speeding railroad train.

Nothing was doing in the Passage. He had just turned the corner into Friedrich Street when who stood before him but Atze!

They ran into one another's arms.

"Man, Chick, how did you get here?" Gunther was greeted with astonishment, as if he had been the one who had stayed away.

At first Gunther felt angry, but all his anger faded before the jovial face of Atze and in the joy of seeing him again. He asked, with a bare attempt at being angry, "Just where have you been?"

But Atze did not answer. Instead he shoved his arm under Gunther's and said, confidentially, "Tell me, Chick, have you got any dough? I'm dead out. And I don't have to tell you I'm hungry!"

Gunther did not want to come out with his five marks right away. So he protested sternly, "Not even a nickel!"

Atze tried to make a sad face, but did not succeed, and then said casually, "Well, then let's just go to the Bear Cellar and Emil will have to put it on the cuff..."

They went to the cellar pub where, the first day of their acquaintance, they had sat at the scrubbed white table, and where there were such gigantic portions of food.

They had hardly finished eating when Gunther told, down to the last details, how he had been living, at first with an undertone of resentment, but then with the babbling joy at being able to pour out his heart to his long-missed friend.

Atze listened calmly. The complaints over the bad days left him cold. The story about the lounges seemed not to please him. Little Mama's conduct was, however, understandable. And the guy who bilked him — well, that was Gunther's own fault: "How come you didn't keep your eyes open?..."

Gunther began to get angry, not the least over Atze's exaggerated Berlin accent. Capable now of the current turns of speech himself, Gunther said,"Man, what's with you! No one here talks like that."

"But me!" said Atze. "Just like that!"

When Gunther began to talk about his last acquaintance, the "boring john" who wanted to find him work and help him, who had begun by talking "nonsense" to him, and then in the end wanted nothing from him, Atze paid attention. At first, he said,

"Ah ha, you swindler! You do have some dough!" Then, to Gunther's amazement, Atze had him tell everything, in fine detail. Atze leaned back in his chair, which he always did when a matter became serious for him, and finally said, with concern and reproach, "Chick, Chick! You still notice nothing. Will you never get smart? The man is in love with you!"

Between them they had discussed nearly everything, but never love. That topic had never come up. Gunther looked at his friend almost as bewildered as in the first days of their acquaintance.

Atze, however, remained serious. He ordered two large cognacs and, leaning back, continued. "There's no such thing as love. At least it's never yet happened to me. But if it did — Chick, pay attention to what I'm telling you now — if one of them was to fall in love with me, I would really take him for a ride!"

With that he got up, paid the check with Gunther's money, and took him home to Little Mama.

3

othing was left but for Gunther to show up at his meeting with Hermann Graff although he did not in the least feel like doing so. For one thing, Atze had ordered him to go, plus Atze had left him only fifty pennies when he left in the early morning. Again, Atze left without saying when he would return.

So in the afternoon, after working the streets unsuccessfully, Gunther arrived punctually at the appointed corner by the bridge. His new friend was already standing there.

Hermann had a hard day's work behind him, which had left him little time to think about anything, but his face lit up when he saw Gunther. *So he did come!* Hermann was downright joyful.

"Well, Gunther, what shall we do now? I suppose it's still too early to eat?"

Gunther thought in astonishment, "What kind of nonsense was this again? Too early to eat? Why? Couldn't you always eat, at any time of day?" He could, at least.

Hermann saw his astonishment and it occurred to him that the boy was probably hungry again. He hastened to add, "But if you want to, we can eat right away..."

They went to yesterday's restaurant and sat at the same table, in the same seats, opposite one another. This time Hermann also ordered something for himself. It seemed to him more tactful not to let Gunther eat alone, although for Hermann it was still too early — he never ate before eight in the evening.

Hermann would have liked to pose a hundred questions to Gunther. How had it gone with him since yesterday? Where had he slept? What had he done the whole day? Had he tried to find work? Had he gotten along with his money? But to begin, he asked none. He had decided to ask as few questions as possible. The boy should have confidence in him (or gain it, if he did not yet have it) to tell everything of his own accord. So he kept silent, and waited.

For the present, the business of eating completely occupied Gunther, and Hermann saw with pleasure that he really enjoyed it. When the boy was finished, he asked, smiling, "Tell me, Gunther, could you still eat another portion like that?..."

Gunther calmly answered, "Why not?"

After the second helping came to an end, Gunther appeared truly satisfied. They looked at one another — Gunther seeing this "odd john," who spent so much and still wanted nothing, and Hermann seeing the fine face, slightly red from the work of eating. Then Hermann asked, all of a sudden, "What are your parents, Gunther?"

Gunther answered hesitantly. "My father," he said, "my father, I don't know. I believe he was a baron ... and owned an estate called Gunth ... that's why I'm called Gunther..." He had already forgotten that, according to his papers, he had an entirely different name. But then he had not yet been asked for papers, and he resolved not to show them either.

"And your mother?"

"My mother was gone when I was still quite small. I always lived with my grandparents."

"His hands," thought Hermann, "that's the reason for those hands ... and for..."

"Shall we go for a short walk, Gunther?"

Gunther looked at the clock on the wall.

"Yes. But I don't have much time. I have to go to my previous landlady's. She still has some things of mine. I also still owe her something..."

"But it's still early—"

"Yeah, sure. But the old woman goes to bed at eight and the house is closed up early. Then I can no longer get in—"

"Perhaps you can just stay there again and sleep there."

"No," thought Gunther. "For if I say yes, he will give me only money to eat with and not another five marks to sleep with." So he continued his yarn, making it up just to get away again quickly.

"That won't do. The room has already been rented again."

Disappointed, but calm, Hermann remained silent as they walked along. On the bridge, he stopped and pulled himself together. Everything should be just as Gunther wanted. Only in that way could Hermann gain his confidence.

"Yes, you're right, Gunther. I was hoping that we would get to know one another better today, but it's probably better for you to go directly to your landlady, so that you don't arrive too late. Take this until tomorrow. Then we will see — you will have more time."

He inconspicuously shoved a bill into Gunther's pocket.

"And tomorrow, do you want to be here tomorrow, about three o'clock at this bridge?"

He listened almost fearfully for the answer. But Gunther promised. They shook hands.

This time Hermann did not look after Gunther left, although he did stay for a while and look into the water at his feet. He was upset and sad. He had pictured the day so very differently. Then he felt so tired that he went directly home and soon went to bed.

"Thank God that's over with!" was Gunther's thought. He was rid of Hermann Graff and he had money. He drew out the bill — again five marks. He could eat nothing more, but he wanted to finally see that interesting film, which he had not gone to yesterday because of Atze. He hoped it was still running today.

On Friedrich Street as he was about to board the bus to the Stettin train station, Gunther was approached by Saxon, a little guy three years older but hardly taller than himself. Saxon had a pale, vicious face and seemed to show up everywhere. He did everything, and therefore always found lovers. None of the other boys could stand him, but no one ever got rid of him. With his long stride and swinging arms, he was on his legs the whole day, and he never came out of the Passage. He knew how to talk and, if not better than Atze, could outlast him. Nothing got him down. He shook off rudeness as a duck does water, and he was so used to beatings that he did not feel them anymore. He always maintained that he had not a penny in his pocket, but he was always flush.

"Chick, where ya headed for?"

Although he was from Saxony — hence his nickname — Berlin had wiped out the friendly accent of Saxon's home. Gunther was angry, but had to answer.

"I'll go with you!" And he followed Gunther to the top of the bus before he could be refused.

Naturally Gunther had to pay for both of them at the movie, and pay again when they were sitting and drinking together afterwards. When Gunther finally wanted to go to his hotel, he saw that not enough was left of the five marks to sleep there.

"Well, what does that hurt! Just come along with me to the flop."

"Where?"

"Why, to the flop, where I always sleep."

The flophouse was a foul hotel whose doors never stood still, night or day. There, along with four others they found three unclean beds, each for two men — Gunther and Saxon together, one mark the night per head. Gunther would be glad if he came out the next day without having caught crabs (or worse).

Early in the morning — for they had to be out of the bed by nine — they were again knocking about together. It was simply not possible to get away from Saxon, so Saxon also learned the story of Gunther's latest acquaintance. Saxon saw it from a purely businesslike standpoint.

"Course ya got to go, when ya get five marks every time."

Gunther realized that too, especially since between them

they did not have twenty pennies. They had to roam around the streets and the Friedrich Street train station, hungry, until three o'clock.

Three o'clock came.

"When will ya be done?" asked Saxon. "You can get it over within an hour. Then let's go to Uncle Paul's, and in the evening to the Adonis Lounge. I'll wait here."

"Who was Uncle Paul? What was the Adonis Lounge?" Gunther knew neither the one nor the other.

"Well, if you don't already know them, then it's really high time you got to know them," was Saxon's opinion.

Now Gunther really was curious. It was agreed that Saxon would wait nearby.

At three, Gunther went to the bridge. What he intended to say to Hermann in order to get away again as soon as possible, he had already more or less figured out.

4

gain his odd friend was already there, and again, joy seemed to come over his serious face as he saw Gunther walking toward him.

In the morning, reluctantly — for he usually spoke with his colleagues and employees only when necessary — he had consulted with the manager of the packaging department, asking if some kind of position was available for a young person, as apprentice, or if nothing else, as office boy. The manager had shaken his head, "Not to be thought of. Everything is taken." It was no secret that from now until summer, a position for a young boy was probably not readily found anywhere. In Berlin there were thousands of young boys around. Here in Berlin was not like in the provinces, though Hermann might not want to believe it. So there was no chance of a position where he might keep an eye on Gunther.

But today he did not want to let Gunther leave, like yesterday, entirely unquestioned. They would be together the whole afternoon, until evening. Hermann wanted to take Gunther somewhere into the open air, and discuss everything quietly and thoroughly — how everything was to be now.

It happened differently. For as soon as he began, "Well now, shall we spend the whole afternoon—" Gunther cut him short: "I don't have a long time today. I have to leave right away—"

"For heaven's sake, whatever for?"

Gunther told him his uncle had arrived, and had written him that he should expect him.

His uncle? He had said nothing at all about an uncle: "I thought you had no relatives?"

"No, not here," Gunther explained, but he did in his province, he told Hermann, and his uncle had written.

"To where did he write? You don't have any kind of fixed address."

Oh yes, Gunther explained. When he had gone by his landlady's yesterday evening, the letter had been there. A letter from an uncle who was coming through Berlin on a trip, and whom Gunther was to meet at the train station at four o'clock. This evening. The uncle was traveling on, but Gunther had to go there without fail.

Hermann became very serious, looking at Gunther as he spoke. The almost blue eyes were looking up at him so innocently that he rejected his every suspicion as wicked and unworthy. But he still remained serious and kept silent.

Finally, while the boy stood waiting before him, Hermann spoke as determinedly as possible.

"Good! If it must be, then go on. I realize that you can't keep your relative waiting. But tell me one thing, Gunther! Do we become friends now? Do you want me to help you and find work for you? Then say so plainly. And if not, then say that just as frankly. I will not force myself on you." Then somewhat softer and hesitantly, he added, "For, the way it was yesterday, and is today — you realize it can't go on like this."

Gunther's eyes, those beautiful eyes, were looking up at him.

To Gunther, the five marks threatened to vanish. "Of course I want to. I'm really happy that I have a friend to help me."

"Good. Then come to my house tomorrow for the whole afternoon. In a pub or here on the street we can't express ourselves as we must. So, will you come tomorrow or not?"

Gunther's eyes looked guileless as he answered. "Of course I will..."

"Come along and I'll show you where I live. I can't describe it. You have to see the house."

"Is it far?"

Hermann looked at his watch.

"When did you say your uncle is coming? At four? At the Stettin train station? It's not yet half past three. No, it's not far. Scarcely a quarter of an hour. If we go right away, you can be at the train station punctually at the proper time. I'll show you the way and then take you to the tram, although it's only ten minutes' walk."

They walked on, Hermann inwardly afflicted, Gunther inwardly angry. But there was no other way. Saxon would surely wait until four, and if not, that was just as good. Both kept silent.

They walked north, to the Luisenplatz, and in fact hardly a quarter hour had passed when they stood at the entrance to the street that ended in a wall. They stopped.

"Note the street, please, and that house, Gunther. It's the last one. There, where the street ends and the wall begins. And be there tomorrow at three o'clock, there at the wall opposite the house. Just stand there. You won't have to wait. I'll be at the window. When you see me, come up and I'll let you in. One flight of steps, to the left. All right, have you understood everything correctly?" Hermann repeated the details.

Gunther had neither listened nor understood. For sure he would never come here and he had only one thought — to finally be free.

Hermann looked at him with concern: "And you will definitely come?"

"Haven't I always come?"

Yes, that was true, Hermann reflected. He had always come — yesterday and today, and punctually. They walked on to the nearest tram stop. The car would come soon. Hermann had time left to say more.

"Today I looked around for work for you. You were right, it is difficult to find work. But we mustn't lose heart."

Hermann laid his hand on Gunther's shoulder. He felt, despite the warmth of the day, the cool, smooth skin of Gunther's cheek on his fingers, and he continued, urgently, as if imploring, so that the boy, keeping still and not moving under the hot hand, heard and remembered the words: "One more thing, Gunther! Listen to me carefully.

"If your uncle, despite his original intention, should stay longer in Berlin and you can't get away, or if something else should come up, so that you can't come tomorrow, then remember that on Monday, and each day of next week, somewhat after five o'clock, I'll go to the bridge, and will wait for you there. Are you listening — each day at five or a little later, on the bridge!"

A tram car rattled up. They shook hands hastily. Gunther felt a paper bill in his hand, and jumped on the tram. Hermann walked slowly down the foggy streets, his head lowered and without looking around him.

This new disappointment pained Hermann more than he was willing to admit. What was this now, this unexpected hindrance, because of "this uncle so suddenly dropped down from the skies!"

He did not want to go out again. The day he had looked forward to was now spoiled. He bought some food for his supper, and walked on home. He sat at his desk and propped his forehead in his hot hands.

What was to become of all this? How was he to find a position for Gunther? How could he support him until one was found? The boy could not just spend night after night in some hotel, which was certainly objectionable, and at any rate not cheap. Gunther needed things besides! That suit, so unsuitable for him, like his shoes, was already worn and covered with spots. And his underwear — from what Hermann had seen of it — was urgently in need of a change. Gunther must have a job; a place where he belonged; a room with regular people who looked out for him...

Hermann made a calculation. If it went on this way, and he gave Gunther five marks daily, by the end of the month that would amount to almost his whole salary. It was therefore unthinkable that the two of them could get along on his salary, not even if Gunther had a position, which probably would be as miserably paid as all apprentice positions.

Hermann lived quite simply, and his innate sense of order compelled him to get along with what he had. But he had one spending trait, like on his first day in Berlin he had stopped at a first-class hotel. Its cheapest and smallest room, though it had cost a couple of marks more, was yet so much better than the best room in a second-class hotel. So, too, he paid a lot for good things, for good material, good underwear. If he went to a concert or to the theater, it was not the seats up in the third balcony that he took. He bought only the most necessary things for himself, but when he bought, he bought the very best because that, he knew, was at the same time economical.

To be sure, he still had a couple thousand marks in the bank, an inheritance from his parents. But that money had to stay in the bank for emergencies, his own unemployment, sickness. Thus he calculated, or at least tried to calculate. Soon, however, he shoved everything away from him.

He did want to help Gunther. He was really fond of Gunther. It just *had* to work out, one way or another. If he was fond of Gunther — and how fond of him he was already! — then he had to put his trust in him.

"I have no reason to doubt his sincerity or to mistrust him," he thought. "That he wanted to go to his landlady yesterday, to pick up his things, was understandable, he really needed them. And this visit today — what was so remarkable about it? Everyone comes to Berlin sometime, why not his uncle?..."

No, Hermann wanted to be glad — glad that he had found Gunther again — glad that he had come, and had returned, and that they had been together, if only so briefly and quickly. Above all, he wanted to look forward to tomorrow, when he would have him here, here in this room all to himself alone! For the whole afternoon! He wanted to think only about tomorrow.

There were all kinds of things to take care of. At first he thought of asking his landlady to set the coffee table for the afternoon for two people, but he immediately dropped the idea. His relationship to her in these first weeks had become ever more distant. They often did not see each other for whole days. In the mornings, his breakfast was set on a chair outside his room, punctually at eight o'clock, and he took it in himself. Then when he came home in the afternoon or evening, he found his room made up, everything in flawless order. Never was there a paper on his desk touched, he never had to ask a question, or for a favor — there was never cause for any kind of complaint or grievance. He fetched fresh water from across the hall himself, when he needed it, and he made his own tea. Punctually on the first of every month, his bill lay on his table. Just as punctually the next day he would leave the amount beside it.

Thus everything was just as he liked to have it, just as he wished. And yet, he felt there was something uncanny about the house. He was here, she was there, in the back rooms, which he never entered — of their number and size he had no idea.

Plus, the house was quiet. Almost too quiet. Hardly a car wandered into the street, where it was difficult to turn around. He seldom heard the doorbell ring. Even then, always only a light shuffle and a muffled whispering could he hear — so as not to disturb him, he supposed. He never saw a soul on the stairs — in this forlorn house on a hidden city street. And then, over there stood the eternally silent, windowless wall.

Before the shops closed, he went out to prepare for the next day. He bought another cup (for Gunther, his from now on, to drink from when he was there), and he bought especially good cigarettes, and a half-bottle of sweet wine (for it would be pretty lively tomorrow!) He came back loaded with parcels, and for the remainder of the evening gave himself over to his dreams.

His dreams were all woven around a blond, young head, and a small, pale, (and already) beloved face; a tender, slim, figure, which soon — soon now! — was to sit there, opposite him, in that chair . . . in the comfortable one there. And this hand, his hand, would again lie against the soft, cool and smooth cheek and might softly caress it. . .

5

Saxon waited patiently, in hopes of a repeated, generous share in a five-mark bill. He would have waited until evening and then half the night, without wasting a word over it, if there was something to be gained. Gunther finally came.

"Well, how was it?" Saxon inquired. "Did ya get it, yes? Well then, let's go on to Uncle Paul's. You'll be amazed. There's not another plate of pig's knuckle for eighty pennies like it in Berlin."

Uncle Paul's saloon lay near the Friedrich Street train station. All the chauffeurs and cab drivers of the whole region, with all the doormen and porters of the numerous neighboring hotels, plus a colorful group of other guests filled the saloon from early morning until closing time in the evening. It was a pure gold mine, and its fame was well founded.

Behind the bar stood the proprietor. Why he was called Uncle Paul by everyone from time immemorial, probably neither he nor any other person knew. His name was not Kruger and he had not the slightest resemblance to the great Boer leader. He had a fat, good-natured pug face, and oversized, red, fleshy hands dripping constantly with beer. He did not know the word tired. He was always ready for a loud laugh, but he could be damned nasty if a bill was not settled the way it had to be — with him!

In the farthest corner of the large pub stood a round table. This was the famous hustler table.

Uncle Paul tolerated the table, its name and the customers at it, because they always ate well and plenty. Nor were they louder there than was usual in the pub, and finally, the little crooks did want to live too. So why not at his place? He was not a crooked father, just a father to crooks, as he laughingly said. The cops came here just as seldom as the johns did. The boys were among themselves, and safe from both.

It was still early in the day and so there was room at the hustler table as Saxon arrived with Gunther. Only a small, runty boy, at most fifteen years old, was sitting there, his nose hardly reaching over the table's edge and so he was not immediately visible. He cried out with joy when he saw the two.

"Where did you come from? Hello Saxon! Hello Chick!" He gave each his little hand, for he knew them both from working the street.

Saxon, of course, could not keep Gunther's secret to himself. "Gunther has got a steady relation. He was just now with him—"

Gunther became angry and poked Saxon urgently in the side. "Oh, leave off the baloney. It's not really a relationship."

They would have argued further, if there had not appeared just behind them three more boys — Tall Willy, Hamburger, and Brown George.

Brown George was a strikingly handsome boy, with thick, smooth, coal-black hair, black eyes, and splendid teeth, which he showed on every occasion, for he laughed easily and often. He bore his name not without right — his skin was like bronze, and the blood shone rosy through the smooth and flawless brown of his cheeks. The gentlemen "didn't matter" to him, and he only went along when need required, but on the other hand, he could hardly rescue himself from them, or from women, and altogether was as lazy as a hippopotamus. Brown George was not without a healthy wit, although not a genuine Berliner.

Hamburger was likewise a handsome boy, but coarser, always in a good humor, however badly things were going for him — and often enough they went very badly for him. At the same time he was always obliging and ready to help, and was armed with such a big mouth that no one lightly opposed him.

There was nothing special about Tall Willy, a tall person, with thick, protruding lips, which he seldom opened, and then only for some stupidity.

Hamburger had just begun to bore the five to death, one after the other, with his nonsense, when Clever Walter appeared and put an end to the flood of baloney. Clever Walter was a personality not to be taken lightly and was thoroughly aware of his worth. Despite the heat he was wearing a thick wool sweater and underneath, up to his chest — one saw their outline — a pair of knee pants that squeaked when he moved. He had a relationship with the daughter of Uncle Paul. He had fathered one child already by her, and a second was soon expected. He thought of marrying her one day and taking over the thriving business, an intention that gave him a special and unassailable prestige in this circle. There appeared to be nothing to hinder him from constantly roaming the lounges and taking whatever came along.

He was talking now, and the others listened silently. Hamburger was leaning against the wall. No one noticed, or seemed to want to notice, that earlier, a pale young man had silently sat down among them without a greeting. They were used to his doing so. Someone might say softly, "Hello, Leo!" but he appeared not to hear it, as he did whatever happened around him.

Of an indeterminate age, but obviously still young — though past twenty — with hollow cheeks and staring eyes, he sat there with a sickly pallor and looked straight ahead, as if he had to consider something that had slipped his mind. Then he slowly took a small box from his pocket, carefully shook a white powder onto the back of his thin hand, and drew it up through his nose. Only then did he look around the circle for the first time.

"Leo, do give me one, too!" he was begged. But he did not hear it. Leo was a tireless cocaine addict. He sniffed cocaine the whole day and half the night, wherever he was. This was already his tenth dose today.

The consequences showed, in his unsteady look, his trembling hands — in his whole absent-minded, unsure, almost shy conduct. Twice committed to an institution, he had each time escaped. Now they left him in peace.

Since cocaine no longer really worked, he was taking stronger poisons — ether and morphine. He would not last much longer, a blind person could see that. But why should he not be allowed his pleasure? Most of the boys took cocaine themselves, if only occasionally, when they were especially flush. It would never have occurred to anyone to say to him, "Do leave off, Leo! You're killing yourself!" — which would not have helped in the least anyway.

A pity. For Leo was a fine boy, from a good family. He had attended secondary school, and in lucid hours could converse charmingly.

He went with gentlemen seldom, with women not at all. He made money through the secret sale of his drugs, which — God knew from where! — he acquired and always carried with him in astonishingly large quantities.

He was the only one who neither ate nor drank anything. His stomach could tolerate nothing more than, now and then, a sip of coffee. Even he did not know for sure how he nourished himself and kept himself up. Everyone liked him.

Thus they were now eight at the table. They all knew one another, and talked one on top of the other. They put in their orders — beer, coffee, cognac; and sausages and sandwiches to eat.

Clever Walter, expectant father and son-in-law of the place, had — no one knew why — a special fondness for little Gunther, and it was he who spoke first to Gunther: "Well, Chick, you here too? How's it going?"

Again, before Gunther could answer, the damned Saxon broke out with, "Gunther's got a steady relationship now, who wants to find work for him—"

For a moment all were dumbstruck, as if they had not heard correctly. Then Brown George cried, "What, work? I'm crying for help!"— and everyone laughed out loud.

"That's really the end of the road!" said Tall Willy, sincerely outraged.

"He must really be dumb!" cried another.

"And you go with someone like that?" asked Hamburger. He was speechless. And when Hamburger was speechless, the end of the world must be near!

Clever Walter, however, looked at Chick (whom he liked) quite anxiously. "You'd better watch out for him!" he said "I wouldn't have someone like that as a steady—"

"He's not at all a steady." Gunther finally got a word in. He did not like being made the center of attention and did not know what to do, the way they all stormed at him. Help came.

Little Kurt, called Kurtchen, or usually Kuddel, who had been the first to sit at the table and till then had kept silent and listened, suddenly stretched his little mouse of a face over the edge of the table and said with his high and clear child's voice: "But I'd write him a letter!"

They looked at him. Clever Walter spoke scornfully. "What would ya write then? Can ya even write?"

Instead of answering, Kuddel began to dig around in his pocket, brought out a crumpled but clean piece of paper, and a pencil stub, which he wet on his tongue, and began to write without a further word. The others no longer concerned themselves with him, but turned to their conversation, which, always, turned on one theme — gentlemen and money.

While Kuddel, unconcerned, diligently and thoughtfully continued to write, the group was enlarged by a new arrival, and the table was now full. The new arrival sat down quietly, said softly, "Good evening," but was not greeted in return.

The newcomer was a strange boy. He was neatly dressed, clean down to his fingernails, and he resembled an apprentice in a large clothing store, or a just-confirmed schoolboy, with his innocent blue eyes and his light blond, carefully parted hair. He wore starched linen and a watch, and carried a walking stick, usually gloves too, which he preferred to keep in his pocket.

His name was Ernest, Ernest Wenderroth (or Wenderotter), and he was the only one of them whose surname was even approximately known here. He was said to live with his parents, who knew everything and allowed everything.

No one could stand him. He was only tolerated. Nevertheless, why he showed up from time to time at the hustler table, no one knew.

For a long time no one had concerned himself about him.

Then one of them spoke. Naturally it was again Saxon, who could leave no one in peace. "Well, Ernest, are you working hard at your bookkeeping? Can you let me have a nickel?"

A nice smile was Ernest's only answer. Ernest's smile impressed no one, not here. They all knew that he never gave nor loaned even a nickel, and they expected his usual answer.

"But I don't have anything myself!"

As for the bookkeeping, the previous winter, once when Ernest had stepped out, someone had taken a notebook from his overcoat pocket. There were hieroglyphics in it that no one understood. Every page was cleanly divided into columns by blue and red lines. Between the lines were separate letters and numerals. For example:

5   8   FBe   XXXII   15

The numbers and letters in the columns were a code which meant, for example, that on the *fifth* of the month at *8 o'clock* in the evening, at the corner of *Bessel* and *Friedrich* Street, Ernest had met a gentleman. The numbers and letters represented the date, time and location. The gentlemen's identity would be represented in the next-to-last column with a secret Roman numeral. The amount Ernest had received was noted in the last column. These last figures, his cash income, Ernest added up weekly, and they must have reached a pretty good sum by the end of the month.

Atze, naturally, had enticed the meaning of the codes out of Ernest in his irresistible way, and of course had immediately passed it on.

"It's a scream!" Atze had said, "and what that dude makes for money — unbelievable!" Atze had said it half admiringly and half enviously.

Now they all knew about the bookkeeping, and they also told themselves that the owner of the book already had a pretty amount in savings. When the savings reached a certain amount, Ernest intended to withdraw from that business, and open up his own — one of a different nature. So much for Ernest Wenderroth (or Wenderotter), and his book.

Atze was not there because he was again not in Berlin; plus Atze never ever went into "such" a pub.

"Atze," Karl the Great had once said, "Atze, the 'refined' [with contemptuous emphasis] is an eighty-penny-boy!"

"Eighty-penny-boy" meant that Atze, the refined Atze, was in secret alliance with the police. Although Atze constantly and vehemently swore that this was the purest slander, and only envy, the suspicion was not erased. The police constantly had a couple of boys from whom they received reports on the other hustlers, as well as on the homosexuals with whom they associated. As a reward they left the "eighty-penny-boys" unmolested. There was much in Atze's behavior and attitude that always fed new fuel to this suspicion.

Nothing was so contemptible to all these boys as an alliance with the police. It was perhaps the only thing that they truly despised. Thus, when along with Ernest's famous book, the name of its discoverer was mentioned, for a moment there lay over the table an oppressive silence. Gunther alone did not yet understand why.

But soon they were shouting and laughing again. Little Kuddel, meanwhile, had continued to write, without anyone paying attention to him. Bent over the table, he wrote zealously, with his nose almost on the paper. Each time a word was finished, a small, red, pointed tongue went out between his thin lips and the lead was moistened on it.

"Are you still not finished!" he was asked.

"Nearly! Nearly!" he said, continuing to write.

He wrote, or drew, every single word in a stiff, small child's writing, and he allowed nothing to disturb him in his work. On his sly gray face there appeared from time to time a cunning and satisfied smile. Whoever saw him thus would have taken him at his word, that he knew his business. He let no one touch him, and yet still got his money. In this he was a little master, and wonders were told of his slyness, with which he managed to win over the johns, again and again.

He was almost finished when suddenly there stood behind

him, as if shot out of the earth, a tall man, twenty-two or twenty-three years old. It was Karl the Great.

In a well-tailored suit of the best material, with his powerful, strong shoulders and his broad chest, his large, regular, handsome, and frank face, Karl stood there and, with a good-natured smile, looked down at the shrimp under him.

"Children, what are you doing here? School work? Show me..."

"One moment, I'm nearly finished," and Kuddel's tongue appeared between his lips.

Karl the Great took the seat that was offered him with obliging friendliness by Hamburger. With Karl sat one who had arrived at the same time, Sailor Otto. Sailor Otto was almost the same height as Karl, but otherwise an entirely different type. He and Karl were the same age and were old friends, but Otto was quite different from Karl in character. What in Karl was restrained power expressed itself in Otto as brute strength. As his name indicated, he wore a seaman's outfit and one sensed under the outfit his muscular and sinewy arms and legs. His exposed breast showed red and blue tattoos — two hands entwined in love, and above them the flaming star of hope. The tattoos on his arms and legs were said to be worse, and those on the discreet and private parts of his body (viewing gladly allowed, but cost a bit), as the blond Lieschen — the little tart who had slept in his arms one night — related, not without moral indignation, were "simply indecent."

Sailor Otto had never been to sea and was even more stupid than Tall Willy, who at least kept silent, whereas Otto continually threw around some expressions he had picked up in Hamburg, such as "boss" and "steward," which he pronounced "stayward."

Otto's reactions were definitely prized more than his words. He was a bitter foe of all open and secret police and therefore also of Atze. When he had one of them, say, at night, in a quiet corner, under his mighty fists, it was something not quickly forgotten. The criminal police knew this too, and preferred to avoid him.

Now he sat there, his sleeves rolled up, his elbows propped on the table, throwing down one beer after another. He could hold an enormous amount, a capacity he had in common with Karl the Great. No one had ever seen those two drunk, even after they had caroused the whole night.

Karl the Great's steady for a long time now was a rich jeweler in Leipzig Street, whose name was never mentioned. One of the boys had once seen him and described him as "a tiny man with a gray hat, trousers with cuffs over patent-leather shoes, and rings on his fingers — you couldn't count them..."

However, one john, a regular visitor to the Adonis Lounge, known and loved as a wisecracker, had not only seen Karl's gentleman, but even knew him.

"A rare cross between a sparrow and a vulture..."

Out of respect for the two grown-ups, who gave the table some dignity, the conversation became somewhat less loud.

Gunther and Tall Willy sat silent, as they had for hours. Leo dreamed on in a blissful drugged forgetfulness. Saxon had fallen into an argument with Clever Walter over the sale of an old pair of pants. Hamburger continued to talk, without anyone listening to him, while the smart little Ernest's blue eyes hung on Karl the Great in continual admiration — *just think, a relationship with a rich jeweler!* Brown George was audibly asleep, sunk back in his chair, showing two rows of splendid white teeth. He had not seen a bed for three nights now.

Up front in the pub there were shouts and brawls, threatening and drunken voices clashed with one another, and were mixed into a confused noise. There was a continual coming and going, especially from the drivers, who could only stay a short while at the bar.

The bar smelled of cabbage and fat. The smoke of the locomotives from the neighboring train station penetrated inside, and mixed with smoke from pipes and cigarettes in a thick haze. The heat was unbearable. But these young people were all completely insensitive to the discomfort. They hardly recognized heat and cold, and were used to noise and stench.

Kuddel's letter was nearly finished.

Kuddel wanted to read out loud, so that everyone could hear

it, but Clever Walter had torn the sheet from his hand.

"I'll read it!" He spoke in a loud, hoarse, but distinct voice, "Dear..."

"There's no name. Chick, what's the name of your steady?"

Gunther, who had been angered by this business the whole time, said crossly, "I don't know. And he's not my steady!"

He really did not know the name at that moment, or had completely forgotten it again.

"It doesn't matter!" roared one of them impatiently.

"Well, all right!" said Walter and began again.

> Dear friend, no john has ever been so brash and dopey as to say that I should work. If you don't want me, you just have to say so. If you want to, we can talk things over, but I won't be made fun of anymore. Do you understand? Your loving Gunther.

They all found the letter very good, and Kuddel reaped praise. He said, quite proudly, "There's still something on the back side."

Clever Walter turned it over and read, "If you give me five marks, however, it's all right again."

That, too, was universally approved. Only Karl the Great was irritated and opened his mouth for the first time.

"Baloney!" he said scornfully. "First you mock him, and then you say you love him. Who is it for anyway?"

He looked around the circle and everyone glanced again at Gunther, who was turning red. He had little liking for this story. It would not have pleased Atze either.

While the letter was being read, yet another boy, tall and gaunt, had joined the table, making a full dozen. It was Corpse Eddy.

Dressed entirely in black, including his derby and his wool gloves, he sat down among the others without a greeting. He had no color on his face. It was as pale and bloodless as his snow-white, long, bony hands. He was even paler than Leo.

"Corpse Eddy, where'd you come from? Out of the grave?" was the expression with which he was always greeted.

He seemed not to hear it. He sat there looking with his black eyes in his white face, from one to the other around the table —

then began again from the beginning, always without saying a word. They were glad when he came. For there was a saying that he brought luck. Always, whenever he showed up, in the street or elsewhere, whoever met him soon after found a rich john. Not because johns ran from his into other arms. On the contrary — many johns who had been with him took him again, and praised his quiet indefatigableness.

Corpse Eddy was truly indefatigable. He could walk the whole night through, until early morning, up and down Friedrich Street, from Oranienburg all the way to Halle Gate, with his long, hard strides — ten times there and back, without becoming tired. With his upright posture, staring straight ahead, he appeared to see nothing and nobody. Yet he saw everything. If he sensed an approach, he calmly turned into the next cross street and stopped. If he was not followed, he just as calmly returned and walked on.

Thus he sat there now, calm and upright, looking from one to the other, from little Kuddel over to Gunther, to whom Eddy gave an uncanny feeling, and on to Hamburger and Karl the Great and back again.

"What are you looking for now?" someone snapped.

Eddy gave no answer. He never answered. But he was noticed.

"Corpse Eddy, where'd you come from? Out of the grave?"

The letter had been read, and now they spoke about other things — about hard times.

You couldn't make anything decent any more, either on the streets or in the lounges. The foreigners were missing, the rich Americans and Swedes, with their dollars and kronor. Brown George finally awoke and heard what was being talked about.

"There's nothing for it," he said yawning, with a deep sigh, "we'll have to use blackmail!"

But that was not to be taken so seriously. For they all knew, when they tried extortion, they themselves got the worst of it. Who still let himself be blackmailed today? Certainly not a Berliner. Karl the Great, tired of all the chatter around him, called for cards. "Now then, are we going to play today or not?"

The cards arrived, the dice rolled. They all played in groups, and the hustler table resounded under the fists of all the small and large hands which fell on it with every trick.

Kuddel's letter was forgotten, swept under the table, trampled into illegible scraps under the young feet. It never reached the one for whom it was intended, and that was perhaps the only thing that was to be spared him.

At eight o'clock the cards were thrown together, the checks were paid — not without many loud arguments with the waiter — and they broke up. Some went to their steady relations, or had a date. Others went to see whom they could waylay in Friedrich Street, the Passage, or they rode to the west — everyone for himself, but all to make out.

Saxon and Gunther headed for the Adonis Lounge. Gunther had been irritated, to be sure, but he did want to go to Uncle Paul's often — it was pleasant there, he felt. Tall Willy crept after them. Karl the Great, however, true as gold, went to his little jeweler.

6

here followed an evening such as Gunther had never experienced before! Despite the early hour, it was very lively in the Adonis Lounge.

It was a Saturday. At the large, round table in a corner, a birthday was being celebrated with champagne and schnapps.

Two females, one with a gigantic feather hat and in a fiery red dress, were incessantly filling glasses — held out to them on all sides — from the bottles in the ever-refilled ice pail at their side. It was the birthday of one of them. Like her companion she was really a man, but looked entirely like a female.

All the boys, large and small, were sitting or pressing around the table to get their share.

Saxon and Gunther, as soon as they entered, were called over by two "uncles" from the sticks who, having been left unnoticed because of the unusual occasion, were not yet taken. Gunther and Saxon sat at their table. The two men, stimulated by the nearby carousing and not wanting to be left out, began to run up a monstrous bill, eagerly urged on by the sly Saxon.

Before the dancing began, with which the evening in the lounge really began, they were all four so drunk they no longer knew what bar they were in, or how many others they went to afterward.

Late the next afternoon Gunther drowsily woke, sat up, and looked around him. He was in the best room in the most expensive hotel in the west. He had not the slightest idea how he got there. His head ached terribly, and he could hardly open his swollen eyelids. But he was able to see that in the bed next to him lay a hairy man, with untidy, gray hair and a long mustache hanging over his half-open mouth. The man was still fast asleep, and snoring loudly.

The man was not one of the pair he had met yesterday in the Adonis! Gunther did not know this man at all, had never seen him before! But then he must have seen him yesterday, or today. He could not remember what had taken place last night. How did he meet this man and get here? Gunther did not have the faintest notion. And how his head hurt!

He climbed out of bed and plunged his head deep into a washbasin of water. Somewhat awakened, he looked around the room.

It was a nice sight! Discarded clothing hung on the chairs, dusty boots sat in the corner, the beds were soiled, and this man lay there and rattled. Gunther shook him on the shoulder, but the brute did not stir.

What time is it! Gunther wondered. *Is it morning! Is it noon!*

From the breast pocket of the man's thrown-off coat peeped a thick wallet. For a moment Gunther pondered the opportunity, but he did not steal. He was a decent boy. He rang the bell.

After a considerable time a young man appeared at the door. In elegant pajamas, with leather slippers on his dainty feet, he came dancing in and looked around at the mess, his hands propped on his strikingly protruding hips. He turned up his fine little nose and said with conviction, "Pooh, you pigs!"

Gunther knew him. It was Josie. Josie's real name was Joseph, but since it would have seemed perverse to call him Joe, he was more appropriately named Josie. He, or rather "she," occupied something like a confidential position at the hotel. Being at the same time porter and waiter, she was glad to be available (when it was worthwhile, of course) as a substitute for the young guests, in case a gentleman arrived without one.

"Pooh, you pigs!" she said again. "And how it stinks here!"

She threw open all the windows. The rotten humid air was mixed with the hot haze of the street that entered the room.

Gunther, still wearing only a shirt, was searching out his things, from the clothing that was scattered around, and groaning as he dressed himself. When he was almost ready, he spoke. "Stop grumbling, Josie. Instead help me get the john awake. I haven't got my money yet."

Josie showed no desire for that activity, and shrugged her shoulders disdainfully.

But then they did try together, by jogging and shaking, tugging and pulling, to waken the man. Nothing worked.

Finally Josie picked up the full water jar and poured it over the snorer's face. That worked. The man tore his eyes open, let out a curse and sprang out of the bed onto both feet. He leaped like a tiger onto his coat, snatched out his wallet, and, sitting on the edge of the bed, began to slowly count its contents, down to the last of the abundant bills, while the two speechlessly watched.

The result appeared to satisfy him. With a grunt he took out a twenty-mark bill and looked at the two boys with his nasty-looking bloodshot eyes, as if he wanted to remember which he had arrived with.

Then he threw the bill at Gunther

Gunther had had enough. He finished dressing and made his escape.

On the stairs he could still hear Josie's shrill voice as she squabbled over the payment.

Outside, in the still and deserted streets of the Sunday afternoon, he thought only about his awful headache. He hailed an open coach and was driven to the Adonis Lounge. There he sat for the next two hours drinking seltzer, with and without raspberry flavoring, in monstrous quantities.

At the same time, not far distant, his friend Hermann Graff was wandering the streets, looking for the name of a hotel that did not exist.

Hermann Graff had waited in vain for Gunther that afternoon. From half past two on, he had stood or sat at his open window, again and again leaning out so that he could see Gunther coming down the street. But Gunther never came.

The heat of the day was unusual for the time of year. It was like a day in mid-summer. Half past three came, and then four o'clock. The coffee had become cold and the mountain of pastry, every piece of which he had carefully and lovingly selected at the confectionary only two hours earlier, had sunk together.

It was almost five o'clock. His joyful anticipation had passed, uneasiness had seized his heart, and he felt only a dull, oppressive fear, as he restlessly paced his room

He felt a torturing, indefinite fear, as of an approaching, unknown disaster.

It helped little that he said to himself again and again that this uncle, who had so unexpectedly shown up, must have stayed on, seeing how badly it was going for Gunther. The uncle probably wanted to help Gunther find a position before traveling on, thereby doing what he not only had a right, but a duty, to do.

Or perhaps — and here fear clenched his heart — the uncle had taken Gunther home with him, to take care of him there...

But then he is gone forever, once more — and irretrievably — lost to me!...

With this thought he felt such a pain that he had to stop and press his hand against his chest.

He could not believe it. Was Gunther, who had been unexpectedly found again so recently, to be torn from him anew through an absurd coincidence? No, he believed, fate could not deal so cruelly ... not with him, not with the two of them...

What was he to do? He had to do something. Sit here longer and wait in vain? — that he could not do.

Gunther, he remembered, once had mentioned the name of the hotel where he slept. It was Pasewalker Hof, or something similar. At any rate Gunther had described the location. It was on the corner of the street that led from the Stettin train station, straight down (therefore toward the south), and at the second crossroad.

He should be able to find the hotel, and it was not far away. They must know something about Gunther there, perhaps his full name and where he came from. If Hermann knew that, finding Gunther somehow was certainly possible.

The hotel was quite near, but even if it were at the edge of the metropolis, if it had been in its furthest suburb, Hermann Graff would still go there.

How empty of people the streets were this Sunday! How hot and muggy! Everyone had fled from town, and was outdoors in the woods or at the water.

He searched for the hotel.

The hotels in the area stood almost one beside the other. In front of the train station they were large and imposing, but in the side streets, smaller, inconspicuous, of third or fourth rate. Almost all had names of cities in northern Germany. There was a Demminer Hof, a Schleswiger Hof, a Holsteiner Hof. But there was no Pasewalker Hof. He entered one hotel after another, pressed a coin into the hand of the porter and inquired. The answer was always the same — no one had heard of a Pasewalker Hof. It must not exist.

He did not allow his hopes to fall. He walked on, up and down all the streets in the vicinity of the train station, in the sultry heat of the afternoon. He read all the signs, and asked and asked.

Tired and discouraged after two hours, he finally landed again in front of the train station where he had started. He could not go on. He sat in the large second-class waiting room. In the high, airy, and quiet room, he sat for many hours, on into the evening. He drank and smoked, stared ahead, and thought about only one thing. Once he said almost aloud to himself: "My God! It's horrible! He's gone. He has been taken from me. He is almost a stranger to me. I hardly know him. I know nothing about him. And I can't live without him!"

7

He clung to one thought yet: *Day after day shortly after five on the bridge...* That's what he had said to Gunther, and in contrast to so many things he had said, the boy seemed to have understood and grasped these words. If Gunther had understood them, if he were still here in Berlin and *could* come, would he remember? And then, if he remembered, would he come?

Only one thing was left for Hermann to do — to be there, on the hour, day after day! That appointment was like a last hope for him. Directly after work, at five — and if possible, somewhat earlier — he would take a streetcar and than walk along the river bank, to the bridge.

The following Monday, Hermann even took off at half past four. He could work no longer. He was at the bridge before the appointed time. His heart was beating. He was unable to stand still in one spot, but walked up and down, letting his gaze swing to all sides, spying from afar every distant approaching young figure, only to see each time that it was not Gunther. It turned six, then half past. Finally he gave up.

Hot and tired, he went into an empty, poorly ventilated summer theater, without eating first. He wanted to deaden his thoughts. When he left, long before the end, he had not heard one word of the rubbish that had been handed out up there; he could not remember one single scene.

On Tuesday he stood for almost an hour at the bridge, as if nailed there. Inwardly he was almost calm. At six he entered the small nearby restaurant, where he and Gunther had been on the two evenings of the previous week. He sat in "their niche."

When the friendly waitress asked, "All alone today?..." he felt he could bear it no longer, mumbled an incomprehensible answer, drank up, and left.

His head was dull and heavy; his heart was empty; his feet were like lead. But he slept that night, he slept deeply.

The next day, Wednesday, he at first hesitated to go to the bridge. He no longer believed that Gunther would come; but he went anyway.

The day was especially hot and the sky was blazing. The whole city steamed, sweated, and stank. His nerves were stretched to the breaking point. As he placed his hands on the railing of the bridge, the iron burned. Nowhere was there a hint of coolness. He no longer hoped...

He felt, gradually, an entirely new feeling rising up in him — rage — against Gunther and against himself.

Gunther had promised to come. Why didn't he come? He should come, however many hindrances he had, however many uncles! What had Hermann really seen in him? Gunther's conduct toward Hermann had been improper from the very beginning. Not that Hermann had asked for much friendliness or even gratitude, but that indifferent, complacent, even condescending behavior, and at the same time Gunther's letting himself be fed and money slipped to him, that was what outraged him. If he had not been so blind, he would certainly not have put up with it! Besides Gunther was by no means as handsome as Hermann had imagined. That pale, almost yellow face coloring, the circles under his eyes, and that odd twitch in the corner of his mouth — that was really anything but beautiful!

And so unclean he was! Could anyone respect and love a person who thought so little of himself? Could Hermann, who was so scrupulously clean and sensitive to these things himself?

The rage he had talked himself into increased, now against himself.

It was all his own fault. Why had he entered into a relation with Gunther? What did he really know about the boy? Nothing, but what Gunther himself, hesitantly and sulkily, had said. It could all be true and could also not be true. He should have quizzed him, down to the bones. Above all he should have had Gunther write his full name, his place of birth, the address of his landlady and hotel. He should have had Gunther show his identification, to know if it all was correct. What was the good of all Hermann's tenderness and consideration!

It was well beyond six o'clock and Hermann was still standing at the bridge, letting himself be taken for a fool by a young rascal. He no longer looked around and quickly walked home.

But there, lying on the sofa as if in a stupor, his rage and his displeasure blown away, he knew that if he should ever see Gunther again, he would treat him exactly as before. He felt entirely in the power of that unique face — of those strange and unfathomable eyes, those pale lips, those slender hands. Only *one* wish filled him entirely: to see Gunther just one more time, just one time more, to apologize to him for these ugly and unworthy thoughts just now!

Humbled and repentant, with no more hope but tortured and striken with anguish from a dull feeling of fear — the fear that some terrible event might have happened to Gunther — he lay there, for hours.

That night he had a fearful dream. In the dream Hermann no longer was standing on the bridge itself, but somewhat to the side, staring into the dark water of the Spree. Gunther's body welled up from the water, sank, came up again and slowly floated past him ... and away ... Hermann woke bathed in sweat. Falling asleep again, he dreamed more.

In his second dream he was standing on the edge of a bottomless abyss, and he saw Gunther falling, deeper and deeper — falling, falling. He rushed after him ... fell himself ... Again Hermann awoke, with a cry...

8

he week following Gunther and Saxon's drunken night
was hardly less dissolute for Gunther. Mornings he found himself
left alone, or sometimes not alone, in some strange bed in a
strange place. Hardly was he rid of one hangover before he had a
new one. He never quite recovered his senses.

Still, a certain regularity came into his days. He usually slept
until noon, if allowed and not thrown out of wherever he found
himself. Then he cooled his hot and muddled head in the dirty
waters of the Spree. A small bathing establishment was nearby,
where all the boys of Friedrich Street bathed for the whole long,
lovely afternoon, ducking one another, carrying on with any kind
of shenanigans they could think of, recovering fresh strength for
their trips and carousing. From bathing they went to the hustler
table at Uncle Paul's, where some of that Saturday group were
always to be found, to eat and drink. Toward evening, the Adonis
Lounge became their regular hang-out.

At the Adonis, Gunther, being a newcomer, never lacked admirers. Every evening he found some new ones. One would try to
entice him away from another, pump him full, promise him
more, and in the end someone usually took him along.
Somewhere. Gunther never knew where the trip was going to end.
He never lacked money, but during the course of the next day
every penny ran through his hands.

Everything would have been fine, but for the carousing. In the lounges of the west — closed to him since the many-sided Atze had once again disappeared — there was certainly drinking, and not too scantily. But in the Adonis Lounge, where they were not so particular about age — and where everything swirled in confusion — boozing was to a certain extent the main event, and a point of honor. The johns even seemed to try to get the boys drunk. If they were not quite drunk at the Adonis, then they became drunk in other bars, from which they were then taken somewhere else, to a hotel or home. Sometimes they were simply left sitting by their johns, now irresponsibly drunk themselves.

The small and still delicate Gunther was unable to hold much and was always soon drunk . Then he suffered the consequences terribly, more than the others. The amount they could throw down like water made Gunther sick. He got so he could no longer eat and even the sight of drinks began to disgust him. He was fed up with his life.

He longed to sleep alone again, all alone in bed, even if it was only in his hole of a room in the hotel at the Stettin train station. But he still had to get johns, else there would be no money the next day for food, bathing and cigarettes. The Adonis guests, like the bartenders, would really have given him the eye if he had refused to look lively and drink up with them.

He was much too weak-willed to say no. He was already too weak to get rid of Saxon, who was a nuisance now and, mostly without admirers himself, lay in wait like a dog for scraps from Gunther's table; Gunther was too weak to simply get up and walk away, or to not go there in the first place.

Thursday he was in a particularly miserable mood. After awakening long past noon, he found not a penny in his pocket. Where had the ten marks gone, which he had received yesterday evening (he remembered it quite clearly) from the businessman from Frankfurter Avenue? The man's idea of a good time consisted of showing up once a week in the lounge, getting each newcomer to his table, treating him to drinks, but not too many, and then quizzing him about God and the world. Every newcomer, but only once each. The boys knew this and knew that ten marks at the end was the rule. Naturally the man was thoroughly lied to, but that hurt nothing. He only listened to stories — they could be true or false . . . an inquisitive person, but otherwise quite harmless.

So where had the ten marks gone? He had once again slept in the flophouse, six in a room, two to a bed. The other five were long gone. One of them must have snitched from him. What a dirty skunk! The filthy cleaning girl stood at the door, broom and bucket in her hand and yelped at him.

He had paid for the night, not for the whole day! March, out!

Where was he to go? It was too early for Uncle Paul's; besides, he had no money. The Adonis Lounge was not open yet. Even the small change needed to bathe was lacking. He felt no desire to work the streets; it had been a long time since he had hit the pavement. Then, too, this was not the right time for it. Besides, he would not find johns, but more likely criminals. They were on their feet the whole day.

He loitered along the parapet of the Spree, discontented and hungry, from bridge to bridge, here stopping to watch the unloading of a boatload of apples; there, how a dog was bathed, and so on to the third, then the fourth bridge. There he stopped. Hadn't he been here often before? Right, and there, standing — actually! — the crazy guy he had met there last week, from whom he always got five marks; the one he had made believe the story about his uncle and landlady, who had wanted to find work for him. Since the last time they were together he had not thought once about the man. God knows, there he was, standing and staring ahead of him, crazy as before.

The man seemed to be waiting for someone. For whom? Certainly not for Gunther. Surely he couldn't still be waiting for Gunther? That was so long ago, it could no longer be true...

No, the man must be waiting here now for another boy, whom he had procured in Gunther's place. There were johns like that, who always picked the same places for each rendezvous because it was the most convenient for them.

Gunther retreated a few steps, so as not to be seen, and stood next to the buildings. He wanted to see whom the man had now. But what if Hermann turned around now, saw and recognized him? The way he looked now? And what was Gunther to tell him, why he had not come?

The man was standing there, near the railing of the footpath that led down to the water, seeing nothing. Just as if he did not *want* to see anything ... How strange he appeared! What was it with him?

An uncomfortable feeling crept over Gunther. He wanted to leave before he was seen. He wanted to go to Uncle Paul's. Tall Willy was probably already there. Gunther had lent him two marks several days ago, and Tall Willy should give back at least one of them or pay for Gunther's meal there.

Gunther carefully slipped around the corner. He turned and saw once more the motionless, sunk-down figure. "Completely crazy!" he thought.

On the way to Uncle Paul's he did not get free of the memory of this unexpected meeting. What was the last thing Atze had said to him? "Go to him! For the man loves you!"

And Gunther had gone to him and had followed Atze's advice to take advantage of him, as much as was possible under the circumstances. Then he had stayed away, because it had bored him out of all patience; because the others had laughed at him with the stupid letter; and finally, because these last days had been much too busy for him to think of other things.

Otherwise the man had been a nice person. To have a relation — a steady one — must also be really nice. Gunther saw that those who went in couples were not bad off — they always had money, a fixed place to live, and clothes, plus they usually did not have to take fidelity too seriously. Above all they did not have to go with just anyone because need drove them to it.

The man had halfway promised to take care of him, and he did look as if he would keep a promise, as if he were serious about it. The man was too serious — not at all like the other johns. In the end, it also came down to one thing — how much could the man make in a month?

Work? Now, that surely depended in the last analysis on himself, and if there were a genuine relationship between them, Gunther would just twist the matter around, so that the question would no longer come up. *That* noise naturally had to stop.

He had to take care of lodging, food, clothing, and a certain amount of pocket money — that in any case.

Gunther's thoughts went further. What if the man had been waiting for him now, his Gunther? What had he said: "Every day . . . this week!" The man would have been there — Gunther calculated, it was already the fourth day, and today too, he had still been watching for him!

Man, Gunther, he said to himself, as the Friedrich Street train station showed up, *if that's really so, then he must be terribly keen on you!*

Should he go there once more tomorrow, to see if the man was there *again*? The thought enticed him. He resolved to be respectable today, and to say nothing to the others about it.

Of course he still had to make some money today. But it was to be only table money. In no case would he go with anyone. He wanted to sleep alone and, if he could, to buy a few things, so as to look as decent as possible: a new shirt, a pair of socks, and a new tie.

At the hustler table were Leo, totally out on cocaine; little Kuddel; and, naturally, the unavoidable Saxon. Then came the two studs, Sailor Otto and Karl the Great, in all their glory. Then, one by one, Clever Walter, Tall Willy, Hamburger, and finally, Corpse Eddy, pale as a ghost and wordless.

The smart little bookkeeper Ernest was missing. After setting aside an amount for a return trip, and after taking care of some other business matters, Ernest had been taken along to Italy by a rich Englishman, with the blessings of his pleased parents. He would no doubt return safe.

The still unsettled argument between Clever Walter and Saxon over the used trousers broke out again. Sailor Otto was losing at cards and therefore was as irritable as a tiger whose tail has been stepped on. He was continually roaring at the smaller ones — they should stop, or he would knock their teeth in (what they were to stop, no one knew, for no one was doing anything to him). Karl the Great finally became angry and bluntly silenced Otto — "The kids aren't doing anything to you, so leave them in peace!" Apart from all that, it was a right cozy evening! The musclemen were playing cards — a nice game called "Hunt me, George" — and the kids were rolling dice for their beers.

Toward eight they all broke up, as usual, to "make out."

9

t was the second time that Gunther not only made a resolu-
tion, but also carried it out — the first had been his running away.

From table money he made eight marks, merely by his
presence, although he drank little and was dull. Then he got after
everyone who still owed him money — which was almost everyone — and requested his money back, unusual for him ("what's
the matter with you all at once, Chick?") He forced one mark
thirty from Saxon, one mark from Tall Willy, and Brown George,
finally, angrily threw him a fifty-penny piece. All the others
obstinately refused him. But now he had altogether ten marks and
eighty pennies.

He slept alone, for the first time in a long while, at his old
hotel. He was up at eleven and went shopping. He bathed until
four and, at half past, was on the bridge.

He had figured out exactly what he wanted to say. He wanted
to be friendlier — but not too friendly. He saw the man coming.

Again, just as yesterday, the man was looking absently
straight ahead. Stopping at the railing, the man laid both hands on
the iron bars. Gunther slowly walked up to him.

Earlier on this Friday Hermann Graff had resolved, since Gunther
had not come yesterday, that he would wait no more, but would
instead take the streetcar directly home. But at the Spree he got

off anyway, and walked his usual route along the river's edge to the bridge.

He was standing at the head of the bridge thinking about nothing. He was not waiting. He was not hoping. He was just standing there. Then he was startled by a light touch on his arm.

Before him stood, in a fresh, colorful shirt, the collar turned down, his hair still damp, smelling of water and youth — Gunther!

Not at all embarrassed, but smiling and looking up at him, Gunther began talking. "You're not angry with me, are you, Hermann?" Gunther hoped he remembered the name correctly. "You're not angry, are you, that I didn't come? I *really* couldn't. My uncle took me with him, on his business trip. I helped carry his bags..."

Hermann heard but understood not a word. Shaken, he stared into the smiling face before him, like the face of someone believed dead, now resurrected. Was it really and truly Gunther? He could find no words. His throat was dry and choked.

Slowly Hermann realized he was not dreaming, that standing before him, speaking to him, was Gunther. Gunther had called him by name, and was smiling, as Hermann had never seen him smile.

At one stroke, all the cares and fears of these past days fell from him. All mistrust and every suspicion also fell away, as did his feelings of indignation, anger, and every doubt of this dreadful week. Only *one* feeling did he have — joy. Joy, so violently flooding over him like a wave, that he was able to smile again. But he still could not find words.

Gunther found them. "But we can't just stand here. People are already beginning to look at us. Shouldn't we walk?"

Nothing was more indifferent to Hermann at this moment than other people, but the boy was right. They could not stay there.

They walked alongside one another and as a matter of course entered their old pub. They sat at their table. The waitress came, friendly as ever. "Now he's back ... and now you're not so sad as the last time, sir!"

Hermann Graff was not listening. Gunther, already over the menu, was ordering.

Then, alone, Hermann reached across the table and took the small hand, still damp from bathing and now quite clean, and spoke with a deep sigh. "I believed I would *never* see you again, Gunther!"

He held the hand firmly, quite firmly, as if he never wanted to let it go. Gunther started again about the uncle. "He absolutely did not want to let me go, but wanted to take me home with him. But I had to come back here, for I knew that you were waiting for me, Hermann..."

It was no longer joy that Hermann felt, it was happiness. An inexpressible feeling — happiness! He had come! He had returned for Hermann's sake! He spoke pleasantly — so very differently. He was smiling. And he called him Hermann!

"And I believed you had entirely forgotten me, Gunther. Did you think about me?"

"Always. When you were so good to me..."

Food arrived. It would have been impossible for Hermann to get down even a bite. But the boy seemed not to have lost his appetite and ate as if he had eaten nothing the whole week.

"You're not eating anything!" Gunther said.

"I can't. I'm not hungry."

"But it shouldn't go to waste. May I?"

Hermann's portion disappeared too. They had to laugh about it, and drew closer together. Gradually Hermann became calmer. He looked at Gunther. He never took his gaze from him. His thoughts cleared.

Painfully it occurred to him that today he had carried away from the office a large pile of urgent proof sheets that he must take care of before Monday. He had voluntarily taken on the work. The press was waiting. The work would have helped him get through the evening, through tomorrow, through the long Sunday. But now everything was different.

He thought it over. Tomorrow, as soon as he was free — and all of Sunday too — he and Gunther must be together. It was better to get the work done this evening. He would have to work half the night, but what did that matter! He could now work three times as fast!

He told Gunther hesitantly. Gunther entirely agreed with him.

"It doesn't matter. Let's see one another tomorrow..."

"I'll tell you something, Gunther. It has to be done today. It's better that way. Tomorrow when I come from work early, let's meet right away and then ride out to Potsdam in the afternoon, stay there overnight and all of Sunday and" — he could now smile too — "see the town and Sanssouci, rent a boat, go bathing..."

Gunther was listening. As long as he had been in Berlin, the whole quarter of a year, he had never gone beyond the city limits. He would be glad to make an excursion. He had gone in a boat only once — on the Spree near the pavilion. But then the others had carried on with so much nonsense, rocking the boat so that it had almost turned over, and he would have fallen into the water, and he couldn't even swim. He agreed to Hermann's plan.

"All right, tomorrow then. And what will you do until then? Where are you staying? You'll also need something..."

But here Gunther made a heroic decision and said, "No, let it go, Hermann. My uncle left me so much that I can get by until tomorrow..."

"That on top of everything else!" thought Hermann, who was touched. And he had been able to doubt *him!* He felt ashamed. But he had to give Gunther something, so it was again the usual. After some resistance, the five marks was accepted — and only too gladly! Thus they separated, and made an appointment.

"Tomorrow at three o'clock, again here on the bridge. Do go to a good theater," Hermann added. "That's the best way to spend the evening..."

This time it was the boy who watched and waved with his hand. Hermann tore himself away hesitantly and with a heavy heart. He had to hold himself from turning back and grasping Gunther in embrace.

Hermann worked deep into the night. The work came easily. As he fell asleep it occurred to him that he had forgotten again to inquire after Gunther's name, his hotel, and many other things. But not for a moment did he doubt that they would meet again. They could talk about those things in the coming days.

Happiness had arrived — they had met again. The boy was changed — he had smiled, had been friendly and almost trustful towards him. And — he had called him Hermann!

A thoroughly honest boy, whom he had severely wronged. But he would make it up to him. They would meet again — get to know one another. They...

With a happy smile he fell asleep, and slept free from all the ghosts of the past days and nights. He awoke and went to work with a happy expression on his face. One of his colleagues asked, quite astonished, if he had received some inheritance!

No, he had not received an inheritance. Something much, much more beautiful had happened to him... In a few hours he would see Gunther again. Happiness makes one so sure.

10

Gunther came — they met in the middle of the bridge.

Gunther was somewhat drowsy, for even though he came directly from his hotel, he had gone to bed late, and had again drunk more than was good for him.

Hermann, also somewhat tired from his work in the night — but happy as never before in his life — was carrying a small hand-bag with the necessary toilet articles for a night.

They would go to Potsdam, to the Potsdam Hermann liked so much. And tomorrow he wanted to show Gunther everything — the old castle, the splendid parks, in the morning; in the afternoon, the blue lakes and bays of the Havel River, and the still woods.

The trip to Potsdam passed rather quietly. They were not alone in their second-class compartment. A loud group from west Berlin was riding with them — ladies and gentlemen. Gunther looked out the window — Hermann was happy.

As always when they were together, Herman looked at Gunther and a feeling of inner joy seized him and he was completely absorbed in Gunther. Hermann desired nothing more than to sit there forever, with Gunther opposite, and look at him. Only once did he bend forward and speak in a quiet voice. "You have dimples, Gunther, when you laugh..."

The boy almost became angry, but said nothing. What this man saw in him! What if the old lady next to him heard, the one in the silk dress with the wobbly breasts, who was staring at them so brashly and inquisitively?

In Potsdam they first looked for an accommodation for the night and found it in one of the lovely old houses on the canal, a house from the good old times. They had a comfortable room, looking out across the water at old trees.

Then they went out to eat. Gunther paid no particular attention to anything — to the distinguished quiet of the streets, the gables and emblems of the simple, yet noble houses, to the church with its famous cupola. He gave good attention to the excellent dinner, which they ate on the terrace of a large restaurant on the water. Underneath them the steamboats glided by, music and the laughter of merry people echoing up to them. They spoke little and only about indifferent things.

Hermann had resolved to allow nothing to trouble these first hours of their being together — not to torment Gunther with questions, not to intrude. Tomorrow they would be together the whole day, and in the long hours of being together undisturbed, everything would come out without pressure and by itself, every question and each doubt could be addressed and clarified. Tomorrow evening they would no longer be strangers, as they still somewhat were today. Tomorrow evening they would be friends, and he hoped, for their whole lives!

Back in their hotel, Hermann shed his coat and vest, opened his little bag, and washed himself carefully, as he did every evening before going to bed. When he finished, he saw that Gunther was already lying in bed — he must have stripped off his clothes and shoes in a jiffy.

Hermann asked, "Are you tired, Gunther? Do you want to go to sleep right away?"

He received no answer. He was just looked at. He began to wonder.

"Well, then, good night, my boy — and sleep well!"

Again there was no answer. Gunther was lying on his back, his hands clasped behind his head, looking at Hermann with his now quite gray eyes, seriously, as if examining him.

Then, when Hermann made no move and asked no more questions, Gunther quickly turned on his side, drew the cover up over himself, and budged no more.

What was this? Was Gunther already asleep? Hermann approached the bed. Gunther's head was almost entirely buried in the pillow. Only a tuft of his dark blond hair showed. He did not move.

"He's fallen asleep," Hermann thought, "how quickly it happens at that age!" He walked to the open window and looked out at the quiet streets, the canal with its black water and the tree tops under him. "How hot it is!" He was breathing with difficulty.

What had that been, there just now! The way he had looked at Hermann before he turned over, so strange, so . . . almost inquisitive. At the same time so . . . superior. Superior, yes, that's what it was. Just as if Gunther wanted to say, "I already know what you want. I know it very well. But you must not think that I have come here with you for *that*. . ."

The look burned into Hermann. How little he knew Gunther! But how was he to know him, after these couple of days, these few hours . . . Strange, that look, and this silence had been very strange — strange, and not friendly.

It burned into Hermann. And was Gunther indeed asleep?

He walked back into the room and to the bed again. Gunther was sleeping — there was no doubt that he was sleeping now. He could not have been quite asleep before. As he fell asleep he must have made a strong movement, which had tossed the featherbed, that horribly heavy featherbed (ineradicable in Berlin) to the floor. For he was lying there now almost naked.

He also was lying again on his back. His short shirt had been shoved up. His legs were lightly drawn up toward his chest. He was sleeping. He was quite fast asleep.

Hermann stood spellbound. How divinely beautiful! Never had Hermann believed that a human being could be so beautiful!

How beautiful were his legs! How soft his thighs and hips! How well-proportioned his still-so-childlike breast! How undeveloped still his slim shoulders, those still-so-thin arms! And how beautiful were those hands, those slender hands, the only part of this body Hermann had come to know, those hands that he had held in his own and which he loved almost more than that face!

That face, however, fully visible now on the white pillow, that face appeared to him all at once strange again. The eyes firmly closed, as if lifeless, now hidden under the long lashes, the slightly open mouth with its white teeth, the somewhat low forehead, and those smooth cheeks — that face, he did not recognize it, he did not yet know it. Only one thing about it was familiar — the corner of the mouth, even now in sleep, drawn up — that corner of his mouth so oddly distorted, in defiance and displeasure. . .

That mouth was the most foreign thing to Hermann in Gunther's face. It was not the mouth of a child, not the mouth of someone still young. It was the mature mouth of an adult, with a trace of bitterness and of experience, of satiety, even of disgust with life — a mouth quite foreign to Hermann.

Gunther was sleeping, but apparently with bad dreams. His breath was labored. What was bothering him? What was he fretting about?

What burden pressed on his small heart, which was beating so irregularly under his breast? So restlessly beating under his hand? He had laid his hand, tenderly and lightly, almost fearfully, on the place where he believed he heard it beating. How brown it was, this breast, how warm and soft!

The breast was brown, a light brown. Like old ivory. *As trite as it sounds, that word fits here*, he thought.

He stood there for a long while, not daring to move, bent over the sleeping boy, looking into the face that he loved like nothing else in the world. He tried to read in the face what he did not understand and could not explain to himself. It remained a puzzle, inexplicable for him. Then, he felt with alarm that his reason was beginning to vanish, giving way to the scent of his body. Quickly, like a criminal, he drew back his hand and walked away from the bed, back to the window.

He was done in. He had overtaxed his strength. If he had stood there, only a minute longer. . .

He grasped the cross-bars of the window with both hands. No

— he would not! he must not! It would be stealing. He was no thief, who stole quietly in the night. He was a decent person. He had always been. *Not in sleep! No, not in sleep!*

He laid his burning forehead on his cold hands at the crossbars. How hot it was, how unnaturally hot!

Each day was the same — scorching, although it was not yet midsummer. Outside, the streets echoed the steps of passersby. Good and satisfied citizens of this town, returning home to their wives after an evening grown late with a few beers. Their ample and ordinary words faded away with their steps. A cat was spitting in its love-path to a neighboring roof. From the square across the way, diagonally opposite him, a clock struck. Then all was still again.

No, not in sleep!

He wanted to awaken the boy, kneel down by the bed, and tell him everything — the whole truth. That he loved him. And that he could bear it no longer!

Would Gunther understand? *Could* he understand him?

That Gunther was no longer an innocent, no longer entirely innocent, he was now convinced. But then, what boy was still entirely innocent at that age!

But what did he know? How much, how little? What? And how was Hermann to tell him? Could it be said at all? Said in words? No.

Then his temples became quite cold again. A voice inside seemed to call to him: "Wake him up! Take him! Wake him with your kisses! Wake his sleeping body, and his sleeping soul, wake them with the kisses of your love, until they both become yours!"

Yet another voice said: "No, let him sleep, let him sleep out his innocent sleep! Don't wake him up! An hour is coming — and it is near — in which he will give you both, body and soul, freely, conquered by your love. And only then is it happiness!"

The voice continued: "For, if you wake him and want to take him — and he twists from your arms, astonished, shocked, and horrified — not suspecting, not knowing, not feeling what you want from him — how could you bear that! Or, if he does not resist, gives himself to you, drunk with sleep and only half conscious, from a feeling of gratitude or thankfulness, and you both stand face to face in the morning, in shame and regret at having seduced, having been seduced — how could you live on after such an hour!"

Again he took control of himself with superhuman strength. He extinguished the gas flame. What did it help? The night was still as bright as the day.

His face averted, he once again approached the bed. He lightly pulled the shirt over the knees and the sheet over the naked body of the sleeping boy.

Then he quickly undressed himself and lay down in the other bed. He wanted to sleep. He *must* sleep. He finally succeeded.

Hermann awoke first. In his sleep he had unconsciously grasped for Gunther's small hand, noticing only on awaking, when he still held it fast in his own.

He carefully released the hand so as not to awaken Gunther, and sat up. His first glance was at the bed next to him. The boy was lying in the same position in which he had fallen asleep, half on his back, but his face almost entirely in the pillow, so that Hermann could see nothing of it; and Gunther was fast asleep.

He felt himself refreshed, and gave himself entirely to the joy of being together with Gunther. What a day today was to be! This day belonged to him. Nothing human or divine was to rob him of this day!

When he had finished washing, shaving, and dressing, which in his case — doing everything with exactness and care — took quite a while, he walked to the bed and laid his hand on the shoulder of the sleeping boy. Gunther did not stir at first, then he grumbled, made a reluctant movement, woke up, and looked around him.

"Good morning, Gunther! Did you sleep well?"

The boy sat up and rubbed his eyes.

"No," he said crossly, as he saw the already dressed man in front of him, and his look became angry.

Hermann laughed. "It appeared as though you did! But come on, lazy bones, get up and get ready. It's almost nine..."

The bell rang.

The proprietor, who had received them yesterday, arrived and asked through the door for their pleasures.

"Well, what will it be, gentlemen? Coffee? Yes? And since it's Sunday, also pastry, I suppose?"

"Yes, of course, that too, and plenty . . . and bread and fresh butter. . ."

When Hermann turned around, Gunther was still sitting in bed, his knees drawn up against his breast, both arms wrapped around them, and Gunther was looking at him again with that look of yesterday evening — examining, as if curious, as if he wanted to get to the bottom of him. . .

Hermann could not figure him out. Just what did he want? He was a strange boy.

While Gunther washed himself, lazily and superficially, and slowly dressed, Hermann described his plans for the day. He received no answer. "He still has the night's sleep in his eyes and senses," Hermann thought.

But when breakfast came, he saw with pleasure that Gunther's stomach, at least, was wide awake. Gunther went at everything, and the mountain of pastries sank down visibly. He still said nothing, and Hermann watched with amusement.

What moods such boys could have!

Then, when they were finished, getting ready to go, Hermann heard the boy behind him stand up, shove his chair back, and say, "I'm going back to Berlin now!"

Hermann turned around. He believed he had not heard correctly.

"What do you want to do? Back to Berlin? What's that supposed to mean?"

But Gunther only repeated himself, and quite calmly. "I'm going back to Berlin."

"But, for heaven's sake, why? What will you do there? Didn't we agree to be together today? So tell me at least, what this is suddenly supposed to mean?"

Gunther's upper lip twitched nastily, but no answer came.

Hermann stood there, likewise speechless, and he knew neither what to say, nor what to do.

What was this supposed to be? What did it mean?

Then fear for the day gripped him. The day threatened to vanish from him. If he had become crazy, this boy who stood there defiantly and maliciously staring ahead, then Hermann must be the reasonable one. For that, he was the older. *I must not become angry too. With love ... With goodness...*

He walked up to Gunther, gripped him with both hands under his armpits, lifted him up, and sat him on his lap. Holding his arm fast around him, his mouth next to his ear, he spoke, softly at first and falteringly, then ever faster and more urgently.

"Gunther, my boy, now listen to me one time! Look, I have looked forward to this day with you today like a child does to Christmas. You have no idea what I've gone through, what I've suffered these last weeks. And now you want to leave. Without any reason — you want to return to hot Berlin, with its dust and its noise. No, my dear boy, you won't do that to me, Gunther, you won't do that to me?..."

He saw how the lip continued to twitch, always more strongly, and he continued, anxiously, imploringly, almost pleading. "Don't you know yet how dear you are to me? Don't you feel it? I never told you, but still you *must* feel it, Gunther — from each and every thing!..." Silence and defiance.

"Gunther, so tell me at least, *why?* Why so suddenly? What has come into your mind all of a sudden? Why are you being such a stranger to me? We want to get to know one another so as to become friends, and how is that to happen, if I'm not allowed to look into you, as in an open book! Why do you not speak? So at least say something, so that I can understand you! Have I done anything to you? Have I offended or hurt you? Come, be good, my dear boy, trust me! Tell me why you want to leave!"

Now desperate over the silence, to which he did not want to yield, his words rushed on.

"Isn't it so, Gunther, you're staying with me today? Say yes, say that you won't go back to Berlin, say yes, my dear boy, dearer than anything!"

He fell silent, exhausted. He found no more words.

During this long speech the boy sitting on his knees had only one thought: "Good God, will this nonsense never stop? Not even a horse could stand this for long! This show has got to come to an end. Was he really so stupid? No human could be that stupid! And now he's even starting up on love! — when he did not even touch me the whole night. What does he think about me then! What did he think about at all? Does he want a relationship or not? Then why did he bring me here?"

No, he was not letting himself be treated so, not like this! ... that had to come to an end, and soon. What had Kuddel written in the letter: if you don't want to have me, you only have to say so! This nonsense, which was always breaking out anew, was enough to make one throw up!

With the cruel pleasure of his age, the malicious desire of youth, which does not yet know true sorrow, and does not know what suffering means — with the malicious desire to inflict pain (not to inflict pain, no, only to torment), he said, as he quickly got loose from Hermann's arms and stood up, "And I'm still going to Berlin!"

Hermann, too, was now standing again. Even while Gunther was speaking, he felt with each new word that it was going past him, was wrong, was not heard and not understood, not in the way he meant it.

He had to begin differently.

He saw that Gunther was serious, but he still understood nothing. Not the least thing.

He had to stop him, stop him at any price. But how? With a desperate attempt at joking he said, "You don't even have the price of a ticket..."

He promptly received the answer, "You will give it to me!"

Now becoming angry himself, over this more than foolish answer, but still with an effort to keep up the joke, Hermann reached into his coat, which was hanging over the chair, took his wallet out, and held it out open to him. "I can give you even more. Here, take it!"

The boy was startled for a moment. But then he calmly reached out with his fingertips, took one of the three twenty-mark bills, drew it out, and shoved it into his pants pocket.

"I'm going now!"

That was too much for Hermann. He moved towards the boy.

"Gunther," he cried, "you *can't* mean that!" Then he saw that Gunther really meant to go, felt deathly shocked at losing him for today — no, not for just today, but perhaps forever.

"You really mean to go. But where will we ever meet again?" He sought to stand in Gunther's way.

Gunther, however, avoided him with a lightning-quick motion and Hermann heard him say clearly and distinctly, as he opened the door and before he closed it again behind him, "If you want to see me again — I'm in the Passage every day."

PART
3

1

The Passage — there it was. In its triviality and its dubious fame, it sucked in and spit out, spit out and sucked in — from early morning well into the night, when the insatiable jaws of its two openings were closed with black iron bars.

The Passage — sucked in and spit out, spit out and sucked in — crowds, crowds, and always new crowds. . .

Crowds of the curious and indifferent, the casual and the occasional, as well as the seekers, amateur and professional in these matters — the native and the stranger. For there was no Berliner whose walk in Friedrich Street had not taken him at least once through the Passage, and no stranger who had not soon left it again in disappointment.

Vice and inexperience, swindlers and racketeers of all kinds, carried on their business there. Cheats and idlers, prostitutes and whores — there was no questionable livelihood that did not find its way there. And the others. . .

There went young people without jobs or shelter, without a penny in their pocket, who did not know what they were to live on but who had heard from comrades that money could be made there, and they offered themselves.

There, too, those who had work went during free hours — young apprentices and errand boys who thought they could improve their meager week's wages, and make quite a day of it at the same time. They needed extra money because they wanted to go out with their "fiancée" tomorrow, or mother had a birthday and they had to buy her a gift.

However, those were not the only reasons. Sometimes, not caring about girls yet, they were looking for a friend who would go out with them on Sundays, and somewhat adopt them — to care for them and understand them, better than their parents in their sad home ... They did not always find what they were looking for, but many good and fine friendships were made there, walking up and down, after the first understanding glance.

There went, in calf-length stockings and colorful caps, pupils from the secondary schools, to get pocket money because they received little or none at home. Some came just to wander around and "tease the queers," by first enticing them and then leaving them standing. A favorite joke, when they saw that one was following them, was to go to the nearest policeman and ask directions to some street or other that was in the direction of the man following them, then, pointing at him, to die laughing when he believed they were reporting him and quickly skedaddled.

Also, sometimes they let themselves be spoken to, going along amiably, letting themselves be offered cigarettes and then, in the nicest tone, suddenly drawing themselves up to say threateningly, "Sir, what is it you really want from me? If you do not leave me alone this instant..." Then they would laugh loudly at the man's terror. Of course, a dyed-in-the-wool Berliner did not fall for this dirty trick. He knew from the first glance and word whom he was dealing with, or he said, rebukingly, only calmly: "Oh, don't talk nonsense, you couldn't do that to me!" and took them along for coffee and pastry, where he then soon found the right way to their responsive hearts.

Sometimes people came just from curiosity, for adventure because it was too boring at home. They came, then stayed away again, having long forgotten everything when their real adventure, with girls, began to completely capture their interest.

There it was, the Passage, a Moloch, sucking in and spitting out, spitting out and sucking in — crowds, crowds of people, always new crowds ... yet always the old same picture.

2

What he had done that Sunday after he had been left behind in the hotel room, how he had left the hotel, where he had passed the day, when he had reached home — Hermann Graff could remember none of it. The day had been as if he had never lived it, though in fact he had paid his bill calmly and had rented a boat, lying in it for many hours under the trees, finally taking the train back home, just like many other excursionists.

The next day he sat over his work, feeling nothing, thinking about nothing. The blow left him numb and unconscious all day.

What first brought him back to himself again was an inner, boundless rage — over the abysmal dishonesty, the monstrous cheek and inconceivable depravity. Everything, every word, every look, every gesture of Gunther's had been false, false, false, plain false! — and he had been so stupid beyond human conception as to believe in him! This rage agitated him for days.

But it did not keep up. Basically Hermann was not a person to become angry over others. He was seldom provoked by the vulgarity of people. They were the product of circumstances. So long as the circumstances did not change, people would also not change. Thus the first rage yielded to a feeling of disgust.

How was it possible for a boy, for *that* boy, to degrade himself so much! How was it possible that eyes, so clear in certain

moments, lips, so childlike, words, so candid, could be so deceptive? How was it possible to give oneself for money? It was really
for money that he sold himself and his body. No doubt things
went badly for him, but must one's aversion not be greater than all
hunger?

Hermann did not understand it. He would never understand.
But, he told himself, he himself had never yet suffered hunger. He
said this to himself so often that even his feeling of repugnance
did not keep up long.

What lasted longest with him was his feeling of suffering an
undeserved offense. What had he done to Gunther, that Gunther
treated him so? Had he not helped the boy? Had he not loved him?
Gunther must have known it. He *must* have felt it! Hermann did
not grasp the reason ... He did not once suspect the truth.

And if it was not true, then what had Gunther said with those
last rude and appalling words? Were they only an excuse to sneak
off — to get away from him? ... No, they were true. Only too
true. Everything fell into place — going with Hermann after the
second meeting, without remembering the least thing about the
first meeting; going with Hermann, a complete stranger, and
Gunther's always wanting to leave quickly — who knows to
where, but surely to another appointment with even more money
to be gained; Gunther's hesitation with every answer to his questions — and then always that characteristic twitch of his upper
lip, as if embarrassed over his own evasions.

Only one thing did Hermann still not understand. Why had
Gunther run away from him on that first day, out of the Passage,
with whose activities, according to Gunther's own words, he
must have been familiar? Hermann did not understand; it was a
contradiction.

But he was finished with Gunther, quite finished. He wanted
never to see Gunther again. If chance should bring them together
again, Hermann would walk past, without a glance or a word, in
silent disdain.

He wanted to forget Gunther. To think about him no more,
no more with affection — there could be no question of that — but
not with hate. Gunther was not worth either. Hermann would be

entirely indifferent to him, like to a stranger whom he had never seen.

Hermann wanted to forget Gunther so completely that he would not even recognize Gunther if they should meet again. But of course he would never see him again. Berlin was after all large. And in the Passage, where Gunther was "every day," Hermann would never set foot again.

3

or Gunther, meanwhile, life went its usual pace. Potsdam was long forgotten. That morning, on his way to the train station, he saw a steamboat that went to Berlin waiting at the bridge, and he had a fine excursion on the water to Wannsee. If he ever still thought about that day, it was not without a feeling of having been personally hurt and deeply offended, and also not without a certain uneasiness. It was probably for this reason that he said nothing about that experience to any of the other boys.

But now, all that was forgotten, and Gunther's days went by again with a certain regularity — sleep in until noon, a long bath in the boiling Spree, for the heat had not let up. Then, dice and food (when he had money) at Uncle Paul's, and finally the lounges. Between times, a short walk through the Passage and down the Linden to see if there was maybe something to be picked up there.

How his day ended could never be known ahead of time — it might be with some new acquaintance in a hotel, or in an all-night café, or in one of the lounges, or even alone.

Times were bad, however. Most of the johns were out of town. With the heat, the few foreigners spent their stay outdoors, and often nothing happened in the evenings. Then one just had to be a bit hungry again. But it was still never quite as bad as before

— the boys helped one another. Thus Gunther's life went along again, up to the day when the big event arrived.

On that day Gunther, after bathing, was sitting as usual with several other boys, sixteen to nineteen years old in the Adonis Lounge. He had not a penny in his pocket, and the others had little or no more. Going to Uncle Paul's was out of the question. They sat around, bored to death, and waited. But it was still much too early — hardly six.

No other guests were present in the Adonis.

Just as Justav lit the first gas flame in the back room, a rental car stopped in front of the lounge. A servant climbed down from the front seat next to the chauffeur and helped a gaunt gentleman in a top hat out of the car. They entered, the servant at a respectful distance behind his employer.

The gentleman, after a cursory glance around, took a seat in the most remote corner from where he could survey the whole establishment, and the servant indicated to the boys who came running up from all sides that they should leave the gentleman in peace. In return they could consume, at his expense, whatever they wanted.

When the first general excitement settled, they did not have to be told twice. The boys sat down again, singly or together, and Justav was kept busy. With shy, curious and greedy glances at the noble guest, they ate and drank whatever they could.

The strange gentleman watched them calmly from his corner. He ate and drank nothing himself. His servant sat up front and drank a glass of beer. In honor of his guest, Justav lit all the flames. He could not do more.

A tense expectation settled over all the tables. But nothing happened.

After about half an hour, the gentleman stood up, tipped his hat politely, and left the lounge without having spoken a word except for a brief whispered exchange with his servant on his way out. He climbed into the automobile outside. The servant stayed behind, drank up, went to the bar and gave Father (as the old proprietor was called by everyone) a fifty-mark bill with an indication that this was to cover the total bill. The change could likewise be spent on those present. Then he beckoned to Gunther, who was standing around him with the other boys, and took him outside into the street.

The car was gone.

Behind them, from the lounge, rang a wildly confused mixture of loud and excited voices, wrangling over the rest of the money.

Outside, Gunther was asked if he had some time.

Naturally he had time.

They went into the first café they came to.

In the café, Gunther was asked his name. And where was he from? It occurred to Gunther that, in the face of such definite questions, it would be better not to give his real name. He therefore drew out the false identification papers that Atze had procured for him and held them out to the servant. With a quick glance Gunther refreshed his memory: he was called Michael Koslowsky.

"Michael Koslowsky," read the servant. After a short reflection he continued. "That won't do, of course. The Count will have to give you another name."

Then he asked how long Gunther had been in Berlin. Here the truth could not hurt, so Gunther answered him: four months. He no longer knew himself for sure.

The man wanted to know whether he had any kind of connections here. Relatives? Friends? Also no "older friend?" An "intimate?"

Gunther responded "no" to both questions. Now the questioner showed his cards.

"The Count is interested in you. You are to live with him. You will have everything that you need, and each week you will receive a generous amount of pocket money. I am the Count's servant and my name is Franz."

Gunther was so astonished that he could find no answer. If only Atze were here now! Never before had he so wished Atze to be present. Finally he brought out with difficulty: "What do I have to do for it then?"

Franz appeared to have been waiting for this question and

only smiled. "Nothing. You have only to keep the Count company, that is, when he wishes it. Otherwise you can do whatever you wish, though nothing stupid, of course. The only condition is that these queer affairs have to stop. You will go, and speak" — with a movement of his shoulder toward the street they had just left — "with no one from that company there. You will go with no one else. You will avoid any new acquaintance and will no longer know the old ones. Otherwise this arrangement is immediately over. And now, decide. You will not be forced or talked into it. Simply say if you will or not."

The boy felt uncanny. If only Atze had been there! He tried to put off answering. "Do I have to go right away?"

"Yes. Why not?"

"But I still have to go back once."

"Why?"

"Someone there still owes me money."

"How much?"

"Eight marks..."

Franz, the servant, laughed out loud.

"And then I still have things in the hotel..."

"Things? What kind of things?"

"Well, another suit. And boots and..." (Truthfully it was two neckties and a pair of worn-out socks.)

"A suit like this one here?" Franz indicated the suit Gunther was wearing, and laughed even louder. Gunther's objections were granted no further answer. Franz said, "Do you know how much pocket money you will get?"

No, Gunther had no idea but he imagined if he had everything there for free, then maybe five marks, or only three. But he refrained from saying anything.

"Fifty marks," Franz said.

The boy's head swam. Fifty marks! And everything else for free! He was speechless.

Franz asked now, "You are a decent boy, aren't you? You don't steal, do you? For otherwise..." he made a movement of his hand across his throat.

But when he saw how Gunther turned red and his look

became angry, he said, "Well, never mind. You don't look like it. And you won't have murdered anyone either, you're too small for that. So, let's go. . ."

Gunther followed, numb. They climbed into the next cab.

4

What followed — at least in the first days — was no longer reality. It was like a dream.

The cab stopped in the Tiergarten quarter before a house that was not large, but like a palace, shut off from the street by a high fence and a small front garden.

Franz unlocked the door himself, led Gunther up the wide carpeted stairs, and then into a luxuriously outfitted bathroom with colorful tiles and a gigantic bathtub of red marble. There he was thoroughly washed from head to foot with wonderful, perfumed soap, a sponge as large as a wagon wheel, and streams of warm water. Then, wrapped in a soft bathrobe, he was given a warm supper in a shining kitchen. Finally, in a small but snug room he was tucked into a gigantic bed, into whose pillow he sank down over his nose.

Next to this room was that of the servant, as Franz told him. Gunther was to sleep as long as he wished.

But how could he sleep! That no harm was done to him, at least not for the present, he could see. But what would he have to do? Well, they surely wouldn't murder him. He just had to wait and see. Tired from the bath and the rich food, he finally fell asleep in the unaccustomed pillow.

The next morning he had to get in the bathtub again. This time his hands and feet were also given expert treatment. After breakfast he rode out with Franz.

On this day he had no time to reflect on anything. He simply fell from one astonishment into another. They went from shop to shop. There were many purchases: a light-colored summer suit of light, soft material, with long pants; a sport suit, coat and pants, with leather belt and six sport shirts that went with it; an evening suit of black cloth, with a low-necked vest, which first had to be measured, since it was not in stock — "to be able to go out evenings with the Count," added Franz, by way of explanation; and yet another suit, a blue sailor-suit — nothing like the common outfit that Sailor Otto wore, but instead like a sailor of the fleet — with open collar and on the cap the insignia of the imperial yacht club. This last outfit suited him best and he would have preferred to wear it right away. But that would not do. For today, the light summer suit was the only appropriate one. The clothes Gunther had worn were simply left behind.

Then there were more purchases: linen, underwear, wool socks, silk socks, handkerchiefs, gloves, ties, a derby, a straw hat, two caps, and shoes and boots, four pairs right off — low, high, calf, patent leather, fine sheepskin, yellow and black. There seemed no end...

Yet, it did end, with a toilet case with a hundred things in it and, as the very last, a fine leather suitcase was bought, into which most of the things were immediately packed before they returned.

Gunther's head no longer swam — he was completely confused. All that was to belong to him! He tried to add it up — that must surely already be a thousand marks! Franz, however, appeared not to be calculating, and he gave evidence of astonishing experience in these matters.

At the end they went to a barber. There his hair was cut — short, in the military manner, without topknot and without the vulgar straight-around cut. Franz also gave instructions here, down to the smallest details.

That evening Gunther still did not see the Count.

"The Count is dining out this evening," he was told.

He had enough to do admiring all the splendid things, and admiring them again, in his room — in *his* room — undressing and dressing again, inspecting himself in the mirror. He could hardly eat or sleep this evening, for all the excitement. It was madness! If he were to tell this to Atze, he would not believe a word of it!

Every day was a dream. Each day a new one — incomprehensible, supernatural. Everything was different, everything became different from what he thought it — as far as he was still able to think at all.

Two days later, in the afternoon, he came face to face for the first time with his new master.

"Franz, out for a drive!" came the order.

Two minutes later a car stopped before the door.

They drove out — the Count leaning back in the leather cushion, Gunther opposite on the fold-down seat wearing his sport jacket, short pants, and black calf-length stockings. He was curtly greeted with a nod, as if they had known one another for a long time already, instead of having just met for the first time. The Count spoke not a word during the trip.

Gunther, of course, kept silent. He would not, for all the world, have been able to bring out a word. He hardly dared look at the man opposite him.

They drove to Wannsee, on the famous automobile road. There they went into the garden of a small café on the water, and sat as far as possible from the other guests. The few steps seemed to tire the Count. While they were drinking their coffee Gunther glanced briefly at him.

How old would he be? He was probably still young, but his face, a gaunt, pale face with sharp eyes, small, long nose, and firmly closed mouth, looked tired and bored. His hair was thin and already slightly gray. The few words he had spoken when ordering had been soft, but very polite.

Moreover, he appeared to be quite content. He breathed in the somewhat cooler air here with obvious pleasure, drank his coffee in small sips, the cup held carefully in his long, ringless hand, and he offered Gunther a yellow cigarette from his golden case ornamented with a monogram. When the boy looked astonished at the quite small, thin — little tobacco and a long paper mouthpiece —

cigarette, the Count spoke for the first time, but as if to himself: "Russian — smoke up in two puffs!" That the Count did, drawing the smoke in deeply and only after a while blowing it out again, then throwing it away. Gunther tried to imitate him. Oh, he could also inhale smoke! But he immediately fell into coughing, and the Count imperceptibly smiled. Then he concerned himself no further about Gunther. But Gunther had indeed noticed that the Count first offered him a light from his wax match, before he used it himself. Gunther still had enough composure to bring out a faint "Thanks!"

The return trip passed by just as silently. The boy, for the first time in an automobile by day (for nights, almost always quite drunk, he had often enough been put in one by his johns), in the open country, had no real pleasure in the rushing trip. He kept silent and looked straight ahead in embarrassment.

In the evening, after a small meal that was excellent and ample as always from Franz in the kitchen (whom Gunther dared ask nothing, for he mostly received no answer), Gunther was allowed to come to the Count's quarters. He had to undress first and was wrapped in a silken mantle.

"Just be tranquil and undress," Franz had calmly said, "nothing will happen to you."

Nothing really did happen to him.

The Count, in light pajamas, was sitting in a deep chair and holding a book on his knees, and he motioned Gunther to the divan opposite. The divan was covered with the black fur of a powerful bear. The mantle had been taken from Gunther by Franz as Gunther entered. He hesitantly lay down and almost sank into the soft fur.

He was close to crying.

For the first time again, since that first acquaintance, Gunther felt fear. Since then, and since he had become acquainted with Atze, he had not been fearful — of no one and nothing. He had gone along with whomever and wherever, and nothing had ever happened to him. Some people had been crude to him and some friendly. Some had asked for this, and others for that. He had said yes, and no. No one had done anything to him. No, he had no more fear. He even had no fear of the criminal police — with whom, to be sure, he had not yet run into conflict. Here, too, he wanted to have no fear. He wanted, at least, not to show it.

He also had no reason at all to be afraid.

Nothing happened. Nothing. None of all the things that usually happened did happen.

The Count looked into his book, looked up, looked at him as he lay there, looked away again, and read further.

"Hot," he said just once.

It was truly very hot. The heat penetrated through the open balcony door, undiminished by the late evening, mixed with the humid fragrance of the flowers and shrubbery in the garden behind the house.

Gunther dared to move and look over at the man calmly sitting there. The Count seemed to notice it.

"Smoke?" he asked quite amiably and indicated the round stool beside the couch. "But don't burn the fur. Asiatic bear. . ."

Gunther only shook his head. No, he had no desire to smoke. He lay motionless. A long pause ensued. The Count smoked, read, looked at him, looked away, read further, and yawned.

In his glances there was no kind of excitement, neither of pleasure or aversion. His glances were completely indifferent, as if it were the most natural thing in the world that he was sitting here in his pajamas, and the boy was lying there naked.

The boy stretched himself out in the soft fur. He half-dozed. He was now quite sure that nothing would happen. At least not this evening. But he did not feel well. After an hour the Count stood up, nodded to him, and went out through the other door. Franz appeared with the mantle, wrapped it around the boy, and took him to bed.

Thus had the third day passed, and so, too, passed the next ones.

Gunther had it truly good there. Always the best food, as often and as much as he could wish. And enough money. Already on the second day he had received from Franz the first fifty marks.

He could do or not do whatever he wished. No one questioned him. No one made regulations for him, and no one concerned themselves about him. If the Count was not at home — and he often was not — Gunther was allowed to go out.

He was also allowed to walk around the house, throughout each of the two floors and in the garden. He sat in every chair but found peace nowhere.

At first Gunther observed all these things that were completely strange to him with curiosity and astonishment. The furniture, the silver, the carpets and drapery everywhere on the walls, the strange and valuable objects on the tables, the beautifully bound books in the tall and sturdy cases. And all the pictures on the walls. Naturally they were a long way from being as pretty as those in the Passage, and with most of them you couldn't tell what they were supposed to represent. But they had no doubt cost a lot of money, like everything here.

He touched nothing. An odd shyness held him back. Everything was so strange, and nothing became more familiar to him over time.

He always returned to Franz in the kitchen. Franz was the only person with whom he could speak. But Franz spoke little and almost nothing to Gunther. Franz had too much to do, his hands were full, and he was not able to spend time on the boy, even had he wanted to.

Franz, there could be no doubt, was the model of a gentleman's servant. He was on his feet the whole day. He shopped, he tended — with the help of an elderly married couple, who otherwise resided out of sight in the basement — all the rooms. He cooked excellently, even when the Count was out. He kept the accounts of all payments, conscientiously and honestly. Franz was attached with obvious devotion and respect to his master, to whom he never spoke other than in the third person. By the Count, Franz was singled out by being spoken to now and then, occasionally even with something like a conversation.

With time Gunther grew accustomed to the silence of the Count on their afternoon automobile trips. The regions through which they drove left him cold, but the rushing speed of the car was always fun.

Sometimes the Count stopped, looked a while at the lakes

and woods, made a broad wave of his hand, and said, as if to himself, "Beautiful!" Often, however, he used another word, which Gunther did not understand — "Superb!"

The first times that Gunther was taken along in the evening were not so easy for him. They went first to one of the large restaurants of a first-class hotel. There, always in a previously reserved corner, they ate things he would never have believed existed, or could be eaten. The Count never told Gunther how to behave, never corrected him. Even at the most comical moments, he remained invariably serious and calm. He seemed not to notice that Gunther ate his fish with a knife or, in the case of lobster, wanted to eat the claws too. He never became impatient or indignant. He was never unfriendly. But he was also never friendly.

Little by little, however, merely through his example, through his calm and dignified movements, his imperturbable way of acting, his youthful companion grew to want to imitate him. Gunther no longer looked around on all sides when they entered a room. He no longer tucked his napkin in his neck. He no longer attacked his meal, but learned rather to wait until the person sitting opposite began. And he learned little by little, if with difficulty, to handle knife and fork — that was the hardest.

He also grew accustomed to answer without betraying the least emotion, when waiters bent over to him with silver platters and asked if they might serve him more. He almost always said, "Yes..." Now he said, "Yes, please..."

He was conspicuous through his natural charm, and many benevolent but always discreet glances were cast, especially by elderly ladies, at his young appearance, so strange in these places. And he made a flawless appearance in his black evening suit, the low-cut vest, and the small, black tie around the stiff shirt collar.

The Count nodded, they got up, and drove to some theater or music hall. There a box was always reserved for them.

What he did not at all understand was that he was to sit in front of the Count. Surely that was improper. But little by little he caught on to the custom, that the young people sat in front of the older ones here.

They watched and did not speak.

Sometimes he heard the Count behind him softly say to himself: "Beautiful!" — or the other foreign word.

"Beautiful, is it not?" And the boy nodded, although it could hardly have been directed at him. This nodding was the first thing he learned from the Count. It was also so very convenient.

Sometimes, after the performance, they went for a quarter hour in some large bar. He never received more to drink than he could handle.

It seemed to be entirely indifferent to the Count if they were seen together. He probably had not too many acquaintances. If they met one by chance, he walked by Gunther and the Count almost like a stranger, with only a slight bow, or his greeting was a brief word and a quick handshake, without a glance at Gunther.

Evidently the Count stayed out of people's way as much as possible. He seemed to tolerate their proximity with difficulty. He overlooked them. Doubtless no one would have dared to approach him, so unapproachable was his attitude. They sat by themselves, not because the Count would have been embarrassed to be seen with Gunther, but because the Count wanted to be alone.

He belonged to society, but society was not necessary to him. He seldom had visitors at home. Only once did Gunther meet his master on the stairs, showing out an elderly gentleman with a hook nose and green eyes which fixed sharply on him.

"My little groom," said the Count perfunctorily. Everyone knew that he had no stable, never rode, and understood nothing about horses, but the visitor betrayed no emotion.

Moreover it did not appear to be the Count's intention for his companion to always keep silent. The Count constantly listened with that certain obliging politeness, and once or twice even the shy and clumsy remarks that the boy dared to make obviously amused him. But he never followed them up, never encouraged Gunther to continue, replied not a word, and so it remained always a rare and one-sided flow of words.

Gunther felt instinctively, too, that never under any circumstances was he allowed to ask questions. Franz had also brought this to his attention.

"The Count does not like to be questioned. What have you to ask about anyway?"

Gunther never once had to answer, for he was never questioned. Never questioned, for example, as to whether he enjoyed what he was eating, whether he enjoyed what they were watching, never about anything in his life. Not even his name. The Count seemed not even to know his name. Since he was never called, he no longer needed to remember what his name was supposed to be. He was glad of that, for he was still angry over the stupid name Michael, when he already had such a nice one.

Gunther knew nothing of a conversation between the Count and Franz, during which Franz had given a report on the first evening.

"He appears to be quite a decent boy. Somewhat limited. . ."

"Just what is his name?"

"Michael. I called him Michel, which seemed to anger him."

"Impossible! Quite impossible! We must give him another name. What was the other one called?"

"Edmund, Count."

"Also impossible. Better to give him no name at all. . ."

And there it remained. Gunther was just not named. His true name was to remain a secret in the house. He only had to be there.

If they spent the evening at home, then after dinner, which the Count took alone in the small dining room, Gunther was always called in and it was just like the first evening — the Count lay on his lounge chair; Gunther, naked, lay on the bearskin opposite him.

The nights were like the days, equally humid and oppressive. The Count read, looked up, looked at him, read further. Sometimes he read verses out loud, in a foreign language, with an odd voice, as if sounding from a distance but very melodious.

"Beautiful, is it not?" he asked, when he let the book drop and stared ahead for a long time.

No, it was not at all beautiful, it was very boring to Gunther who had understood not a word. He twisted this way and that. He lit a cigarette, careful that no spark fell on the fur, threw the butt into the ashtray next to him, and was bored with it all. Or he lay on his back, his knees drawn up and crossed, and played with the pink toes of his feet in the air, until the Count stood up with a nod. Sometimes Gunther had fallen asleep from sheer boredom. Then Franz came, took him in his arms, and carried him off.

Again and again Gunther thought, especially in the first weeks, "Is it just to go on like this? What does he actually want from me? Just to always look at me?" It seemed to be so.

The Count wanted to have Gunther about, spotlessly washed, well dressed, and talking as little as possible — in the afternoons on excursions, just as in the evenings at dinner and in the theater.

The Count wanted to look at him, stretched out there, illuminated by the soft light of the wax candles in the high chandelier, whose reflections played over his naked body. Nothing else.

"Like a dog," thought Gunther sometimes. "Just like a dog. Only a dog is called and sometimes petted." Gunther was never called . . . Never even touched.

One evening, during dinner in the Adlon, the Count, as if by chance, reached into his pocket and laid a case down before him. "Open it," his nod said. The case contained a gold wristwatch that Gunther had wanted so long. He had to put it around his wrist himself. It was difficult at first. But the Count did not help him. It was as if the Count shunned even the least contact with him.

"Pretty, is it not?" — the boy, who had turned quite red from joy, heard the Count say. He did not dare to thank him out loud.

Gunther felt wounded in his pride. The Count had not so much as given him his hand in these almost three weeks. Why was he disdained? Like once already — where had that been? — oh yes, that time in Potsdam, by the monkey, the one he had run away from. Why was he disdained? The man must know whom he had before him — who he had been, when the Count himself picked him up "from there"! . . .

On this evening when, as usual, they were again together in the garden room and Gunther was lying on his fur (happy over his watch, which now formed his only clothing, yet angry), he saw how the Count made a movement, as if he were searching for something. Then he knew that it was a glass of liqueur that he wanted, and he sprang up, before Franz could be rung for, in order to bring it.

He brought it himself. He remained standing near the lounge chair. He was excited.

He saw how the Count brought the glass to his mouth, tipped and emptied it, and set it down again. And how he then, as if astonished, looked up at him. Gunther remained standing where he was.

But an expression which he had never before seen on the Count's usually indifferent face caused him to crawl onto his fur again. It had been an expression, not of repugnance, but of unconcealed aversion to seeing Gunther standing so close to him. He threw himself sulkily onto the fur, ostentatiously turning his back to the Count. He bit his lip. He could have cried, as on the first evening, but not from fear.

He did not see how the Count complacently looked at his tender, slim back, and longer than usual — in just the same way he looked at his paintings. Nor did he hear the Count murmur to himself, "The devil knows where the rascal got those hands and feet! If only he were not so hopelessly stupid!" Else Gunther would have been able to say to the Count that he had them from his father, who had perhaps also been a count. As for his stupidity — what did the Count know about it, seeing he never spoke with him? However, Gunther never again repeated this, his first and only attempt.

Otherwise everything was fine, if it had not been so horribly boring. Again and again he asked Franz whether he might not be allowed to help with something or other.

"Just let it be. I'll do it myself. Besides that's not what you're here for..."

And when Gunther continued to linger: "Go on out. Have fun. You're got money. Only," Franz raised a warning finger, "only — not there..."

"But if the Count is waiting for me?"

"The Count never waits," said Franz indignantly.

So he dressed — for the first time — in his splendid sailor suit, took a taxi, and rode to the largest and finest motion picture house in the west. No one would have dared to ask the member of the imperial yacht club in the box if he was eighteen years old.

But one could not always go to a cinema. He felt bored, prowled through the rooms, to Franz in the kitchen, and looked at him so long, he was thrown out again.

"Go on out! Why are you always sitting around here? You can do whatever you want. Go and have fun..."

One day he had not seen the Count for twenty-four hours. He questioned Franz.

"The Count is on a trip. But don't worry, you can stay on here. The Count will come back..."

"When?"

"The Count never says how long he will stay away."

5

I f the many free hours before had been boring enough, they now became unbearable. Gunther could no longer endure being so alone.

If he had believed that Franz would now have more free time for him, he was thoroughly mistaken; Franz's fiancée immediately appeared on the scene and strutted around the house.

Gunther could not stand the red-haired female. She looked at him askance, always disdainfully, and made offensive remarks to which he could not reply.

No, he could stand it no longer, this whole crazy life! Was it even living? No one to whom he could tell anything! Ever and always alone!

Never before, since he was in Berlin, not even in the first days of the futile search for Max, did he feel so abandoned as now — now, when things were going well for him, beyond all measure, when all the other boys would have burned with envy, had they known.

But they did not know; he was not allowed to tell anyone. That, however, would really have been the greatest pleasure — to relate this experience. To tell it at Uncle Paul's at the hustler table, and in the Adonis Lounge. He would have been the hero of the day!

He thought about Atze again and again. How astonished Atze would be! Would Atze again be in Berlin? Surely. It was already a long time since the morning on which he had vanished once again.

He could stand it no longer. Should he go to Little Mama and ask? That was still surely allowed him. Little Mama was certainly not queer. And then, too, Atze was perhaps not even there and he would come into no temptation.

Just to be able to drink coffee with Little Mama and tell her would have been a release from everything that was beginning to oppress him. After all, he was not in prison here. He could come and go as he pleased, and now he had plenty of time. He struggled with himself and his last scruples.

After three days, however, he climbed into a taxi and rode to Sonderberger Street by the Humboldt Wood. He wore his light summer suit, carried a cane and gloves in his hands, and naturally had his watch on his wrist. He looked like a prince and felt like one.

Little Mama opened the door.

"Chick!" was all the fat woman could say. He asked for Atze.

Yes, Atze was there. "He lies in bed the whole day and sleeps."

Atze actually was still lying in bed, although it was bright afternoon. But hardly had he seen Gunther than he sprang up onto both feet. He looked at him. Then, right away master of the situation, Atze spoke.

"What did I tell you: What love won't do!"

At first Gunther did not understand. With the Count, indeed, there could be no talk of love.

"You seem to have a fine relationship! He keeps you good, eh?" asked Atze, no longer able to control his curiosity as he pulled on his pants.

Gunther continued to look at him speechless — for what could Atze know of the Count?

"Your john with the five-mark bills."

Only now did Gunther grasp what Atze meant — the goof in Potsdam. He waved his hands scornfully.

"Oh, not that one!" — and he began to explain.

Gunther told his story while Atze dressed. He talked while Little Mama brought pastry and made coffee. He talked while the three sat at table, drinking and eating. He talked in a veritable intoxication of joy, to finally hear himself speak once again...

For the first time since Gunther had known Atze, Atze was speechless, becoming quite silent and reflective. Gunther's tale was new even to him. He was lost, but he would never have admitted it. So, collecting his thoughts, once again the Berliner dumbfounded by nothing, Atze spoke. "He's a special kind. They're called voyeurs in France. They get it off merely from looking!"

Then, he turned to Little Mama, in a triumphant tone. "Little Mama, what did I always say? Chick is a winner!"

They remained together for a long time and it was a fine evening. Every detail was talked about, again and again.

As they were breaking up, however, and Gunther said they really should not have seen one another, and would probably not see one another again soon, Atze said pompously, "You can't mean it. For one thing he's away, out of town. And secondly, you're just not to go with others. You don't have to any more. You don't need it. And after all, what does fidelity mean? He doesn't even love you. The other loved you..."

"What other?"

"Well, the one with the five marks..."

"But he never did anything with me either..."

"Just for that reason," said Atze decisively. Then Atze, who not so very long ago had asserted that love was nonsense and did not exist, added, "Just for that reason. *Because* he loved you. But again you don't understand, Chick, and you will probably never understand, because you don't know life like I do!"

They did decide to meet again. Naturally not in lounges, or where there were streetwalkers, but in private.

Fifty marks a week! I won't let them get away from me so easily! thought Atze. He had already decided right away — it did not require Little Mama's understanding look — to participate in his friend's good fortune to the best of his ability. His last words,

however, were only to repeat again (for even he was still numb):
"Man, Chick, *you* are a lucky dog!"

They met again and again during the next days, at first in neutral
streets and establishments. Gunther paid as a matter of course,
after about half of his savings had been first taken from him.

"Just think, Chick, what all you owe me in tuition!"

Then, when it became boring for them and they wanted to see
old acquaintances again, they met in queer bars, but only in the
afternoon hours. To be sure, Atze kept Gunther distant from the
gentlemen.

"You see, things are going good!" he said, "and why should
that goofy servant ever come here..."

On the fifth day they intended to meet in the Kleist Lounge,
at four o'clock. Since Gunther wanted to show off his tuxedo,
which Atze had not yet admired, he changed at home beforehand.

Then he strolled in this impossible costume of black evening
suit with low-cut vest, top hat, and patent leather shoes, in the
early afternoon — to the secret amusement of the passersby —
from the Tiergarten quarter to Wittenberg Place, for he still had
time until four. That Franz, who was struck by the change of
clothes, was following him, Gunther did not suspect.

He had hardly entered the still quite empty bar, however, and
had just greeted Atze, when the servant appeared on the scene.
Franz did not make a long speech.

"If you want to pick up your things, you can come along right
now!"

Gunther, startled and disconcerted, hardly had time left to
whisper to his friend. "Go to Little Mama. I'll come afterward..."

Franz went ahead and the boy followed, completely ashamed.
He wanted to keep his things.

He got them. While he collected and packed them in the
leather suitcase, Franz stood nearby, in shirtsleeves and red servant's vest, watching each piece with sharp eyes, although Gunther did not think about taking anything that had not been a gift to
him and therefore rightly belonged to him.

This time the boy carried his bag down the stairs himself, and

Franz followed. Conscientious as always, he had strictly kept to his master's order: "If the rascal shows a longing for his earlier life, let him go..."

Happy to be rid of the useless eater and inconvenient loafer in such a good way, he opened the iron door to the street and, without a further word, closed it behind the outcast.

The boy was by no means the helpless lamb he had been at the beginning. For one thing, he had money, still more than seventy marks, and he had a great number of possessions. He went first to a hotel at his old familiar Stettin train station. But instead of his former hotel, he went to one of the large ones, opposite the train station entrance, where he took a room on the first floor up in front. Six marks a night.

Then he went directly to Atze and Little Mama, but there he was badly received. The two of them, having felt sure they had set a good trap for the weekly fifty marks, covered him with reproaches.

"Why didn't you pay more attention, you fathead!" Atze cried.

But Gunther also had a ready tongue now, and used it. Was it not he, Atze, who had misled him into going to the queer bars again?

Thus they quarreled for a long time until Gunther, becoming tired of it, simply walked away, not to return.

For the second time that day he stood in the street, no more discouraged than before. The affair with the Count would have had to end sometime, that he understood. In the long run life there would have become simply unbearable.

Over cake and whipped cream in a café he counted his money and found that it was even more than he had thought — over eighty marks, for the fourth week had also been paid in advance. Enough, therefore, for at least two or three weeks!

But even when it was all gone, he would not go with anyone for under fifty marks, now that he made such a good appearance.

or young Hermann Graff, these last weeks had gone by neither slower nor faster than others, but no longer in the calm of earlier days. He wanted to forget. As if forgetting were easy!

He had his work, and he did it. He came home, then went out again for a walk. When the heat let up a bit — but it hardly did — he went for long strolls. He stayed at home more rarely. He had there what he wanted — quiet and solitude — but he no longer felt at ease in his room. It became ever more foreign and uncomfortable.

Not that he had any complaints about his landlady. On the contrary, no one could be served more punctually and silently than he was. His breakfast stood before the door, his room was made spotlessly clean daily. Never did he discover a sign of improper curiosity. Never were the papers on his desk moved from their place. He himself, meticulously tidy, could not have done better.

Nor could it be her person, for he never saw her. Days could go by without a sight of her, and when that occurred, their meeting was limited to a brief greeting, and now and then the most necessary words.

But her entire appearance was strange and unpleasant — the black, staring eyes, her stern mouth, her hard, cold face, even the invariably black dress, and the whole attitude of her gaunt, bony figure. He still had no idea how she lived when she was out of the house, or there in her back rooms. He did not worry about it, but it was uncanny. Had she known better days and was it a terrible bitterness that she now showed?

Thus little by little a breath of chill came between these two people, who in living habits so resembled one another — who lived here next door to one another. A chill breath that, with time, became a no longer concealed aversion and thus, at least on her side — he sensed it vaguely — became plain hatred.

Basically Hermann Graff had a clear and cool head. He was slow in his decisions, but once they were made, he stubbornly carried them out.

He knew his orientation. He knew how it stood with him. He still read a great deal, but did not trouble himself for an explanation when there was nothing to explain. What was self-evident, natural, and not in the least sick did not require an excuse through an explanation. Many of the theories now posed he held to be false and dangerous.

It was love just like any other love. Whoever could not or would not accept it as love was mistaken. The mistake reflected onto those who were mistaken.

They were still in the majority, those who were mistaken. And therefore in possession of force. But they were mistaken there too, for force never has power over human sentiments. The most human of all feelings — and the strongest except hunger — was love.

Since that terrible struggle with his passion, which a young pupil in his home town had awakened in him (that pupil, whom he had so often seen, but hardly spoken to, with whom he had never made friends, because all circumstances forbade it) — since that life and death struggle he had been afraid of himself. Never again in his life did he want to go through that hell again.

Besides, a certain shame had always prevented him from giving in too much to his feelings or conceding a larger space in his life to them. To betray his feelings to others, or to even show his feelings, to speak about them, would have been completely impossible for him. It would have seemed to him inconceivably ugly.

Therefore, in calm hours, when he rendered an account of himself, he knew why he had at first been so frightened over the impression that strange boy had made on him. When he saw the boy again, Hermann felt how passion threatened to seize him once more and become master over him.

Then, later, he knew he could no longer evade it. He no longer tried to smother and kill it — that, too, would be against his nature. He gave in to it. His passion lived in him, became a part of him. And not the worst part.

But now — after the terrible disappointment of that Sunday — he struggled again, with the whole strength of his will. He must remain strong. He must finish with Gunther, he must forget him. If he could not, he was lost.

At first he believed in his victory. Then he saw, from day to day, how much he deceived himself. He wanted to forget, but could not. It was too late.

He knew there were supposed to be people who could love only once in their lives. Once and then never again. Did he belong to them? he asked himself.

Doubtless not. It was not the first time he was suffering. When he was still quite young, still almost a child, before puberty, he had been fond of a little school companion, with a shy, but entirely fulfilling tenderness, and he had cried bitter tears over him, which hurt as only a child's tears can hurt.

Then, years later, had come that other experience. He was almost a young man, his love still a boy. That experience, which had stirred the depths of his soul, and had brought him near to madness — even today he could shudder when he thought of those hours of torment, bitterness, despair — that experience with the home-town pupil, which none of his associates had even suspected, he kept in his heart as an eternal secret.

What was it now this time? The same? No, entirely different.

He had become older, yet was still so inexperienced, so foreign to true life, so out of human contact.

This time was entirely different. This was a longing, not so much for friendship, for understanding, for trust — it was much more a desire for his self, for those hands, that face, those eyes, that — body.

He did not admit it to himself at first. But in lonely hours he began to suspect that it was so, when in bed he stretched out his hands. For whom were they reaching, if not for Gunther? What was it he yearned for — for his words? No, for his voice, for his nearness. To have Gunther with him — it would be enough, it would be everything!

He wanted to forget him, and could not. He suppressed his thoughts by day, only to have them become dreams at night, which frightened him when he remembered them. Nothing helped.

He now thought about Gunther by day. Always, wherever he walked or stood, he saw Gunther before him. He yearned for him. Immeasurably. With a longing that drove him mad. All other feelings — of rage, disgust, disdain, anger, and bitterness — were absorbed into this one feeling of longing, perishing as if they had never been.

It triumphed, that eternal creator of everything good and best in us, the mother of all geat art, the only home of all lonely or all not quite ordinary people. It also triumphed over him.

Again — as on that Sunday afternoon, when he believed he had lost Gunther for the second time, when he had wandered about, looking for him, not finding him, again, as on that afternoon in the hall of the train station — he said to himself, with almost the same words: "It's terrible! I know him now! He is no longer a stranger to me. I know who he is. I should hate and despise him, and cannot! For I *love* him!"

7

Gunther did not indulge himself in dreams for very long.

He was allowed to be generous wherever he went, looking the way he did. He was constantly asked about the story with the Count, and everyone crowded around him to hear it again and again. He became quite wild when they touched on it. Then he gladly treated them to whatever they wanted. The eighty or ninety marks were spent not in three weeks, but in three days.

His tuxedo had to submit to fate first — that he would surely no longer be able to use. The second-hand dealer was of the opinion that it couldn't be used at all: "What young person wears something like that?"

He received only thirty marks — it had cost four hundred. The sailor suit was next in line, and after it, the gold wristwatch.

He got somewhat more for the sailor suit from a boy who had made out well the evening before and wanted to go to Hamburg. The boy could put such a thing to good use there. Gunther lived for two days from that sale.

Saxon eagerly took care of the watch. He faithfully promised to bring back to Gunther at least a hundred marks, but he showed up with only sixty — he had already taken out twenty as a commission for himself, which he naturally kept quiet about. When Gunther became seriously angry, Saxon's opinion was that he should be happy to get so much. Who would have believed that it wasn't stolen? Only he, the clear-headed Saxon, knew how to wangle it.

From the sixty in the evening, Gunther, on waking up in the morning, had only twenty. The boys had got him drunk, and Gunther was left to pay the whole bill. Two days later, when he had paid his hotel bill, and moved with his suitcase to his old hotel, he had exactly five left. But the worst was yet to come.

True, he no longer gave a loan to everyone who begged him, now that he himself had nothing, but in the evening he let a new arrival talk him into taking him to his room. "I'm new here," the newcomer had explained. "I have no place, haven't yet made anything, and don't know how to do it..." Gunther was basically a good-natured boy, and the memory of his own first days did the rest. A rickety sofa had been placed in the room, since it was too shabby for all the others. It was all right by him if the newcomer slept there. Gunther paid for him, and gave him some of his supper.

When Gunther awoke in the morning — alone — the stranger was gone, and with him Gunther's suitcase — his beautiful leather suitcase! — as well as his light summer suit, and his all but last pair of shoes. In their place were hanging the rags the stranger had worn. The old waiter, in his usual and indifferent way, knew nothing and denied any responsibility — "Why did you bring such a crook in with you?"

Gunther, however, was again out in the street, and wearing everything he now owned — the sport jacket with knee-pants, and in his pocket a couple of marks from yesterday's table money, given in appreciation of his tale of the Count by a delighted john, susceptible to such cock-and-bull stories. Playing the cavalier for fifty marks a night was now out, and he had to return again to the Adonis Lounge, drinking and going with the guests only to pick up the five marks that had become the rule there. Thus the circle had closed. It was the old life — sleeping and loafing by day, carousing and love-making through the night.

But neither the days nor the nights pleased him anymore. In a certain respect a change had taken place in Gunther. He washed himself more often and more thoroughly, when this was possible. He cleaned his nails — which never would have occurred to him before — and he even went around with the thought of buying himself a toothbrush, to get rid of the awful taste in his mouth in the mornings.

He now often sat apart from the others and brooded to himself. He was not drawn into everything that came along, as before. He felt for the first time a certain disgust at the life which he had so quickly been pushed into again. He did not feel well.

He had never liked this life, never really liked it. He had gone along with it, because he had no alternative.

He had had to take part in the dissolute drinking bouts, listening to the dirty jokes, joining in the laughter, but mostly without understanding and not really with the boundless delight of the others, who never got enough of hearing and passing on obscenities. What certain gentlemen wanted and desired — which was also taboo among the other boys and seldom tolerated — he had always refused, and they had never brought him to it, not even through the promises and flatteries. What he himself had felt had never gone beyond a very weak outward stimulus.

Certainly, among the many gentlemen he had met there were one or two whom Gunther's particular kind of conduct attracted, men who assumed that more was behind this constant, quiet passionlessness of his. But when they saw that at bottom Gunther really was indifferent, they soon gave him up and turned to the others, who were more vivacious and entertaining. No one had ever taken a deeper interest in Gunther.

It would hardly have been possible for anyone to do so, for at the core of his being, Gunther was without interests. He read, at most, dime novels, never a good book, never even a newspaper. He almost never took part in a conversation, he mostly kept silent or listened with boredom. The only thing able to captivate him was the moving pictures of the cinema — the more exciting and impossible, the better.

He had — like his Count — tired blood in his veins. That came from his father. What made him so indifferent to his life, indifferent to life altogether must have come from the mother he never knew, the former maidservant; yet he did not have the robustness that allowed her to make her way in the world.

Certainly, however, the feelings that sometimes now tormented him came from instincts inherited from his father's side. What the Count had noticed — Gunther's fitting into a completely new atmosphere, into an atmosphere of wealth and splendor — that, like his slender hands and feet, his walk and entire bearing, was part of his heredity, a part blocked but coming to light again. It was a part of his heredity that could be absorbed by that other part, from his mother, yet not without leaving a residue behind.

He no longer liked his life, and wanted another. But what could that be? It was a difficult question. He did not think of work. Out of the question. Who of his sort worked? He had to go to the lounge, take to the street. The struggle with the next day was an ever new, never resting one.

He also went again to the Passage. That was always a matter of chance, but still mostly not without result.

On one of his Passage afternoons, he saw him there again, the man who — according to Atze — "had loved" him, the one with the five marks, with whom he had been in Potsdam.

Gunther did not recognize him at first, and only saw him because he suddenly felt a look, a strange look, half frightened, half sad, and serious. He recognized Hermann again by this look.

Gunther separated himself from the others he had been standing with around the entrance, and followed him.

Naturally the man didn't love him any more, he assumed, but if he tried it yet another time? He needed five marks so much. Not a john the whole day ... Hermann couldn't do more than chase Gunther away. The man would probably leave him standing and walk on.

He followed Hermann, but at a distance — just enough to keep sight of him. Gunther was not sure of himself. He did not possess the impudence of the other boys, who immediately chatted up each man.

The man would have to look around and see him. Then Gunther would go up to him and ask if he still remembered him. But the man did not look around.

Hermann was walking with sunken head, as if heavy thoughts were oppressing him, just like that earlier time he walked his path through the streets toward the north.

He surely did not recognize me again, even though he looked at me, the boy thought, and followed him further.

Finally they were on Hermann's street. Gunther recognized it again. He stopped and looked down it after him. The man who "had loved him" vanished into the last house.

8

Gunther turned and walked back to the Linden. *So, nothing came of it.*

But he had to have money today. It was Monday, and nothing was happening at the Adonis Lounge. He let his eye travel over Unter den Linden, looking boldly into the eyes of the passing gentlemen he supposed were "so" or "could be so" — the boys acquired a remarkably sharp eye for this — and finally remained standing at a shop window where a small, rotund man, who had doubtless just looked at him and had walked closely past him, now stood as if waiting for him while observing the display.

Gunther positioned himself near the man, likewise looking over the things in the shop window. The small man looked at him from the side, smiling encouragingly, it seemed to Gunther. Then the man slowly walked to the middle promenade, where he stopped again. Doubt was no longer possible. Gunther likewise crossed over. When he was close to the man, he heard the usual remark.

"Well, little guy, out for a bit of a walk?"

He followed the man to the other side of the street. There the man suddenly grasped him on the wrist with two iron fingers. He heard the man speak again. "Just come along, my boy!" The voice was no longer friendly, as it had been before.

Gunther tried to free himself, but could not. The iron pressure on his wrist only became more painful. He was drawn into the entrance of a building. There Gunther flared up.

"You? Who are you? And what do you want from me?"

The small man quickly flipped his coat collar back a moment. The boy saw enough — a cop!

"Don't be so fresh!" the cop spoke again. "And show me your papers!" The pressure on his wrists loosened somewhat.

It occurred to Gunther just in time what Atze had said. "Just don't become fresh! There's no point in it. Always act as if you don't know nothing from nothing..."

His papers? He had them. He always had them with him. They were false, but were papers. He pulled them out.

The policeman checked them over slowly and carefully. Then something about them seemed to capture his attention. With a nasty smile on his beardless mouth he gave them back.

"I'll let you off for today. But don't let me catch sight of you here again, you young scamp, you!" And while he was sharply eyeing the street again, he added, already half walking away, "I'll recognize you again! You can count on it. We'll see one another yet another time!" Leaving the boy standing, he hurried across the street with the small, quick strides of his short legs, obviously after a new and more important victim.

Gunther rubbed his aching wrist. Arrested! Him! Then he made a wide arc around the Passage

In the evening there was absolutely nothing to be done with him. At first he sat for an hour alone in a corner and brooded. Whoever came close was rebuked, "Oh, leave me in peace!" And when Saxon sat next to him and said comfortingly, "Chick, what's the matter with you? Are you sick?" Gunther would have liked to box his ears. He ate a sandwich and slept in his hotel, paying beforehand with the last of his money.

He did not fall asleep immediately, as he usually did. He lay awake for a long time and tossed about. He could not get the day's meeting out of his head. For the first time he saw Hermann in a different light.

He decided Hermann was really a nice person, always clean and well dressed, with money and a permanent position.

He reflected that he had been mean to Hermann, that time in Potsdam. To run away, even to take money first, when nothing had happened! Of course Hermann had also acted stupid. He must have seen, if he had eyes in his head, who Gunther was — not a boy who was looking for work, but for something entirely different. How he had believed everything right off, even that story about the uncle!

But perhaps the guy simply had no desire that evening, and everything was to come the next day.

And now it was over ... For otherwise, he would surely have turned around toward Gunther at least once, to see if Gunther was following him. But it was as if he had not even seen and recognized the boy.

Atze had so firmly asserted the man loved him. There must have been something to it, for otherwise he would not have waited all those days, almost a whole week, every day on the bridge. He did say, too, that he loved Gunther — it was precisely that which had made Gunther so angry that morning...

No, it was over. Hermann would no doubt be able to love only respectable boys, not such as Gunther ... But then why had he looked at him so sadly?

Was he angry? His look had been so strange, so ... so serious. But not angry. No, he wasn't angry. *If he had been angry, he would have hauled me out of the Passage and called me to task for having run away and for the twenty marks.*

Too bad that it was over. Once, Gunther had wanted a relationship with him. Now he wanted it again. It would have been just the thing that he now needed so badly — a good friend to take care of him, support him, and at the same time leave him his freedom. How would it be if he did attempt it once again?

Gunther had to begin. Lying no longer helped. He had to win Hermann over. And a slight suspicion of truth began to dawn — what if Gunther had started something that time, or even earlier, and had not waited for Hermann to make the first move? Many men wanted that. Had he not heard often enough, not only from

Atze, that he should be more accommodating? Gunther wanted to try once more.

He now knew where Hermann lived. He also knew when he came from his job for home — at five. So a quarter or half hour later he had to be on his way.

What else was he to do now? It was over with Atze forever. The lounges in the west remained closed to him. He was sick and tired of the Adonis Lounge. And — worse — he was no longer allowed in the Passage and its surroundings, the Linden and Friedrich Street, after being arrested and warned today. He would have to be on guard against letting himself be seen there again! Then it was over for him — he knew that! He was angry with himself — he should have been able to see that that cop was no john. To be taken in so!

He was unable to fall asleep. The whole day thunder had rolled and lightning flashed. But still no rain came, none for weeks now. The heat in his small room was unbearable. Even when he opened the window, it did not help, for it was the same outside, and it also always stank so much from the courtyard. He twisted about in the pillows. He thought further about Hermann.

Yes, he wanted to try once again. Tomorrow. At five. But not on the bridge, in another way. But if — and so it appeared — Hermann was still innocent? Then — and with this thought he had to laugh to himself — "then I will just have to seduce *him!*" Laughing to himself, he finally fell asleep.

9

In Hermann's feelings a definitive change had taken place in the past days. He no longer blamed the boy, but only himself. He realized how falsely, how completely falsely, he had conducted himself and acted.

The boy could not understand him. He was too young for that. He did not know what love was; he could not know. He had doubtless never met with it. He had never heard from his father; hardly remembered his mother, out there in the world; his grandparents, old people ... And here? Whom could he possibly have here, who took even the most superficial interest in him?

The environment in which he grew up, even more, that in which he now found himself — (Great God, what kind of environment that must be!) — must have choked off all his better and finer sentiments. The struggle against hunger and need had hardened, dulled, and embittered him. The filth all around him had rubbed off on him!

Thus this man, still so young and ignorant of life, spoke to himself, again and again, in an effort to find excuses for his loved one. In the end, he was almost on the point of admiring Gunther, that in spite of everything, Gunther had held his own, had still remained at times so childlike in his glance with those gray-blue eyes, so charming in his nature.

He, he alone was to blame, or at least mainly to blame. Why

had he not taken him in his arms? Why had he not spoken to him, as doubtless everyone spoke to him, in the only language that he was able to understand, only with an entirely different tone, a more affectionate and understanding one? Why had he not been entirely different to him?

Everything would have then turned out differently. Insight would have come, even if there was no understanding. A kind of friendship would have slowly grown up between them, even if not really a true friendship, which could only consist of mutual respect. Even perhaps with time, a long but beautiful time, something like an inclination — even if, of course, not love, for one could never feel love for a street boy.

Such were Hermann's thoughts now, and he brooded deeper and deeper in them until they were replaced by others, which tormented him so that he found no peace. If he had acted differently to Gunther from the beginning, he would perhaps have been able to rescue the boy, to lift him out of the mire in which he was sunk, have still been able to rescue him at the last moment! He sought to acquit himself from this guilt of omission, and could not.

This self-torture, however, also gave way to a feeling of helplessness and fatalism. No, he could not have been able to help him. It had been too late!

And finally this last feeling gave way to one that stayed and stayed — that of longing for Gunther...

Last of all, however, in these hot days and humid nights which made the blood boil, this feeling of longing changed itself into a new and final one — desire!

Now he lied to himself no more. What was every love — and he loved him, still loved him! Loved him more than ever before! — what was every love in its deepest base but the burning wish for possession of the beloved object?

What nonsense did people talk about a love of souls! It did not exist. It was the sentiment of weak, eccentric, sick people! The healthy person wanted and had to possess what he loved, not in helpless dreams of longing, but rather in the warm reality of life. Everything — he lied to himself no more — that he felt for Gunther had been nothing other than this one burning wish: to possess him!

He remembered the first evening after their first reunion, the evening after their quick parting in the garden on the Spree. He was prepared to sacrifice his life's salvation to be allowed just once to enclose this strange and tender body in his arms!

That's how it was, and not otherwise. What had his fearful struggle been basically? Where did the unrest of his days, the nightmares of his nights, come from? And this tormenting longing, what was it except this one unfulfilled wish?

He deceived himself no more. He had arrived where he should have started from, if he had not been so obsessed, not been blind and deaf, not been such a complete fool!

"To him!" cried out in him. But where was Gunther now? Lost, again lost, and through his own fault!

The scorching heat of this summer was no longer bearable. It crept into the blood, fatigued and stirred up again. It boiled in every vein, in the veins of the people who crept through the streets with glassy stares and tired movements. It seethed in his blood, too. It cried out for Gunther! Day and night!

He felt with a frightening clarity that he could no longer continue to live this way. He had to have another human being with whom he could talk, with whom to share, whom he could think of during his work, in the many and long hours of his solitude.

Gunther was gone, lost. So it had to be another. One who, even if not a friend, filled the place of friendship. Someone he could enclose in his arms, to calm and cool his boiling blood. But where to find him? Why, only among the boys — there!

He had not the least idea how these boys lived, what they did and how they carried on. Of course, things went badly for most of them. Many probably felt comfortable in their awful occupation.

But among them there must surely be some who, perhaps, had entered that life, without knowing what it was, and who now wanted out again, who longed for a helping hand. If he could find one, one not entirely corrupted and lost, the boy need not be good-looking or especially bright. If the boy only pleased him to the extent of being beside him, having him close to himself . . . as long as he was just not so crude, so cheeky, so dirty and common, as those he had seen in the Passage on the first day...

Since that time when he had looked for Gunther, in vain, Hermann had not been through the Passage again. He went in — hesitantly, with a secret reluctance.

The rascals were standing around the entrance, impudent and provocative. Again, people pressed around, again the crowd was as stifling as in a hothouse.

His gaze roamed over the faces of the young boys; it was warily, impudently, familiarly returned. It was impossible — quite impossible! Not even *one* face attracted him. There was not *one* that did not repel him!

He must constantly think of Gunther and *his* face! Not that he hoped, or feared, to see it show up. Gunther was long gone. He could no longer be here. How would it be possible to stand around here for weeks and months, walking up and down, without completely going to ruin or becoming mad? It appeared even physically impossible — no body could stand that for long. Not to mention a youthful and still so tender body as Gunther's.

But he thought about him — as he always thought about him. He thought about how he had seen him for the first time. How he had stood there, how Gunther had run away...

Again and again Gunther's face shoved itself between these other faces, these faces so different and strange.

When Gunther had said those dreadful words: "I'm in the Passage every day!" — that was not to be understood literally. He must indeed have come here often. Now, however, he was surely no longer in Berlin. Or he was corrupted, dissipated, hopelessly depraved. Gunther was no longer here. He could no longer be here. It was impossible.

Again Gunther's face stood between him and these other faces, now so plainly palpable that he could bear it no longer and hurried out.

He wanted to go there no more. He could not bear it. And yet he went there once more, and then a third time. But always he left immediately. Today, already the fourth time in two weeks, was to be the last time, he had decided.

He no longer knew what still drove him there. Yet he did know, but he no longer accounted to himself over it. It must be the obscure urge in his blood in these hot days.

This time he approached from the south. The Passage was not very lively. Everyone was sitting outside on the chairs and benches, for the intense, yellow heat under the glass roof was simply unbearable. Guests sat in front of the café and spooned their ices. Music sounded soft and sleepily. He stood still for a moment, then walked out the exit to the Linden. There, in a group, stood Gunther!

Hermann recognized him immediately. Gunther was wearing an entirely different outfit — a sport jacket with short pants and a leather belt, his thin calves in black socks. His shirt was open at the breast. He was wearing no hat. He had become much, much taller. Nevertheless Hermann recognized him immediately, still ten paces distant.

Then the beat of his heart stopped. His feet might carry him no more. But he continued walking. He walked up to the group and looked Gunther full in the face.

As if drawn by his presence, by this look, first from behind, now near and on him, Gunther turned and they briefly looked one another in the eyes.

It was Hermann who first turned his gaze away and walked on out and down the Linden. He was thinking nothing. He had not a single thought. He walked on further, along the Linden. Then, without knowing to where, he crossed over.

When he came to himself again, he realized what had happened — the unexpected, the unbelievable, the paralyzing. He had seen Gunther again! He walked in the direction of his room. It would have been impossible for him to turn around and look back. Only when he was alone in his room, after he gulped down a glass of water, did he collect his thoughts.

He had seen him again! But not as he had imagined, disreputable and tattered, but rather entirely different.

Gunther had looked much fresher, healthier, and far stronger. And he had become tall, so oddly tall. It did not seem to be going at all badly for him — the almost new outfit, the colorful shirt, his whole unconcerned and not in the least depressed attitude.

And how he had looked at him! Hermann's heart, which had stopped, suddenly began to beat madly. How Gunther had looked at him! He had returned his gaze with not a trace of surprise — not friendly, not unfriendly, without any impudence or provocativeness — no, entirely calmly, almost indifferently, as if Gunther wished to say, "Well, here you are again too. How's it going with you?" And only a bit, just a little bit, had his upper lip twitched.

Gunther had recognized him. There could be no doubt about that; he had recognized him again. Hermann's heart beat madly.

He felt unable to stand. His limbs were like lead. His nerves twitched and twitched to the breaking point. The sultry room threatened to suffocate him.

Finally he stood up. He threw open the window, but from outside came such an oppressive air that he closed it again. The small piece of sky he had just seen over the wall opposite was sulphur yellow, with red stripes that appeared to be burning.

He threw off his clothes and, in the bathroom across the way, let the water flow over him. It scarcely refreshed him. Stretched out on the sofa, he soon broke out in sweat again from every pore. He was unable to eat. Only drink, constantly drink. Water mixed with cognac.

How beautiful he had been! Never had Gunther appeared to him so beautiful.

Where had he been all these weeks? Always there in the Passage? Perhaps. And how might things have gone for him? Apparently they were going well.

How Gunther had looked at him! The moment now stretched for him to a full minute, when he pictured to himself the slightest movement, the slow turning toward him.

How was he getting along? And where was he now? At this moment — where and in whose arms?

He lay his head back and spoke softly and passionately to himself: "I do not know where he was and where he is. But I have seen him again. I now know where I can find him. He was there today, and will be there again tomorrow. Every day I'll go there, every day until I find him again. And if I have to go there every day for a whole year, I'll go. For I must see him again. Others have had him. Others have him every day. I, too, must have him!"

He continued, with firm decision: "I'll go there again tomorrow. Tomorrow — and then every day. Right after work. I'll be there about six..."

Then with a repressed and terrible vehemence: "If I see him, he must come with me. No matter whether he will or not. Others have had him. Others have him — each day. I, too, will have him — finally have him! For I have a right to him, greater than all these others. A greater right, because — I love him!"

In the night, too, when a storm continued to threaten — the thunder rolled and the lightning flashed, and the heat outside, like that within, was oppressive — these thoughts returned again and again, thoughts so foreign to him before, thoughts, not of his brain, but rather of his stirred-up blood, his twitching and over-taut nerves, and again and again he gasped into his pillow: "Tomorrow! Tomorrow I'll see him again! Tomorrow you will be mine! For you are beautiful, like no other, and I love you!..."

10

Hermann did not need to go to the Passage. As he turned into the street to his rooms the next day, about five-thirty, a dirty little boy ran up to him, shoved a note into his hand, and ran away again.

He opened it with astonishment and read the words painstakingly written with pencil, "Can you fergive me?"

He did not understand at first. Then he looked up. There opposite, on the other side of the street, Gunther stood. Gunther, for whom he was searching, for whom he would have searched today, tomorrow, and every day until he found him — there stood Gunther!

Gunther slowly came over the street and up to him. He stood before Hermann and looked at him. Neither of the two spoke a word.

They walked, side by side down the short street, entered the house, the apartment, his room. The door closed behind them.

Hardly were they alone when the boy threw his hat onto the nearest chair, bounded to him, wrapped his arms around his neck, and sought his mouth.

Hermann reeled and breathed with difficulty. He thought he must sink. Then he gave in. A god would have given in. He was no god. He was only human. And — he *wanted* to give in.

Outside, the storm finally broke out. The scorched walls hissed. The clouds broke and the rain roared down in streams.

When they came to their senses again, they were sitting on the sofa. Gunther slowly removed himself from the arms that were holding him as if they never wanted to let him go again, and he walked to the window. When he opened it, the rain sprayed into his face and he quickly closed it again.

Turning back, he again lay his head against the breast of his friend, snuggled up close to him, and said, as he looked up at Hermann with an impish smile, "You could have had that long ago, if you had not been so dumb!"

PART

4

1

An odd relationship arose between the two. On the first day, while they were sitting for a long time next to one another in a close embrace, Gunther had set out his conditions.

"Naturally we'll see one another more often, and if you want, we'll stay together. But I must be free. Being always just with you would in time be boring for both of us. I'll certainly always come to you. You don't need to be afraid any more that I'll stay away. So, do you agree?..."

Hermann had only half listened. Never in his life had he believed a human being could be so happy, beyond all measure, superhumanly happy, as he was. He promised. He would have promised anything. He would have promised within twenty-four hours to fetch the moon from the sky.

Gunther continued, saucy and serious.

"See here, you have things to do, too, and must work. You need only give me what you can, I'll certainly be satisfied with it. So it's agreed, and you don't ask me about anything else. I can't stand being questioned..."

That, too, was promised. Hermann was thinking at that moment only of how wonderful was the profile of Gunther's red, somewhat arched lips. They were to be his, his. No, they were his. He pulled Gunther to himself and kissed him, and was kissed in return.

Everything was transformed. Never in his life would Hermann Graff have thought such bliss possible, as there was in these first days. They were a dream, a dream of happiness and bliss! ... Incomprehensible ... quite incomprehensible!...

Waking in the morning was a joy, unknown since the days of his innocent childhood. Work was play, and even waiting was the ardent, agreeably painful happiness of an hour, for hours of a greater happiness...

For his fear, his fear — will he return? — had vanished. He returned. He would return.

The world was transformed, the people, everything...

In his office he was asked again, "You must have won the lottery, haven't you?"

He had won it. Finally.

Only at their third time together did he dare place a condition from his side too. But it had to be. He did it almost timidly.

Struggling, he said, "I will not question you, Gunther. It is to be as you wish. But — you must understand what I'm saying now — then you are never, never to tell me where you are coming from and where you are going. You must understand. I couldn't bear it. If you believe you can't live otherwise — I am not your guardian and am not to make rules for you. Only I am not to know. And the past — well now, we want to let the past be buried, speak about it no more, think about it no more. You understand me, don't you? Come on!"

And he drew Gunther to himself.

Gunther had listened, but not very accurately. He by no means understood everything. But he understood this much, that he was to tell Hermann nothing, and that was all right with him. One surely did not always have to tell everything right off. Thus, a pact was concluded between them.

Besides, there was enough to do in these first days. What all had to be taken care of! There were so many things to be purchased. Gunther could no longer go out, with the weather getting cooler, in the light summer outfit which he was still wearing. A warmer, darker one for the winter was absolutely necessary; also an overcoat for the really cold days, which no longer seemed distant. And sturdy shoes and warm underwear, and everything that went with them besides, so as to fit him out again.

They went from shop to shop, selected, conferred, and bought. It was an entirely new joy for the older man — and naturally, with every new piece, a joy and happy surprise, too, for his beloved boy. Of course, it was not all done in a morning and with uncounted hundred-mark bills, as that time with the servant Franz. But in return it was much pleasanter.

Not that Gunther's new friend kept an account. He would have been ashamed to do so now. To add it up — now, when happiness had come to him! It was necessary, and so had to be. Thus he drew from the bank what was needed, and only after a long time did he add it up, to see if it was much or little. It was much.

Then, too, a room had to be taken care of. However, Gunther had already made arrangements. He had grown tired of always sleeping in a different bed and in miserable hotels. He had moved in with an acquaintance, a very decent boy "who works and only occasionally joins us." They lived with a nice old lady who looked after them. Gunther needed to pay only half and had at the same time company, if he ever felt alone. "Feel alone!" thought Hermann. "Am I not always and at any time here for him?" (He forgot that he was occupied during the day.)

He did not say it. He only asked if he might not be allowed to see the room sometime, in order to see how they lived together. Not that he wanted to come there often, he added immediately, already fearful again. Only, what a joy it would be for him to make their new and surely bare room really comfortable. (He would also very much have liked to see the other boy at least once.)

But Gunther would hear absolutely nothing of this. He even kept secret where it was and the name of his roommate.

"I certainly can't take a gentleman up there!" he said. "What would my landlady think of it?"

As if I were one of these "gentlemen," the rejected man thought again. But he now said nothing more and regretted already that he had even asked.

The room, and having a roommate, was not a hoax. Gunther no longer lied at all, simply because he did not need to lie any more. He was truly serious about changing his life in a certain respect. No more lounges and no more Friedrich Street. Chance also came to his aid.

Through one of the other boys — boys became acquainted with one another like dogs — he had fallen into quite different circles from those in which he had moved up to now.

He moved in closed circles, of gentlemen who did not cruise the street in order to look for boys to have a good time with them. These circles were supplied — one did not exactly know how — one boy just brought another along. Each was at first carefully examined, to see if he was trustworthy, before he was granted the honor of being accepted.

They came together, at first, to be in company — "among themselves." A gentleman who already had a young friend brought him along. Those who had none, hoped to find one there.

Faithfulness was taken seriously only in certain cases, but then it was taken very seriously. There were scenes — petty jealousies, disputes, tears, separations, and reconciliations.

They were all more or less well-to-do people. Wholesale merchants, attorneys, artists — all the higher professions were represented. Most of them had to be very careful — especially the married ones.

All were polite and friendly among themselves and with the boys, and the tone remained altogether within the bounds of outward decorum and never became common. They took a deep interest only in their current favorites. How deep this went, however, mostly eluded observation at their gatherings.

They met by preference in their homes, if that was possible. They gave invitations and were invited in return. Sometimes they organized formal parties, which were merry and loud, without degenerating into orgies.

It was like a secret fraternity with unwritten laws, which, therefore, were all the more strictly observed.

They were "nobility" who, if they gave someone a cigarette case, did not wish to have him believe it was silver when it was only nickel alloy. They were generous, without exactly being extravagant. And during the day they gave themselves to their work.

Gunther felt quite at ease in this new society. He did not have a steady relationship and he did not find one. He also preferred not to, now that he had his Hermann.

And, oddly, the gentlemen were fond of him, took him along — now this one, now that one — but always they dropped him again. There was no jealousy or argument over *him*. "Hermann really doesn't need to be jealous," thought the boy. But Hermann knew not the least thing about all this.

There had to be a reason for this, and it was probably in Gunther's coolness and lack of sensuality. He was found to be good-looking and trustworthy, but boring.

He no longer suffered any kind of need. He always had money in hand, sometimes quite a bit. But it ran through his fingers. He had no more cares, and needed to have none for the next day. And even if he did — he knew now, of course, to whom he had recourse *always*, and at any time, for help.

Thus they slowly grew accustomed to one another. Naturally Gunther could not come by day. But from five-thirty on he was expected. And with what painful longing, with what tormenting restlessness, with what anxious doubts, still: "Will he come today or will he stay away?"

When he came — this joy! — then Gunther was either already at the corner and went right up with him, or he stationed himself at the wall opposite, and softly whistled with the whistle that, in the first days, they had practiced with so much laughter. Then the window flew open, he went up, the door was already standing open, and he was in the arms that embraced him as if they had not just yesterday held him.

Then they would eat in the room first, or in some decent restaurant, and spend the rest of the evening at the circus, at the Wintergarten, in some cinema — whatever Gunther wished.

Or sometimes Gunther "had to leave soon." In giving this

news, which always cut Hermann to the quick, Gunther sought to make a sad face. Sometimes he stayed, only to start up unexpectedly. "How late is it already? I don't have any time more." Then he would leap up, give Hermann a quick kiss, and make a hasty departure. He never said where he was going. He never promised to return. He never said when it would be. And he never stayed overnight.

For one thing, Gunther's real life began only in the evening, when "the other gentlemen" had time. Then, too, Hermann also did not want it, as gladly as he would have kept Gunther with him. He had taken the room for himself and himself alone. Even if his strange landlady would (as he supposed) have noticed nothing, it would have seemed to him a breach of contract and thus have gone against his sense of justice. He had to grit his teeth when Gunther himself — he had nothing else planned for the evening — once harmlessly said, "But do let me stay with you until early in the morning," and with his impish face added, "I could sleep on the sofa..."

So were the days in the first period, when Gunther *came*. But there also were those days when he stayed away completely. One day, two...

Then Hermann, waited, restlessly walking to and fro, again and again going to the window in fear of having missed the whistle — or standing there, staring at the wall. Then he waited — one hour, two, into the third — until his stomach reminded him that he must eat something, and his heart told him that, for today, it was useless to wait any longer. Then, downcast, he walked around the corner to the small, quiet inn, or he got out food he had previously bought, to gulp it down with a cup of tea which he made himself, not bitter or even wounded — there was no helping it — but still sad and disappointed, latching onto just one thought: "Tomorrow! Tomorrow he will certainly come, since he didn't come today. If it were only tomorrow already."

Tomorrow would it then be: "Do I have time today? Today let's stay together the whole evening. Where shall we go?"

Or would it be: "I've just quickly come up to tell you that I can't stay today. You're not angry with me, are you?"

No, he was not angry. He was never angry. How indeed could he be angry with Gunther!

It required the patience of an overpowering love to endure this waiting, this insecurity, the long hours of disappointment after hoping in vain. Only the certainty that Gunther would return gave the young man the strength to get through them.

And Gunther *would* return — of this he dared grow more convinced daily. The security lulled his tormented spirit again and again.

The boy was glad to be with him, without doubt. He saw it in the way Gunther flew to his neck after entering. He saw it in the way Gunther, little by little, put off the hour of departure and obviously left unwillingly.

And why should Gunther not be glad to be with him? He was always greeted with joy, as if they had not seen one another for God knows how long. There were always sweets ready for him. There were always *the* cigarettes that were just then his favorite brand (a new kind every three days). Everything was always as if it were there just for Gunther, and he was never questioned!

Where was he better looked after than there, with a good friend whose concern and kindness never tired? There he was not only welcome, he was longed for, whenever he came. There he was ruler: over each feeling, over each thought.

With the natural cunning of his years, Gunther had soon caught on to this. It flattered his youthful vanity to see himself so desired, so loved. He let himself be pampered, spoiled, courted. That was just right. Everything revolved about him and him alone. So it should, and must be.

It was precisely this that Gunther had wanted, and had found nowhere else; this was what the other boys, so far, did not have. Never had any person, not even approximately, been like this to him.

A feeling told Gunther that it was better not to speak of his friendship to any of the other boys. Either they would laugh at him or he would be sounded out, and envied. So he kept silent. If he was questioned about where he had been, or where he intended to go, where he had got this new outfit and these new boots, well, he was making out, what concern was it of the others! And the best part was he could come and go without ever being questioned. He was never nagged. He absolutely could not stand constant nagging.

And Hermann? What had he to say about Gunther's life? Nothing — he knew nothing about that life. Hermann kept his promise. His only fear was that he could break down, and lose him again.

He had grown patient, infinitely patient. He resigned himself to sharing Gunther since he could not completely possess him. He could not have Gunther entirely for himself alone, as his dream had been. He lived now only in Gunther. He was himself only in Gunther's proximity. If he was not always happy, still in some hours Hermann was completely happy.

Only at times, in the first weeks, were the old feelings stronger than himself. Then it could happen, when Gunther was sitting on his knees and was holding him fast, his arms would become limp with the thought, *Who held him like this yesterday?* His arms would fall, the boy would slide and look up at him in surprise.

"What's the matter with you now? You know, I can never figure you out. Sometimes like this, sometimes like that. Not at all like—" Like the others, he had wanted to say. But he did not say it. He, too, thought of his promise. And also of how good he had it here. That was not be thrown away!

Then his friend gave up thinking and doubting. He forced himself to. It served no purpose. Things were like this and could not be otherwise. One argument, one demand, one simple question would be the end. Only in this way could he keep Gunther. Only in time win his love, which would then belong to him alone, offered freely and of Gunther's own accord. The hour would — it *must* — come! His love would compel it.

Gunther was standing behind Hermann and looking at the work, the crossed-through words and the incomprehensible signs drawn with red ink on the margin of the long paper strips. He had become bored and was standing with his hands on the neck of his friend, trying to get under his collar. He knew Hermann liked that. Hermann continued working.

Gunther pretended innocence: "Well now, Manny. That's really your name."

What, he still didn't know the abbreviation for mannikin?

No, and he found it silly. One could call a dachshund that (or at most a tactless wife her husband), but not a person.

"Now, don't get upset. I won't call you that again, if you don't like it."

Gunther resolved to call Hermann that again at the next opportunity. It was always good to know what would make someone angry. Actually, he really did not want to anger Hermann, for during those weeks he had truly formed a kind of dependence on this kind, always patient, always loving friend, who was so entirely different from all the others.

With Potsdam, however, he did prefer not to try any more.

"Are you still angry with me about Potsdam?" he had asked. But here, for the first time, Hermann truly became indignant, though not angry.

"Just keep quiet about Potsdam!" Then immediately Hermann became nice and calm, but serious. "All that should and must be forgotten between us!"

Gunther sensed how much the mere mention hurt his feelings, even if he did not understand.

Things became better as the weeks passed by. Rarely did Gunther now stay away a whole day, and when that did happen, it was clear that he himself felt bad about it. Moreover he would now spontaneously give an explanation: he had had an appointment; a "date"; a chance meeting with some acquaintance or other "from earlier," who then did not let him go.

"Don't be angry with me!"

No, Hermann was not angry. He was never angry. He could not be angry with Gunther.

The weather was awful. After the long, extraordinarily hot

summer came a changeable September, then a cool and rainy October, and now it was already November, with the first snowfalls and cold, gloomy, sad days from which the last sun of the year crept away.

Then they did what they both said was best, namely not go out at all. Rather they lit the lamp, prepared their own meal, and made themselves comfortable in the warm and quiet room.

The greatest thing for the boy was, having eaten till he was full, the first cigarette in his mouth and — after a little chat — to sprawl on the old sofa and get snug in a blanket, his legs drawn up and his arm propped, to be able to read to the end a wonderful thriller, while Hermann read printers' proofs at his desk and now and then looked over at the breathless tension and reddened cheeks of the reading boy.

For Hermann, however, the greatest happiness was to sit beside Gunther, take his head in his hands, and to look into those unfathomable eyes, whose color he still did not know because it was always changing; to inhale the fragrance of his hair and lightly and lovingly caress it anew, until the cheeky rascal laughingly blew the smoke of his cigarette into Hermann's face.

It was an odd relationship between the two, and it remained so. At bottom each would have been glad to break their contract, but neither dared to. In the many hours of these days they became closer. But the final trust was missing. Always there remained a barrier between them, which they were never allowed to cross. One not allowed to ask, the other not allowed to tell how he lived. And what stories he could have told!

Thus they kept their silence more and more — Gunther content as it was, Hermann happy just to see him so often, to be allowed to have him for hours, but always with the secret fear of losing him.

At times Hermann thought, "It's really comical. We have already been together so long now, almost daily, and at bottom I still know nothing about him — not how he has lived nor how he now lives. Ask him just once! Try it at least!" But again and again he left it undone.

Even if Gunther no longer resented questions, if he answered, what would Hermann hear? Quite shocking and strange things, which he would not comprehend and which would fill him with indignation or disgust. And which surely could help nothing, but instead harm their love. It was better the way things were. It was better that the veil between them not be removed.

That here and there a word raised the veil, like a breath of air, was unavoidable. Thus it happened one day, spontaneously, that the story of the Count was told. Surely he was allowed to tell *it*, thought Gunther to himself. It was a case of "nothing happened."

So Hermann heard it, astonished, upset and — since unfortunately he entirely lacked the expertise of the all-knowing Atze — without understanding a word of it. The man had probably been crazy. But still — it was bad enough that something like that existed. He gathered from the confused and incomprehensible tale that his darling must have had it very good there in many respects, better than with him, and this pained him. But then he heard also that with him it was really much cozier. This pleased and comforted him again.

Their conversation was otherwise mainly limited to what was immediate — how it was going for Gunther; where they wanted to go today and whether they wanted to go out at all; what he needed . . . to then end in mutual silence or in a mute embrace.

For — Hermann soon had to accept it — his little friend had no interests at all. In no one and in nothing. What was of such burning interest to other boys of his age — sport, adventure (even a little affair with a girl, which he would gladly have forgiven) — all that left Gunther completely cold. He practiced no sport. But of adventures he still had enough experience. He did not concern himself with girls, however: "Oh, the old women! They're all so silly, and also cost much too much money!"

A good play or one of the better films bored him. Excursions were now automatically forbidden. He did not know how to entertain himself. And when once a good book was substituted for his everlasting thriller, it was soon shoved aside with a yawn: "What nonsense!"

To resign himself to doing without an intellectual communion, and to take pleasure only and repeatedly in his bodily presence, always newly enchanting, in his smile and his sweet voice (which remained sweet, even when he talked nonsense) — what was left, except this?

Nevertheless Hermann sought again and again to get behind the puzzle, which was no puzzle and therefore had no solution. For it perhaps was the discord of the teen years: eternal change and becoming; defiance and devotion; wanting and then again not wanting; moods, moods, moods ... Who has ever understood it? Who can understand it — the puzzle of those years?

At times, in clear hours not troubled by passion, Hermann said to himself in the face of this unbounded indolence: "But he is really stupid! Simply stupid!"

And then again after one of Gunther's remarks, "No, he's not either! A stupid boy never says anything like that!" Then, too, there was the entirely characteristic way in which Gunther at times expressed himself. He was often droll, and much that he said pointed to an acute observation and a precocious — *acquired where?* — knowledge of human nature.

Besides, who was Hermann to judge! He was no doubt quite boring himself. Must he not appear stupid to Gunther often enough, with his lack of knowledge of people, plus his inexperience?

He had to love Gunther. Nothing further. And that he did. More and more every day ... Life without Gunther would now seem unthinkable to him.

Gunther was not stupid. Even if his questions were not always intelligent and showed only the level of understanding natural to his years, they were still of a childlike grace — questions of the kind one is always glad to answer for children.

Gunther asked one day, quite unexpectedly, when Hermann was again looking at him as if he never wanted to take his gaze from Gunther's face: "What is it you like so much about me, Hermann?"

The man found no answer at first. "Yes, what is it I like so

much about him?" he asked himself. "Everything, everything!" he
thought. But he could not just say that. So he said then, after a
while, smiling: "Look angry! — So. For then there appears," — he
laid his finger on the upper right corner of his mouth — "then
there appears this little, white tooth..."

Atze, too, had said that once. Only he had expressed it differently: "Man, why do you always screw up your mug! You can
see right away when something is wrong with you! Just get rid of
that. Otherwise the johns will believe you want to bite them..."

"Are you, too, glad to be with me, my darling?" Gunther was
asked in return, in a good hour.

"Yes, sure," came the answer. "With you I'm secure. With the
others you never know what they will suddenly want from you.
With you, I know that you want nothing. Just like with the
Count..."

And at Hermann's look, Gunther continued. "Only what I
myself want," and pressed closer to him.

"Just like with the Count..." Hermann thought bitterly.
"Only with the difference that he was completely indifferent to
you, whereas I love you!"

Gunther then more intimately embraced him.

"Yes, only what *you* want! In each and every thing! *Your* happiness only!"

"You're so quiet, Hermann," Gunther often said.

Happiness makes for quiet, Hermann thought. "Speak, you
speak! I gladly hear you speak..." Hermann said.

"Me? — but I have nothing to tell..."

And, as always, the unspoken lay between them like an invisible wall.

On the fourteenth of November they celebrated Gunther's six-
teenth birthday. Long before, Hermann had tried to find out what
he wished for most.

"Do tell me something, so that I can really delight you, Gunther," he begged again and again. But the boy did not want to tell him. "It's too expensive for you..."

Finally it did come out: "A wrist watch ... a quite simple one ... naturally not gold, there's no question of that ... a simple, silver one..."

Hermann searched for a long time until he found what he wanted — a plain, silver watch, held by a light-colored leather band, which Gunther would like and which would look nice on the brownish skin of his wrist. Hermann was looking forward to the day, more than the boy himself.

"You will come?"

And this time he had the courage to add, "And spend the evening with me?..."

It was granted.

Yes, he would make himself free, Gunther swore — and he honestly meant it.

"Make himself free? From what and from whom?" thought Hermann.

The day came and a loaded table awaited the birthday boy. It was covered in white and decorated with flowers and sixteen candles. On the table also lay all the things that must delight a young heart — this heart also, which knew so little of the joys that moved others his age. There lay neckties; gloves; a walking stick (which he had always wanted); a cigarette case with many cigarettes of his latest favorite brand; and finally a book, with suspense, adventures, and strange fortunes — by which Hermann secretly hoped he could force the thriller a bit into the background. There lay a wallet, also wished for, to carry the papers he never showed, but always carried with him in a dirty envelope. There lay shirts and underwear, again so much needed.

At his first glance Gunther thought that the one thing he most wanted was missing. But it was *not* missing. As Gunther regarded everything in silence, the watch was placed around his wrist. As Hermann did this and then kissed the slender, beloved little hand, and felt Gunther in gratitude fondle and caress his cheek, he was happy, perfectly happy...

"You have outdone yourself, Hermann." And then a soft: "You are good..."

They celebrated, at first with chocolate they made themselves and cakes and pastries in such mountains that even Gunther fought against them in vain.

They celebrated further. Outside. At first in a cinema. Not exactly in the one to which Gunther would have wished to go, but rather — he had to sacrifice something — to one of the largest and nicest, a true palace, and they saw a wonderful reproduction of human longing, human courage, and unbending will more adventurous and exciting than any fantasy they could imagine. They saw a ship of explorers strive toward the unknown distance; saw them spend the winter in the eternal ice; saw an expedition of a few with their sleds and dogs through the ice and snow toward one goal. They saw their disappointment and return, and finally the gripping end — the despair and death from extreme exhaustion. As Hermann sought the hand of his darling beside him and, deeply affected, pressed it, the boy said, "But none of that is really true..."

They celebrated further. The high point, the birthday dinner, was yet to come. For that, one of the best and most distinguished restaurants in a large hotel was selected. A moment of wondering whether the boy might feel strange and uncomfortable there was banished.

Hermann did not need to worry. Gunther did not appear at all astonished, or even impressed. As they sat down at the reserved table, he said perfunctorily: "I've been here a couple of times already..."

Hermann was dumbfounded. "Here?"

"Well, sure, with the Count. We always ate over there..."

Nor did the surroundings for a moment affect Gunther's appetite, and he altogether conducted himself almost more confidently than Hermann in the strange place. It turned out to be a lovely evening.

When it came time to order champagne, Gunther again proved himself a connoisseur. He spoke of sec and dry, and named brands of which Hermann had scarcely heard.

"But you don't know anything at all," Gunther remarked after making the selection.

At the end Gunther declared himself so full that he could no longer walk. Since it appeared that Hermann, too, who could obviously tolerate less than Gunther, was somewhat tipsy, he allowed Hermann to take him in a cab to a spot near his room from which, alone but happy, he trotted home.

It was an odd relationship between the two, and yet it became better day by day.

The gifts for his birthday had pleased the boy, indeed touched him as far as this was possible. They must have cost a lot of money, and he knew indeed that his friend was not well off.

He followed Atze's advice badly — he did not take Hermann for a ride. For one thing, it was not in him to do so. For another, he did not need to, at all.

He was quite content with what he received and he was constantly receiving something, without even expressing the wish. The "others" had to take care of the "other thing." To get out of them what there was to get was self-evidently a matter of honor (and not all that easy). They had it. And besides, that's what they were there for.

Thus the boy lacked nothing, and he wished that it might stay that way always.

Hermann had given up reflecting about him. Gunther was still a puzzle to him in so many ways, and he remained such. He did not comprehend why Gunther still wanted to go away from him — there, to where Hermann could not and should not follow. Two souls must dwell in his breast, the inheritance of his mixed blood — from his father, his spirit (and thoughtlessness); from his mother, his robust indifference to enduring life, wherever it led, this indifference to life altogether — his splendor and his grime. But Hermann gave up reflecting about Gunther.

He said to himself: "I have never been happy. But I am still young. I, too, want to be happy once. I can be so only in him, and only if I take him as he is — with all his delightful charm, with all his secret depths and shallows. I may not question him. I will not question him. I will live in him — in his smile, which for me is like no other human smile; in his breath; in the sweet scent of his youth; and in his heart, as far as it is mine! And I will be content with what he wants to give and can give me."

Thus he thought, and he was happy.

Then one day, eight days after his birthday, Gunther stayed away.

2

He did not come on that day, nor on the next. He stayed away. The first day Hermann Graff was only sad. "Now he is already starting to stay away again," he thought. But the next day brought his old uneasiness.

It had been weeks since Gunther had stayed away two days in a row. Just what could this be? Hermann waited until nine o'clock, then went out and walked the steets aimlessly for a long time. He slept badly during the night.

With the third day, anxiety invaded him.

What could it be? What had happened? Something must have happened? But *what!* With fear, however, also came the feeling that something must be done. But *what!* He found no answer to his own question.

As he sought further for an answer, he realized in plain terror that he had none. What should he do? Where should he look for Gunther?

He knew neither where Gunther lived, nor with whom he lived. Somewhere up there, in the northeast of the city — toward Weissensee. Sometimes, when they had gone out for the evening and he said he wanted to go directly home, Gunther took a bus in that direction. Hermann was not allowed to accompany him. Thus Gunther always rode away unquestioned. Only once, on Gunther's birthday, had Hermann been allowed to take him in a cab, but even then only to the neighborhood of Gunther's room, which still certainly lay further on. Gunther was like that — always with a certain joy in secrecy. It came with his life.

Should he go there where he had found Gunther — in the streets? The streets were many and long. To Friedrich Street with its Passage? But no — Gunther was no longer to be found there. Since he had once been arrested there, his fear was too great that he would be apprehended again and not let go. This fear was not a pretense — it spoke through each of his words, as often as the conversation turned to that area. Even when they went out together, they always, at Gunther's request, made a detour around the feared streets. So, not there. There last of all!

Should he search in the bars, the lounges? Hermann was unfamiliar with them. Not one did he know even by name. And there, too, he would not be found. He no longer visited them, since he no longer made his acquaintances there.

These acquaintances, however, what kind of people were they? Hermann had no idea, he knew nothing about them — not their names, not where they lived, not how they might look, and not what they did...

He knew nothing about Gunther, nothing! He did not even know his last name!

Lulled into security these past weeks, Hermann had lived from day to day with Gunther, sure of being allowed to see him again, if not tomorrow, then the day after — sure that he could no longer lose him again. As if it had to stay that way. As if it could not become otherwise.

Unbelievable carelessness! Inconceivable stupidity! Criminal recklessness! Now he accused himself.

True, Hermann had not been allowed to question Gunther. His promise, their agreement, bound his tongue. But he should have got out of him, with care, with kindness, with promises, yes, even with cunning, what he wanted to know and must know!

Yet, all would have been in vain! Not with cunning and persuasion, not with love and kindness, with nothing in the world would Gunther have let be known what he did not want to tell. Hermann knew him that much — in that respect Gunther was like all boys — or at least the majority. What they did not want to tell, they did not tell. Had Gunther noticed prying, he would have been cross. No, he would have become mean and angry, and in such a state, he might have decided never to return, to stay away, and Hermann would have lost him again, and forever!

Hermann knew nothing. He could only sit in his room and wait, which he did. He waited.

The first days, he did not go out again after work. He bought his food earlier, but he hardly touched it. He lay there, stretched out on the sofa, hands clasped behind his head, staring at the ceiling. He thought about only one thing — will Gunther come today? Will he come again?...

He listened — for the little whistle down below to call him. Had it not just sounded? He sprang up and dashed to the window. But everything was empty below in the street, as empty as the wall opposite. He walked wearily back. He lay there and stared. It became dark.

It occurred to him that he must make a light — a sign that he was home and waiting. Otherwise Gunther might believe he was out and walk on, not venturing to come up. Hermann lit a lamp and placed it on his desk by the window.

Then he lay down again in the half-shadow and stared: waiting, waiting, waiting ... The day came to an end. It was evening — it turned nine, ten o'clock. The day had ended. Gunther had not come. *Tomorrow* ... Tomorrow came. But not Gunther. He did not come. He was gone.

On the sixth day, the end of the week, Herman realized there was no sense in continuing to wait. Gunther did not come because he was *unable* to come. He would come no more. Something terrible must have happened to prevent him. But what? *What?!*

Was he sick? Then he would have sent a message, would have had Hermann summoned to come and take care of him — by the friend with whom he lived, by the old lady in whose house he lived. Or, if he was in a hospital, from there some kind of message would come. No, he must not be sick. Gunther had left that last time completely healthy. And then, did a boy ever get sick? That never happened.

Was he away with someone else? That, too, seemed hardly likely. Gunther would have told him, or at least would have written. That Gunther should just stay away, without a word of explanation or of farewell — Hermann would not and could not believe it of him. No, Gunther would not do that to him. Perhaps, if their relationship had slackened instead of becoming closer; perhaps, if they had seen one another seldom, not as recently, almost daily. But as it was — no, he was not a mean boy, and conscious cruelty, which so many boys did possess, lay far from Gunther. That time in Potsdam, true — but that was now long ago, and even then there were excuses. No, his Gunther would not just walk away forever — Hermann would not and could not believe it.

Besides, with whom could he be? Who would take him away so suddenly, from today to tomorrow? A second Count was not easy to find, and never had Hermann noticed that any of Gunther's current acquaintances were taking a deeper interest in the boy. From his words, from the whole way he led his life — gifts, non-appearances, evasions — surely Hermann would have noticed. His heart would have told him. Like the needle of a magnet, Hermann would have sensed any turning away. No, that was not it either.

So could it be the one thing left — had they apprehended him? For the second time, and this time inescapably, so that he had been unable to send word and even now could not? The only thing that argued against this was Gunther's repeated protestations that, since he no longer walked the streets or went to the lounges, nothing could happen. Yet, it could only be that!

Hermann's fear became so great that he could no longer endure it. He *must* do something. If he only knew *what!* He thought for a moment of going to the police, but realized immediately the folly of such a step. Even if they were able to give him information, they would bluntly refuse to. The registration office? Herman was unable to give them any particulars, not even Gunther's full name.

He even thought of a private detective agency. There they would not be crude and insolent but would take as much money as possible, and naturally not help in the least. There they tried to catch husbands *in flagrante delicto* and unfaithful wives, but not street boys who had run away from home. Nothing, he could do nothing ... However, since he could no longer endure this waiting, he took to the streets.

He crossed through the Passage, again and again, with long and hurried strides. But it was empty these icy winter days, and no people were standing around its entrances, not even a boy. He walked up Friedrich Street and down again, in the insane hope of seeing that one face, the one he was seeking. He searched in the west. He searched everywhere. He walked so long that his feet no longer bore him, and he staggered home.

He sat there again, often until morning dawned, more hopeless from day to day. And always he had this fear lying on his heart like an iron fist, then grasping for his throat to choke him, until he felt no longer able to breathe.

Then, after hours of complete despair, he was driven out. He tried to deaden himself. He went to cinemas, but saw nothing, to concerts, and heard nothing. He went to theaters, only to get up and leave again.

He sought the old places of memory, where they had met, where they had been together: the bridge over the Spree, where at first he so often and so long had stood in vain; the little restaurant where they had sat for the first time, and then so many times after that; these and other places of memory, and each only tore the wound deeper.

At home and alone, it was the same. There in that large chair Gunther's small, tender body had cuddled and there he had lain on the sofa. The sofa was Gunther's favorite place. From there his clear and sweet voice had sounded to Hermann over at his desk, impatient, begging, coaxing, to stop working and come to him. His feet had walked on this old rug — he was everywhere, everywhere! Yet gone ... gone forever!

Another week passed, now a third ... But it did not get better. It became worse and worse.

"I should not continue to think about him," he told himself.

"I must forget him. I must!" He told himself this again and again, and knew that he could not — not for a moment could he forget.

What did it help, that he tried to reason this through: "It is all past. You will never see him again. He is forever lost to you!" He did not believe it. He could not and would not believe it.

What did it help, that he forced the thoughts: "You cannot continue to live like this. It is impossible. Try to find another friend. Even if it is not love, hardly even friendship" — (how much these thoughts resembled those earlier thoughts when he hardly knew Gunther, wanted to forget him, and even then could not!) — "it would be a living being, with whom you could talk, whom you could help," — what did it help that he told himself this, only to immediately see how absurd this thought was, and how entirely impossible.

In such hours he had a horror of himself as a traitor. He had a horror of life, of this life which stole Gunther from his side. He began to hate it with a wild and gloomy hate, as he now hated those who led it — the fortunate ones who could lead it.

Since he found no forgetfulness and could bear the memories no longer, he sought to deaden himself in work. He brought work home with him in piles and buried himself in it. He no longer went out. He sat over work until his aching eyes gave out and his pen fell from his hand from fatigue.

This went on for a week, until he was forced to quit, no longer from fatigue, but from disgust. In the long run his thoughts were not frightened away or killed in this way either. They came again, oppressed and tormented him, scattered and always concentrated themselves anew into one thought: *him!*

Now he did not go home from work at all. Directly after closing he rode out of the city. Anywhere, it was all the same, only out of the city.

At some station or other he got off, strayed for hours through dark, bare woods and along the banks of the wide lakes, aimless, until he came to another station, from which he rode back. He walked in all weather, in rain, storm, and wind, through wetness, mire, and snow, until his body gave way under him. Then he sat for a long time in a lonely forest inn, the only and unwelcome guest, in a cold corner, to later often wait for a long time on an empty train platform. He came home late, soaked through and muddy, but — thank heaven! — tired enough to drop. For that was what he wanted — to become tired, dead tired, so as to find forgetfulness in sleep.

He never knew where he had been. It had been dark everywhere, dark and cold. In the woods, in the suburbs, in the strange inns. And in him. Then that, too, failed him.

Now there came spontaneously so deep a fatigue that he could no longer pluck up courage for anything, hardly for his daily work. He still worked, but mechanically and indifferently.

In his office people shook their heads over him. They did not understand him. One time he worked day and night, voluntarily and unasked — then again he left everything standing and lying around. He was earnestly advised to visit a doctor or take a vacation.

He laughed inwardly. A doctor? How could a doctor help him? One must have trust in a doctor, must be able to trust oneself to him. He had no one whom he could trust.

Sure, if it had been a woman he was suffering over — how they all would have understood him! Then his passion would have been great and sacred, and his despair noble. ("Unrequited love" — in innumerable books, celebrated, described, justified, and understood.) But since it was only a boy, this was madness, if not a crime — the only cure to be locked up in a cold-water treatment institution for the insane. He had no one to whom he could talk.

Fear and despair alternated in the third and fourth weeks, to ever new exhaustion. Nothing brought him comfort, or hope. He had none left.

He was no longer capable of reading. It required too much effort. He could no longer work. He did not know what he was writing, and he could stand people no longer, hardly even the mere sight of them. But he still did not lose his self-control among them.

Only it was now no longer the calm superiority of his guard, but rather a tortured summoning up of his last strength, never for a moment showing them how he felt inside. A last pride held him erect. But their laughter, their conversation, even the impersonal and indifferent shoptalk, all drove him mad.

His fatigue was as deep as that after a long, severe illness. He stayed home again in the evenings. But he no longer lay on the sofa or bed, staring and listening; he just sat in a chair, arms on his knees, his head propped on his cold hands, looking straight ahead at the floor for hours — too tired to stand up, too tired to even move.

At times he talked to himself. Then it was mostly the same words, the words of a little poem that once, in spring, shortly after his arrival in Berlin, he had read and never forgotten. He did not know whose words they were. He did not reflect on what they meant or were intended to say. It was their sound that lulled him.

He thought he remembered that the little poem was entitled "The Day." No — "Call" had stood over it. He recited it to himself again and again.

> Longingly called, you're never there
> With me by light of day.
> Bright is that light, but back to you
> I cannot find my way.
>
> Bathed in the light of early morn
> You stood before me there,
> Walking for hour on hour with me,
> The day with me to share.
>
> Fragrance and light and luster fly
> From farthest heights above.
> See them entirely made for us,
> Just made for joy and love.
>
> Why are you never there for me,
> By me when day is bright?
> Why are you never truly mine?
> You come in dark of night.

> Empty of joy and light you come,
> A shadow-figure face.
> Fool and mislead by empty walls
> And vanish with no trace!

He said the stanzas again and again to himself. Above all, the two lines:

> Why are you never there for me,
> By me when day is bright?

"Never more — not by day, not in the night — never more do you come, my beloved boy, never more do you come to me, never more!"

Call? Every call for Gunther was in vain and silence the only answer.

Finally, the last, poor comfort of these strange words also failed. His memory held them no longer. They disintegrated and, of the empty, meaningless words, now even robbed of the sweetness of their sound, only the final lines remained for him — "Fool and mislead by empty walls. . ."

They alone he spoke at times to the cold and mute wall opposite his house — "And vanish with no trace. . ."

Without a trace! Without any trace!

The days passed. How many? — he did not know. The year was coming to an end.

He required sleeping pills in order to sleep. Then it was a leaden sleep, and he awoke with exhausted limbs and a heavy pressure in his temples. And he never fell asleep without the single wish that remained to him — that it be his last sleep, from which no awakening followed.

Gunther was gone! Hermann did not know if he was still alive. And that was the most terrible of all — that he did not even know that! "If I knew he was dead," Hermann often thought now, "I could think about him more easily."

He had nothing of Gunther's. All that he possessed of Gunther was a small, woefully bad picture, taken on some occasion by an itinerant photographer in the street, a tintype for thirty pennies. He had kept resolving to have a good picture taken of Gunther, but in those blissful weeks of carelessness and unconcern for tomorrow he never carried it out.

That small, hardly recognizable picture, and a dirty, half-torn scrap of paper, on which was written in a childish hand, "Can you fergive me. . ." was all that he possessed of him.

3

It was Christmas Eve. He dreaded the holidays. Again he took work home with him, stacks of proof sheets. That they would help him, though, he no longer believed.

A snowstorm such as there had not been for years swept through the streets, accumulated into mounds, swirled around the corners, and pressed through all the crannies. In his street the snow piled up almost to the height of the first floor, the height of his window.

The entire city lay under a thick white blanket, with the soft white sheet of the sky over it. He did not work; he just sat there. In the evening he went out. He walked down Friedrich Street toward the Linden. He was at the Passage.

For some time the Passage had taken on an entirely different appearance, outwardly and inwardly. Sold to a large business corporation, it was first cleaned up. Swept out were the dubious ladies of Friedrich Street and their pimps. The whores and the boys were persecuted until they gave up and sought other places for their activity. Day by day, from early morning until late evening, the criminal police patrolled along the hall and took away any boy who walked through more than once. Raids were made in the evening and at night, during which the Linden and Friedrich

Street — and with them, of course, the Passage — were closed off within a certain radius. Anyone who could not justify his presence there was loaded into a truck and, amid shrieks and howls, hauled off to the police station. There were roundups.

The johns, both those who were always there and those who only came occasionally, naturally stayed away. All that was left, as the remains of a vanished splendor, were a couple of poor, half-starved hustlers who suspected nothing of the change in the situation and still strayed there, only to be sent back out again forthwith. Only the public, although reduced in numbers, was still the same — the petty bourgeois public with the provincial air, who shoved through and were amazed that there was nothing more to be amazed at. Even the wax-figure museum had to close its doors. The moth-eaten dummies of the waxworks, the crowned criminals as well as the uncrowned, were carried from their pedestals into the light of day, and the great as well as the small disintegrated to dust and mold.

The café in the middle had become a restaurant, from which music no longer sounded to divert the strollers, and the shops did a bad business. Their proprietors changed or left.

The famous Passage even had its name at the entrance taken down and had become a street like any other. Berlin was one sight the poorer.

Of all of this Hermann, who now stood before it again, naturally knew not the least, nor did it interest him. He had not been there since the days of his final despairing attempts to find Gunther, when he had run there, then finally realized that he would no longer find the boy there.

Now he was standing there again. He did not know why. It was already late, about nine o'clock; all the shops were long closed, no theater and no cinema was playing. The few restaurants still open were empty on this one evening of the year. Hermann walked on, toward the castle.

On Unter den Linden light still shone from the window of a wine cellar. It was one of the few old wine cellars from the good old times, visited by regular customers and appreciated by connoisseurs. He entered.

Today, however, only two gentlemen were still sitting in the warm and comfortable room, each in his corner and as far as possible away from one another.

The newcomer, too, selected a similar place and ordered a bottle of wine. He was unable to eat; as usual he had no hunger. The waiter, a son of the current proprietor who was serving his apprenticeship here according to an old custom, brought it to him. He was still as young as Hermann.

"You will certainly want to close soon," Hermann said tiredly.

"No, no, sir," sounded the friendly answer, "we'll stay open, even if no one else comes. Don't let it disturb you at all."

Hermann poured himself a glass and drank the good and warming wine. "I will remain sitting here," he thought, "I will drink this bottle up, and then another, and perhaps still another ... until..."

But then he stood up suddenly, without having drunk the first bottle, paid, and hurried out. A frantic restlessness had come over him.

Where was Gunther? — Where was he this evening, where? — It was as if Gunther were calling him. With a beseeching and helpless voice — he was calling him. He now heard Gunther calling quite clearly. Where was he? He must look for him again — there!

Through the thick snow he quickly walked the first few steps to the Passage, as if chased.

Now he was in the hall. It was absolutely empty. Not a soul, not a single person was in it on this evening at this hour. It lay there — forlorn, desolate, dead.

In the middle the snow, which the storm had driven through the chinks in the glass roof, had piled up. An icy cold streamed through from all sides — from above, from both entrances.

Hermann, walking through it alone, reached the southern entrance. Here, too, there was no one. Through the fallen snow stamped, like ghosts in fog, muffled figures, reeling, hurrying, and disappearing, shadows of the night...

Hermann was standing at the exit. Here they had seen one another for the first time ... here Gunther had stood, alone, nervous, unacquainted with everything, innocent, on a spring day, a day full of sun and sky-blue ... From here Gunther had fled from him. When had that been? Years ago, months ago, yesterday?

What lay in between? His whole life. Their whole life — his own life and Gunther's. Hermann shuddered within himself. Gunther was not there. Where was he?

He walked back. Still, not a human being. "Nothing," he thought, "nothing in the whole world can be so comfortless as this forlorn place of dubious pleasure, of desire, of vice. Nothing! — Oh, yes: *one* place — my heart!"

He came again to the Linden entrance. Here, too, Gunther had stood, no longer alone, no longer innocent and therefore no longer fearful, but in the circle of the others, experienced, all too experienced in everything, and had looked him over when he caught sight of him: on the hot summer afternoon he had looked at Hermann and not moved ... And then he did follow him, to come to him!

He turned and walked down the Linden, still, white, and empty of people. There behind him — that cave, it was his grave. There it lay. From there had he just now called him. But now his call had become silent...

Hermann walked home. Here, too, all was quiet. No light in the windows, as there was everywhere else today. This house, this cursed steet, in which even the children were afraid to play, was passed over by all joy, all celebrations of life. Only pain and suffering came here, as they had come to him. And death! Why did it not come today? And why not to him?

In his room he stood at first and stared blankly ahead. His arms hung down limply and his coat slid down from them.

Then he said to himself: "It is at an end. I will never see him again. For he is dead. Only as a dead person may I still think about him..." And suddenly, as if hit by a blow, he fell into the chair at the table. There he lay, his face buried in his hands, in the final hours of the evening.

"Weep," he thought. One may weep for a dead person. It is all that one can still do for him, even if it is of no use to him and he does not know. But Hermann was unable to weep. Since those first bitter tears as a child he had no longer been able to weep.

He only groaned at times, the way a poor, forsaken and forlorn person groans when his dearest thing has been taken.

Only one comfort still remained for him — one thought: "Now nothing more can come — for this is the worst!"

He did not know that the last and worst was still to come.

e got up late and dawdled away the hours, something he had never done before. Outside, the snowstorm blustered through the streets and the flakes swirled around his window.

He ate in a wine cellar at the Weidendamm bridge. With difficulty he found an empty table — he was surrounded by festive activity, laughter and cheerfulness.

He walked home again. His room had been made, as always. These days, too, he knew of and saw his landlady as little as usual. Was she at home? What did it matter to him!

He did not work. He wanted to read, but as often as he took a book in his hand he let it fall again. He walked around, picked up objects, looked at them as if he had never seen them before, and laid them back down again. A lighted cigarette went out. He crushed it, without knowing what he was doing.

The full understanding of the complete senselessness of his life without Gunther stood suddenly before him. For what was he living? Why should he still live on? He felt incapable of suffering any more. Joy had gone from his life, the short joy of a few weeks. Now suffering, too, was going and his life was robbed of its last meaning.

"End it!" he thought. Go to him, the dead one, lie beside him, and sleep in peace!

Go — but where? There was no horror of death in him, but

also no longing for it. Without a longing, a self-imposed end was — he felt — not possible. Therefore he must continue to live.

He walked around again, picked things up in his hand — his pen, an ashtray, a glass — and considered them with the same long and absent gaze as before, as if he had never seen them. He walked to the window and looked out.

The snow had stopped blowing. Everything was white out there, white powdered the opposite wall, empty, cold, and withdrawn. Hermann stared out at it.

There, where the rain gutter ran down, he had always stood. Now the place was empty. No, it was *not* empty. Was he not standing there — there at the gutter — was he not standing there? ... No, his senses must be deceiving him. It could only be a shadow. He stepped back into the room.

"I'm becoming completely crazy," he thought. "I am already..."

"Fool and mislead by empty walls..." For the first time in weeks he said the words again to himself.

Then he suddenly laid his hands firmly against his temples. No, he had not deceived himself!

With a wild leap he was at the window, tore the casement open, cried out, dashed down the stairs, was over there. He caught the collapsing figure up in his arms. He carried him over the street, up the stairs, into his room, and let him slide onto the nearest chair. He slammed the doors and window shut, then stood before him.

He stretched his hand out, as if to make sure that it was truly he, and immediately drew it back again. A couple of times he even ran around the room as if mad.

Then he knelt down before Gunther, who sat there with closed eyes, his head sunk down on his breast, his arms hanging down limply as if lifeless. He took the ice cold, white hands in his own, and breathed on them. He found his first words.

"Gunther, where did you come from? What has happened? Gunther! Gunther! Do speak, please, say just one word!..."

No answer came. Again he ran helplessly through his room — what ever should he do! — then knelt down before Gunther again.

The boy lay there as if lifeless, his eyes closed. Desperation gripped Hermann.

He took Gunther again in his arms, carried him to the sofa, covered him with all the blankets he could obtain, tore them off again, and began to undress him. First his shoes and socks. Water ran from them over his hands.

Gunther's feet were ice cold, like his hands, ice cold, frozen, bloody in spots. He rubbed them, rubbed and rubbed. He looked into Gunther's deathly pale face, into a gray, strange face.

"My God," he thought, "he could die here under my hands!"

He tried to think. He drew Gunther onto his breast, let him go again, breathed on him, and rubbed, rubbed again and again.

"Gunther, my Gunther, do speak, please, say just a word," he whispered, "tell me that you still live!"

The boy, lying as if dead, let everything happen. His head fell again and again against the breast of his friend.

"No, this won't do!" Hermann thought.

It occurred to him that he must still have some cognac in the cabinet. He rushed there, grabbed the bottle, and filled the first glass he came to. He skimmed the yellow liquid between Gunther's bluish lips. Another sip. . .

He waited anxiously for the effect. The glass shook in his hand. Finally! It seemed to help. After about five minutes the boy opened his eyes and looked at him.

"Hermann!" he said softly. "Hermann!" Then he fell back again.

He lived! He lived! "Yes, my darling, be still. Don't talk. You are with me. . ."

Now yet another sip. The glass was almost empty. What should he further do? He tried to consider. Was it warm enough in the room? Yes, it was warm. He must first get Gunther out of his clothes, out of the wet, cold clothing.

As before with the torn, almost soleless shoes, the dripping socks, so now he began to undress him completely. Piece by piece he drew the rags and tatters from the body lying there motionless — the jacket, the pants, the wool shirt — everything soaked through down to the last fiber. A horrible smell arose from the bundle, which he rolled up and threw into a corner.

Again he rubbed his feet, his hands, his breast. Now Gunther lay there naked. He covered him in the blankets, up to his neck. Gunther's eyes were closed fast, his lips lay pressed together.

Hermann ran around — made hot water on the stove, fetched a pan from the bedroom, and his large sponge.

When the water was warm enough, he uncovered Gunther again and began to wash him, infinitely carefully, as if he could hurt him with each light movement. The boy appeared to feel nothing. Hermann washed his legs, his breast, his neck, and his face. He stroked his hair smooth.

"Gunther! Gunther!" He whispered again and again, but the boy continued to lie there motionless.

Later, when there was nothing more to do, Hermann looked at him and a sob choked his throat.

How emaciated he was! All the ribs of his slim, sunken-in breast stood out, his shoulder bones, the joints of his arms, everything so thin, so wasted, fleshless, and his skin so gray, so bloodless...

A horrible thought flashed through the man standing there. With as gentle a movement as possible, he took the body — lightly as a feather — and turned him over. On his back, from which the shoulder blade projected sharp and hard, there were no traces of mishandling — of beatings.

After he had drawn over him one of his own shirts, Hermann let Gunther down again and covered him anew — thick and tight, so that only his face still showed. He did not know what to do now. He sat beside Gunther and watched him anxiously. His gaze never left the face on the pillow. It was still gray and lifeless, but it did seem no longer so deathly pale. He bent over to his mouth.

He was breathing. There was no doubt; he was breathing. He lived. Hermann shoved his hand under the cover and laid it over his heart. It appeared to beat. Weakly, but it was beating.

He considered again. No, he could do nothing now but wait, until life had returned. Hermann felt how his own heart beat like mad and his knees trembled. He sat and watched Gunther, anxious, waiting.

After a quarter of an hour, the cheeks there before him appeared lightly, quite lightly, to redden. His cracked lips, too, were no longer so bluish as before. He reached for his hands. They were still cold, but no longer quite like ice. Again he bent over Gunther. His breath seemed to be coming stronger.

He listened. Gunther appeared to be sleeping. But did he not just now speak? What had he said? Hermann had not understood it. He listened, again closely bent over, tense.

"Hunger!" — it was only a whisper.

Hunger! Hermann spoke close to his ear.

"Gunther, do you hear me? Are you hungry? Do you want to eat? What do you want to eat?"

Then he saw the boy open his eyes and stare at him. Faintly but clearly Hermann heard him speak again.

"Food!..."

"Yes, food! Of course. Whatever you want. What do you want to have, my boy?"

He looked around helplessly. He had almost nothing in the house. Nothing of what was necessary now.

Gunther was now awake. He lay motionless, looking at Hermann with large and quite dark eyes. But he spoke not a word.

Hermann pulled himself together. He laid his arm around the pillow and said, "Gunther can you hear me? Do you understand what I'm saying? Can you stay alone a moment? Only five minutes. You know no one will come. I'll go around the corner quickly and buy something. Just for a very short time. I'll be right back!"

The boy appeared to understand. He nodded wordlessly.

But Hermann still hesitated. Should Gunther be left here alone? Surely. Who could come? Never did anyone come here. No one knew that Gunther was here with him. What could happen to him in those couple of minutes!

It was surely not only the cold, it was his losing strength from hunger. Food — that was now the main thing. Food — Gunther had just said so himself.

Yes, he might go calmly. But where could he get anything today? All the shops were closed, today and tomorrow, for Christmas. The pub in the neighborhood, where he often ate, occurred to him. A kind old waiter was there. He would help.

Once more Hermann glanced back at the room before he left. The lamp was burning peacefully on the table by the sofa. The boy lay there sleeping again, as it appeared. Nothing disturbed the quiet of the room.

He lived. He was rescued. He was breathing calmly.

He reached for his handbag. It was the same one that had accompanied the two of them that time to Potsdam and had not been used since. He left hesitantly. But he would be right back.

He had hardly closed the apartment door behind him when light, inaudible steps glided over the corridor. They stopped before his room.

Then the latch was softly pressed down and two black, sparkling eyes looked into the room, glancing over the disorder in the room, the table, and the figure, brightly lit by the lamp, of the sleeping boy in the pillows on the sofa. She lit up with satisfaction. Then the door closed again just as quietly and a tall, lean black figure disappeared again, and soundless steps glided back through the hall.

Hermann had luck. The old waiter in the pub, which still had very few customers at this early afternoon hour of the first day of the holiday, gave him everything he wanted — cold cuts, butter, sausage, a loaf of bread, a couple of eggs, and a bottle of red wine, more than his bag could contain and almost more than his overcoat could hold.

When he returned to his room, he found everything unchanged. Gunther was sleeping now and obviously soundly. Hermann could not bring himself to wake him. Food was necessary when he awoke, but sleep was now the best medicine. With sleep, warmth would return, and with it, strength and health. He is not sick, Hermann told himself. Only tired, dead tired.

He took the lamp away from the table and carried it to the

desk, so that the sofa lay in half-darkness. Then he arranged the things he had purchased on the table and brought plate, knife, and fork, so as to have everything ready when the boy awakened. When everything was done, he sat down again beside Gunther.

Color had now returned to the sleeping boy's face, indeed it appeared as if he now had a fever. Hermann felt his forehead — it was hot and sweaty. His hands were burning, and his body in the pillows was warm and moist. Hermann became calmer.

Only now, as he was sitting beside Gunther again, listening to every breath of new life, there came to him for the first time in this hour — (only one hour had gone by — not possible!) — there came to him for the first time the thought that he had him again! It was not a joy, nor an ecstasy — it was something still incomprehensible.

He did not yet ask himself what had happened.

He did not yet ask himself anything. He only knew that he had him again! He was again with him! He was lying there! He lived!

Gunther slept and slept. But Hermann was glad to see it. It was the healthy sleep of recovery. And in the long hours of the dying day, of this quiet evening, of this long night, in which Hermann sat almost motionless beside him and hardly looked away from his face, he forgot what he had suffered for him, he forgot everything, everything, as if it had never been, in the one blissful thought: "He is again mine! I have him again!" Hermann scarcely moved.

Only once did he lay his temple to Gunther's hot forehead, as if to make sure that he was not dreaming — that it was reality. And then he watched further — calm and composed. Gunther was sleeping and continued to sleep.

Morning broke, the lamp went out for lack of fuel, and from outside the white radiance of the light on the snow came into the room. The watching man could only indistinctly recognize the pale face in the blankets and pillows. Hermann had not been able to sleep.

Now he spoke to himself. This young man, who never had anyone with whom he could pour out the joys and suffering of his heart, no mother and no friend; who had always been alone with himself, with everything that lifted him up or depressed him, now softly spoke to the boy who was lying there, and who was the only one in the world he loved, to him who could not and did not hear him, he spoke — softly to the small face in the pillow before him:

"I loved you when I saw you for the first time, on that spring day in which you fled from me in fright. I loved you in thought, weeks and weeks. I loved you when I saw you again and you were a stranger to me. I loved you when you disappeared, hated you and yet loved you all the more. I loved you when you came to me and became mine, in every trait. I loved you when you were lost to me once more. I loved you when you laughed; when you sulked; when you were indifferent (to me and to everything). I love you today, as you lie here before me, so very much changed. I will always love you! Nothing in the world have I loved so much as you! Nothing will I ever love so much, nothing!"

Only in the morning, tired out after the sleepless night and from the terrible excitement of the previous hours, did he fall asleep, in his chair and in his clothes, and he only awoke toward noon, the noon of the second day of the holiday.

5

t was Hermann who woke first. Gunther was still sleeping, calmly and soundly. "Let him sleep," Hermann thought. Then the first thing he did was to renew the fire in the stove.

In this connection, too, he had made himself independent of his landlady. Next to the stove lay always a neat pile of briquets.

His coffee stood before the door, long grown cold. In the house the usual quiet reigned. He wrote a note and laid it on the chair in front of the door:

"I am not going out today. Please wait until tomorrow to make the room." An hour later the chair and note had been silently taken away. He was certain not be disturbed today.

After he had washed and changed clothes he began to put the room in order. He straightened up the chairs, opened the windows for a quarter of an hour, after convincing himself that the sleeping boy was well covered up, hung the discarded clothes to dry and air, ate something himself, and waited again.

About two o'clock Gunther woke up. He had slept for twenty hours. He looked around astonished. Then a happy smile flew over his features. He stretched out both him arms: "Hermann!"

They kissed one another in a first, long kiss.

Gunther wanted to talk.

"First you must eat, my darling, You must be starved. Then you can tell me everything, everything. . ."

They ate and drank. Gunther must have been starving. But

his friend noticed how slowly he ate nonetheless, so different from earlier, as if he wanted to taste each bite like something long denied him.

"Should I get up or may I remain lying? I'm no longer sleepy, but still so tired."

Hermann pressed him back into the pillow. Then they began to talk. Hermann Graff drank in every word he heard.

This is what he learned in the long hours of this second afternoon, not in a connected story, naturally, but rather with questions in between, repetitions, and additions, and which gradually formed into one picture.

On the day that Gunther had been there for the last time, about five weeks ago — an ugly, rainy day — in the house of one of those gentlemen whom he and other boys frequented, there had been a tremendous scene. The police, apparently on the denunciation of someone who lived in the house, had broken in and arrested everyone present.

The gentlemen and the other boys — better-class boys, secondary school pupils and salesmen's apprentices, not those from the street — had been let go. The police did not want a new scandal; they had enough of scandals. Even the man who lived there was left unmolested. He was a painter and made his atelier available for such gatherings, though nothing at all had occurred — they had all sat around quietly and told stories. In this circle he was a quite well known panderer, who had already had countless clashes with the police, but had been declared in court to be mentally inferior and therefore not responsible, so that, as he constantly proudly stressed, "nothing could happen" to him. The others got off cheaply.

Gunther, however, had been taken away. At the central police station it was determined that his papers were false and he was not so unknown there as he had thought; from the Passage and the lounges he was only too well known to many an undercover agent. He was also known as one of the many young friends of the vanished and undiscoverable Atze.

After three days he had been transported to — there! But at

this point in Gunther's narrative, nothing further was to be brought out of him. There — there it had been simply terrible! He began to cry and Hermann, who was seeing him cry for the first time and could not bear it, questioned him no more, but rather sought with all his might to calm him.

There was only one hope left there — that of escape. This was agreed on with one of the older boys, with whom he had become intimate, only the right opportunity never offered itself. Until the evening before yesterday — Christmas Eve. With the preparations for the holiday, which was celebrated even there, the watch was not so strict. Early in the afternoon, when it was already dark and the heavy snowfall favored their plan, they had stolen away, climbed over the wall, and — each with one piece of bread in his pocket — had made their way toward Berlin.

They had hiked hour after hour through the ever thicker falling snow, always along the highway, among the white trees, until he, the smaller, was too weak to go farther. By good luck, they were near a village and they found a hayloft, where they ate their bread and were able to rest for a couple of hours.

Then, long before morning broke, they were on the way again, through snow and cold, on and on, until Gunther collapsed completely and the other had to carry him on his shoulders. At daybreak they were still far from Berlin. He had to drag himself alone. Farther! Always farther on!

Then the terrible snowstorm broke out, which made everything around them almost invisible. If his companion had not known the way so well — and always found it again by certain guide marks — they would never have reached here, but rather would have sunk into the snow and frozen.

Finally, however, they did arrive, about noon, in Mariendorf. Now just over Tempelhof and on to the Halle Gate. There his companion had begged from a passerby and received twenty pennies, so that in the nearest coffee shop they were able to drink two cups of hot coffee.

After that they had separated — the other had gone to distant relatives, who would perhaps take him in and hide him; and Gunther — he had come to Hermann . . . He had dragged himself as far as the wall. Then it was all over.

How long, then, had he stood there opposite? Hermann could scarcely bring the question out.

Gunther could not say. It might have been a half hour, but it could also have been an hour or two.

Why, then, had he not whistled, with their signal? Why had he not come on up?

Whistle? He was not able to whistle. And come up, that he had not dared. They had agreed that he was not to come up alone. . .

And then — Gunther looked straight ahead — "then I didn't know either if you were angry with me, because I did stay away, and if you still wanted to know anything of me . . . You could also have another friend and he was perhaps up there with you right then. . ."

His listener could say nothing, ask nothing. What he heard constricted his throat. That was all so horrible, completely horrible. Only at the final words did he smile bitterly. Another!. . . How little Gunther knew him! He could say nothing.

He took Gunther in his arms again. He kissed and caressed him, his hair, his slender cheeks, his hands . . . Then finally he found words and gave them to him — the good, old, long-unaccustomed words of friendship and of love. All the while, the boy only looked at him with a begging, almost downcast look, as if to say, "You won't send me away again, will you, now that I'm here with you again?" This look shook Hermann even more than everything heard. No, he would not send him away.

They ate and drank again — there was more than enough of everything there — and this time the red wine, too. Then the boy slept again for an hour while his friend walked quietly around the room and, in this thoughts, did not get away from what he had heard.

On awakening Gunther was fresh, as he said, but he did still prefer to remain lying — "if I might."

It was already late in the afternoon and the street lay in darkness. But they did not light the freshly filled lamp. They both felt so much at ease in the twilight.

Only once did Hermann ask, "Would you prefer to go out? Will it not be too boring for you to stay alone with me the whole day like this?" He was thinking about earlier — how restless the boy had always been, unwilling to stay long in the same spot.

"No, stay here, stay here! It's really so nice and comfortable here. And so warm." And with a slight smile for his impractical friend, "I can't go out. I just can't go out in the street any more in these rags, and with you at that. . ." That was true; and Hermann had just not thought about it.

They talked again together, in a way they had never talked together before. It was as if they had only today really found one another, as if every barrier, each last barrier between them, had fallen. As friends, they talked together — in deep trust and understanding, and one word led to another. Everything had become so entirely different from earlier.

When Hermann looked at him — and he did nothing else — Gunther appeared so changed, so much quieter.

When he was full and had laid aside knife and fork, had he not said, "I thank you, Hermann. . ."

He thanked him. When had Gunther ever said thanks to him? And now as Hermann again drew Gunther to himself and looked at him with a long gaze, he heard the boy say:

"You know, Hermann, you don't look at all well either? You have not been sick, have you?"

Hermann had to turn away. When had the boy ever asked about him, about his health? No, he was not sick. Only, *how* he had suffered for his sake, he could not tell him. And he, his darling, would even now still not understand.

They smoked, the boy in his pillows, the other in his deep chair, and smiled again and again at one another happily. And repeatedly Hermann had to stand up and walk over to him, as if to convince himself that they were together again — that it was not a dream, this new happiness!

Finally, however — it was already evening — they also talked about what should be done now. Gunther had already figured everything out in his fashion.

"You know, Hermann, naturally I'm gong to stay in Berlin now, and with you. For where else am I to go? I'll look for work, so that I won't be a bother to you, and will surely find something. . ."

Hermann was astonished. Work? He was talking about work. How he had changed! Hermann was surprised and believed him. But was Gunther safe in Berlin?

Safe — oh, he was surely safe, Gunther explained, as long as he walked the streets no more, nor went to the lounges, which he would no longer do, of course. He would now only associate with Hermann and not with any other man. He was finished with that. If they no longer saw him anywhere, he was entirely safe. No one would ask for him anymore. There were already so many who had run away and were never found again. People were glad when some were gone. About the two of them — Hermann and himself — nobody knew anything at all. He had never, but never, talked about Hermann.

Then Gunther brought out a very curious story, which he himself had heard from one of the boys in the summer, a boy from Hanover. The boy had run away from a state institution in Westphalia (also in winter, the one before). He hiked three days and three nights, and when he reached Hanover his own mother did not recognize him, the way he looked. He was left in peace there, for fourteen days. Then he was brought back, but the next spring he was out and away again, this time here to Berlin. He had an earlier friend here, a gardener who had a small apartment — a small room and a tiny kitchen, but secluded. He had lived with him a half year without registering and everything had gone well. When the gardener came home from his work in the evening, the boy was spending the night out. When the boy returned in the morning, it was time for the gardener to go to work and the boy lay down in the bed and slept till evening. The bed always stayed nice and warm, and never cooled off. That lasted the whole summer. . .

And then? That he didn't know. But it did go well for so long.

Gunther, unfortunately, had no such friend, with whom he could have a similar arrangement.

They both sat and considered. What could they do? First, however, the most immediate things had to be taken care of.

Tomorrow — tomorrow, Gunther stated, Hermann must help him get another outfit and find work. Also tomorrow Gunther had once more — but only this one more time — to see the boy with whom he had escaped. Gunther had promised, and he did really want to see how it was going for him, and whether he had been well received by his relatives. Perhaps Hermann could also help the boy find work, alone or together with Gunther. For going back — he would not go back, not at any cost!

To have to go back — that was the one constant fear that now controlled Gunther. He trembled when he merely pronounced the word "institution." Anything, but not go back! Not in there again!

This fear, Hermann thought, alone will guard him from sinking back into his earlier life, if he should ever again be tempted. But Gunther seemed to attach no more importance to all that which had once charmed and attracted him. He now talked about that life as if it lay forever behind him, finished and forgotten. Repeatedly he said that now everything must and was to be different.

Thus they talked and talked, considering each detail. His clothes — well, he had to wear them again early tomorrow, but only for a while, until new ones were obtained. They were brought from the window, to be dried out on the stove.

The hours ran by and Gunther became almost cheerful, while over Hermann there came a peace such as he had not known for an eternity. While his darling lay there, chatted and smoked and let himself be served and waited on, Hermann realized again how changed Gunther was.

Not only outwardly — his short-cut hair and his frightful leanness (how he would feed him!) No, he seemed to Hermann inwardly transformed too. Even the tone of his voice had become different — no longer so bright and loud, instead much more subdued and affectionate. His movements were no longer so violent and impetuous as earlier, but so much more tender and snuggling when he drew Hermann close. And his kiss, his kiss rested longer and more responsively on Hermann's lips than ever before. . .

Even his attempts at joking were new, as Gunther now sat beside him and passed his hand over Hermann's hair.

"Are you still angry with me about Potsdam?" Even these words, with which Gunther had always been able to anger Hermann, were not so meant, and were just said to cheer him up a bit, so that Hermann answered merely, "Oh, my poor boy!"

Thus it turned into night and bedtime, the day came to an end, and for both of them it was as if they had never spent a more beautiful day together.

In the night, when they separated with a last good-night kiss — Gunther to sleep on the sofa and Hermann in his bed — in the night Hermann heard a soft voice beside him.

"I want to be with you, Hermann. . ."

He lifted the small, light figure in the much-too-long shirt up to him.

And in that night, as they lay in close embrace — Gunther with his arms around the neck of his friend, and the man with his around Gunther's nape — in this night the boy gave himself to him as never before, not in a sensual frenzy, but rather under the clumsy words of bashful love, which thinks only about making happy that which it loves.

6

t was almost eight already when they released their arms from one another. They had to hurry for Hermann to be at his office on time. He would come late at any rate, but would not be the only one today, on the third day of the holiday.

The morning was gray and frosty. The wind had died down. The snow lay firm and hard.

While they drank coffee and Gunther put on his dry but stiff and hard shoes, they discussed the day.

As soon as when Hermann came from work — since he wanted to take off early, at three-thirty — they wanted to meet. Where? Well, the best place was again at the bridge. They wanted to go to their old pub — their regular pub — to eat and then look for a room or some kind of lodging for the coming nights.

They walked to the first men's shop they came to in the nearest street. It had just opened and the salesmen, the two holidays still on their minds, were cross and unfriendly to the early customers. A suit was picked out in haste. It fit badly, but there was no other there. Then a warm, wool shirt, underwear, and a hat. Finally, in the nearest shoe store, a pair of shoes. Everything in a hurried rush.

Then Gunther was newly dressed, from head to foot. He himself had insisted that the cheapest possible things be bought: "At the beginning, until I have work..." The old rags were not even kept.

Then it was farewell until afternoon. The streets were empty. Everybody appeared today to be getting out of bed later.

"Till then, what will you do?"

Hermann need not worry, Gunther assured him he would sit somewhere safe, in a pub or in a cinema, where it was warm ... And then at three he would be at the Adonis Lounge to see his friend.

"But you won't go inside, for heaven's sake?"

No, of course not. Gunther would just station himself in the vicinity, so as to be able to observe the entrance, from which his friend would come out precisely at three as he had promised. First he would look up and down the street, to see if all was safe. But at that time, when the lounge would have just opened, no police had ever been there.

Hermann pressed money for his meal for today in his hand. He saw how Gunther hesitated. He knew Gunther had yet another wish.

"If it's not enough, just say so!"

"No, it's really much too much. But, Hermann, if you will be so good — and it's the last time — and give me something for my friend, too ... You see, he really did rescue me in the night and yet doesn't have anything himself..."

He was thinking of someone else! *This he would never have done before*, thought Hermann, and he fulfilled Gunther's wish with inner joy.

The street was completely empty of people. It was high time for Hermann to go. An indefinable fear rose in him. He bent over.

"Gunther, my darling, I implore you, be careful! Don't do anything stupid! Think..."

The thin arms were laid around his neck.

"Be completely calm, Hermann, I'll be quite careful. I'm not going to do anything stupid..."

They kissed quickly. How cold his lips were again!

Then Hermann tore himself loose: "All right, at three-thirty on the bridge..."

At the corner he looked around once more. The boy was still standing there on the same spot, looking after him. How badly the suit fit! He waved to him, and it seemed to Hermann as if he smiled sadly.

How small he looked! So pitiable, so shy and fearful! So entirely changed! His poor boy! And again the indefinable fear rose up in him. He wanted to go back, to say something else. Anything — he did not know himself what — only just a last word. But he forced himself to walk on.

They were to see one another only once more.

PART
5

1

At the office he saw that, in spite of his lateness, he was still one of the first. He was angry at himself. He need not have hurried so much.

Hardly had he begun to work when fear again rose up in him. He laid down his pen. Everything had been wrong again.

They should not have separated today. He should not have let Gunther from his side for one minute today at any cost. What if something befell him? In vain he sought to calm himself.

What could happen? In the few hours? What indeed could happen to him? He was surely no longer the person he had been, the unconcerned boy who lived from one day to the next! This terrible experience had entirely transformed him. Gunther himself now lived in perpetual fear. Hermann had seen that.

He worked on wearily. Toward noon he could stand it no longer. He abruptly asked a colleague to substitute for him. He had a headache and had to go home.

"Hangover from yesterday," said the man, groaning himself, "understandable. Just go on and sleep it off..."

Outside it occurred to him that he must go to the bank first and withdraw some money. The expenses had eaten up the entire salary for the month that he had taken in advance. On the way to the bank a new thought came to him.

"Withdraw the total amount right away! It must be about two thousand. Take it and go away with him, this very evening, leave everything behind (what was there indeed to leave behind?) Go away with him, abroad, look for some kind of work there. Live with him and never leave him again! Only in this way will you be safe with him, only thus can he be entirely yours!" And he fantasized further: "Early tomorrow we could be in Munich, by evening in Switzerland, or Italy, in safety, in peace and happiness . . . Yes, Italy, there it's cheap and lovely . . . nice and warm. . ."

Then he saw how completely insane all that was. He withdrew only two hundred marks — oh, it had not been two thousand for a long time! — and he stood again in the street, unsure what he should do now until three o'clock. His inner unrest became ever greater. Why had he let Gunther go? Why had he gone to the office at all? Why this eternal consideration for others, this damned, idiotic conscientiousness! Must he, then, ever and always do things backwards? Always just the wrong thing! Would he never get smart!

"Not a step should I have let him take from me, not the smallest step!" He said it to himself again and again, already half despairing.

And the fear that he knew so well gripped him again, this bewildering, paralyzing fear, and chased him through the cold and empty streets. He found quiet nowhere, not in the pastry shop, where he sat before a cup of coffee, and not in the restaurant, where he tried to choke down a bite.

By two o'clock he was already on the bridge where he had so often stood, waiting, as now, for him. He knew Gunther could hardly be there before three-thirty, if he met the other boy at three and then hurried on.

The bridge lay deserted. Today it seemed that not a person had gone to work. The dark water of the Spree was covered with floating chunks of ice. The Reichstag building stood like a pale, gray shadow against the white winter sky.

As he stood there he felt how paralyzed with terror he was. It was now three. All at once he knew that waiting was entirely in vain! He felt, distinctly, that Gunther would not come. Not because he did not want to come — because he was unable to come.

Again — he knew not what — something terrible had happened. Gunther would not come . . . They had him again!

He stood there, no longer waiting for Gunther's arrival, only for the appointed time to arrive — because it had been agreed that he was to be here. It turned four o'clock. His hands were like ice. His heart was like ice.

Meanwhile, Gunther had been in a cinema on "the Mint" (Münzstrasse), which was full to bursting, despite the early hour, and one could cut the air with a knife. He only wanted to sit in the warmth and hardly looked at the pictures.

Then, on his way back, he had eaten something — two garlic sausages, a couple of dry rolls, and a glass of beer. He wanted to cut down expenses. He wanted to proudly report to his friend how economical he had been and to account for every penny. He still had almost two marks of the three he had received, in addition the whole ten marks that he wanted to give the other boy.

It was almost three when he arrived in Elsasser Street, close to the Adonis Lounge. Carefully he looked around. There was nothing suspicious. He stationed himself opposite, on the other side of the street, and looked across.

The lounge was open. This he could tell from the rolled-up shutters and the lights, which in the dark bar on a gloomy day were already lit. Except for a couple of boys he did not know, no one went in. No one came out.

It was already past three. Why did his companion not come? Oh well, he might at least walk over.

He did, carefully, and stationed himself beside the entrance in order to see the one he was waiting for as soon as he came out. That way he could keep an eye on both sides of the street and make off if anyone he did not trust should approach. Inside, except for the couple of boys and the proprietor, there could be no one.

His feet were freezing in the new and too-narrow shoes. He stamped from one to the other. Why did he not come!

No, he would not go inside in any case, even if he froze here outside. But how long should he stand here, when Hermann was certainly already waiting on the bridge? He would have preferred to go. If the other boy did not come, it was his own fault. Gunther had kept his promise.

Just as he was about to turn and go, the door opened and the awaited boy appeared — but not alone. At his side was a tall, strong man with a brown mustache that hung over his red face, and with piercing eyes. He held his companion securely by the hand.

Arrested! Gunther wanted to run away, as fast as he could, but he had not yet turned, when behind the two popped up another, a small, round-bellied man with a familiar face. Quickly he grasped Gunther — that pressure of two iron fingers, which Gunther knew. The man was saying in a friendly tone: "And here we also have right off the other one. You can just come along, sonny. Didn't I tell you we would see one another once again!"

2

A t ten minutes past four, Hermann Graff left his place on the bridge and strode briskly north. Not to his house — he turned instead toward the Weidendamm Bridge and walked up Friedrich Street to the Oranienburg Gate. There he stopped indecisively.

Early today, when they got up, he had once again had Gunther precisely name the lounge where he wanted to meet this companion at three o'clock — the Adonis Lounge, on Novalis Street.

Hermann easily found the street. But where was the lounge? He walked up to the nearest patrolman and asked. The man looked at him in astonishment, and he seemed to draw himself up.

Then, however, he carried out his duty. He raised his right hand, and with its white glove pointed down the street and uttered — as if in the future to have no more such questions — "Number twenty." With that he majestically turned away.

Hermann now easily found the lounge. It was a pub with one window, not distinguished in any way from thousands and thousands of others. He had never been in such a pub. He had no idea what took place in it. But he was at the right place. "Adonis Lounge" was spelled in large, white letters on the plate-glass entrance. It must be open. Light came from inside.

He opened the door, threw back a curtain, and was in a small front room, bordered on the right by a large bar. In a corner, opposite the entrance, stood a tall stove. At several small tables were seated figures, hard to recognize in the dim light of the room, but apparently juveniles.

He hesitated a moment. Then he walked up to the bar where an old man, apparently the proprietor, was busy, tipped his hat, and asked, "Excuse me, does a young man named Gunther not patronize your place?"

Before the old man could turn around and answer, Hermann was surrounded by boys who had jumped up from their tables. They were without exception young lads from sixteen to perhaps nineteen years old. Six or seven. They had heard the name and outdid one another in offering information.

"Gunther? The one with the Count?"

"Do you mean Chick?"

"But he hasn't frequented this place for a long time now..."

"Shut your trap, what do you know! You do mean Gunther, don't you, the one from the Passage, with the sports jacket?"

They were all shouting in confusion. However, they were all more or less agreed that Gunther had not been there for a long time and the third speaker, therefore, had been correct.

Hermann did not know what he was to do under this storm of information. But then, a small runt with a lean, freckled face shoved himself eagerly between all of them, as if through their legs, then looked up at him excitedly and said eagerly and definitely: "I know where he is!"

But he obviously did not want to reveal his knowledge in front of the others, who were standing around the newcomer still filled with curiosity.

He took hold of Hermann's arm and drew him into the larger room lying farther toward the back. There he chattered eagerly on. "I know where he is, and I'll tell you. But we want to sit down first. Here..."

The others remained behind.

This back room was much larger than the front room, still empty of guests and barely illuminated.

A young waiter in a white apron followed in their footsteps

and asked what they wished. The little boy, after a quick glance at the guest, who only nodded as if everything were entirely indifferent to him, ordered.

They were sitting in a dark corner. Hermann still spoke not a word; he just looked at his companion. The boy began speaking.

He knew Gunther. He knew him well. "I just now saw him. Just a half hour ago when I arrived. Just as I wanted to go in, they were standing in front of the door. The cops and Gunther. From there they took him away. It's all up with him — him and another, bigger boy. There were two of them. One held him like this" — he made a motion around his wrist — "that's how they took him away. And he had on an entirely new suit..."

His listener did not yet quite understand. "All up with him"? The cops? He only felt: *The worst has happened!* And this little chap knew about it...

The waiter — Justav — returned, bringing beer, coffee, and pastry.

"Have you maybe a cigarette?"

No, Hermann had no cigarettes on him. But they must surely have them here? Ten? Yes, as many as he wanted. If the waiter would only go away again!

Finally the cigarettes arrived and now they were left in peace. The other boys had sat down again in their places around the stove. The guest had made his choice and could not be disturbed. That was a sacred rule here.

The little boy had to tell again what he knew, and he did it eagerly. His listener understood — they had caught Gunther; he was taken back; everything was at an end!

He was not astonished. He was not even shocked. It was as though he felt nothing. His heart was like ice. The little boy, who saw how the stranger — never before seen here or elsewhere — spoke not a word, but only continued to look at him, and he talked on and on.

It was really unheard of bad luck! Formerly the cops had never come so early. But this was probably connected with a blackmail and attempted murder on Christmas evening, and they were looking here for somcone who was supposed to be connected with it. Well, to be sure, they had not found him here. The other boys, however, who were here every day, were, of course, all known to them. They didn't even question them further. Only the boy who had escaped from the institution and was just on the point of leaving, him they had an opportunity to pick up. And then, too, poor Chick, who was standing outside, and with whom, as he had related, he had gotten away on Christmas evening. . .

"But that Chick, too, had to be standing outside just then. Such bad luck!"

The little boy was finished.

"Where is he now, then?" the boy heard a hoarse voice beside him ask. While he had already eaten his coffee and pastry, despite his long narration, and was already on his fourth cigarette, the man had still not touched his glass of beer. Chick must really mean a lot to him!

"Where? Well, first to the central police station once again, and then back to where he had come from. . ."

The boy did not like the constant stare that remained fixed on his face. An odd john! And now he spoke not another word, nor did he ask any more questions. It often happened that a boy was inquired about here. But this man seemed to be unacquainted with such things, otherwise he would probably not have asked where Chick was now. It couldn't be the Count, could it? A Count must surely look different. He observed the man furtively.

Then he saw how the odd guest drank up his beer with one draft, shivered as if it had been poison, and looked around absently in the now more brightly lit, empty room.

"Can one not drink something warm here?" he heard the man ask.

But of course. A hot rum grog? Might he also drink one with him?

"Justav, two grogs!" was cried to the front.

They came. The little one drank, looked at the man sitting beside him, considered, and drew up closer.

Of course he was a john. Only johns came here. Only johns were interested in boys. Gunther was unfortunately under arrest now and would not come back so soon. Then the man would just have to look for another. How would it be if he tried to replace him? A quite nice man. He seemed to have money, else he would not have let him order so quickly whatever he wanted. Things were going so badly for the boy, too. The johns never took after him. At most once it was late in the evening, when all the others were already taken. Because he was so small. And so ugly — he knew it too. He wanted to at least try.

He drew himself up quite close, so that their arms touched. He laid his hand on the knee beside him. He lightly moved his hand higher. The other apparently noticed nothing. He appeared to see, to hear, to feel nothing. He constantly stared straight ahead. Like Leo always did, when he took cocaine — but this was no cocaine addict.

Now the man looked at him and shoved the groping hand under the table away. Completely indifferently. Absently. But not angrily. The little boy understood. Nothing doing here. Not for today.

It seemed as if the guest wished to get up and leave. But he sat right back down again in the chair and remained seated. He seemed only now to comprehend what he had heard. He looked again into the small, precocious face.

It was ugly, lean, and strewn with freckles. But his eyes looked out slyly, and he was obviously older than he appeared. Experienced. What he said, too, was quite reasonable. He had moved away again somewhat and was stirring the steaming glass. Their arms no longer touched. No one was concerned about them. It was as quiet up front as here in back — as if everyone were sleeping.

Hermann pulled himself together. He had to negotiate. He must learn whatever there was yet to learn. But then...

The little one was ready to give any further information he could. Even if nothing would probably develop between them, something would surely come of it for him. (And, God knows, he had to take whatever came!) At first he asked whether he might drink something else and received the impatient answer: "But just order, sir, whatever you want!..."

That was a super answer and was deemed worthy of a new call for Justav and a generous order. But things still did not move on. The man made not a sound. So he had to start.

"Please don't continue to say 'sir' to me. We're all familiar with one another here, even the gentlemen who come here. And they call me by a little kid's nickname, Pipel. Because I'm so little. But I'll soon be eighteen..."

"He's eighteen ... And he's called Pipel..." thought Hermann.

They sat together still longer, over an hour here in their corner. Pipel conducted himself very decently from now on. He had understood.

Questions and answers came and went, all about only one thing. Pipel answered to the best of his ability, and entirely honestly.

After Justav was paid and had received more than the usual tip, Pipel was asked if might not be given something, too. He might! When three marks were pressed into his hand he was certain: "A Count he isn't , but a real gentleman." He wanted to keep the man well-disposed toward him!

Between them, they agreed to meet here every day from now on. Pipel had to swear that each and every day he would be here at this hour. Pipel would do all he could to learn where they had taken Chick. All the boys who escaped from institutions came here at some time, even if only for a moment and only at times when there was nothing to fear from the cops. Among them, there would surely be one, sometime, who knew about Gunther, perhaps who even came from the same institution. Pipel would then question him and would make an appointment, where they would meet, so that Hermann himself could hear what he had to say. Pipel and the other one were then each to receive immediately twenty marks for good and reliable news. He — what was his name? — Hermann would come here every day, about five-thirty or six, to hear if anything had happened.

All this was agreed to. Hermann was leaving for today, to return again tomorrow. Pipel was elated — every day food and drink and respectable table money (even if, of course, not three marks every day). Plus, he could look forward to a further twenty!

"Now don't forget to come!" was Pipel's last word.

Forget to come!... thought Hermann. What else did he have to do from today on except one thing, find Gunther again! Find him and rescue him!

Alone with the other boys Pipel was stormed with questions as never before. But he answered little. He wanted to earn the twenty marks for himself alone.

Hours afterward, late in the evening, after walking around a long time in strange streets, Hermann Graff stood at the window of his room and looked over at the bare wall. His lips were pressed together, his teeth clinched.

In his brain there was room for only one thought and it did not leave for a moment — it ruled so that no other feeling, not that of pain, not that of longing, not that of despair, not that of fear, could contend with it.

"I will and I must have him again, now, when he is mine — mine as never before! I will not rest until I have him again! I alone have a right to him — I alone!

"You shall not succeed in taking him from me again! You shall not succeed! And if I must perish over it, if we both perish in it — I will have him again. Living or dead!"

3

very day when he came from work — usually directly, sometimes after going home quickly first — Hermann Graff walked to the Adonis Lounge. Each evening Pipel came to meet him, either regretfully shrugging his shoulders, or under the pretense of some insignificant news, drawing him into the corner jealously, then not budging from his side any more.

Naturally everyone there now knew why Hermann came. The prospect of earning twenty marks excited them extremely (for this, of course, did become known) and the name "Gunther" became a battle cry. Every escaped state ward, everyone who was only suspected of coming from an institution, was stopped and interrogated. But no one knew anything of Chick.

When Hermann arrived, the lounge had not been open for long and was still quiet. Only the front room was lighted. The boys were sitting around the tables, boring themselves, waiting for evening when things picked up.

They passed the time playing cards or gossiping with one another. Or they sat dully around the stove and warmed themselves, glad, for today, no longer to need to go out into the cold and wet. On such days they spoke of the Passage with contempt.

Guests were seldom here at this time. Only an odd-looking man, who was said to be a poet and writer for the newspapers, was often there, sitting among the boys and chatting with them — nice, clever, and sympathetic. One saw from his bright and serious face that he must have gone through a lot.

At odd moments another, younger, taller man came in, already half drunk and in the first stage of cocaine intoxication. He would drink, standing, always the same thing — a glass of beer and a large cognac — go out, and return in an hour.

Around this time things were still quiet. When a couple of people went at one another with loud words, they were hushed again right away.

No one needed to eat anything, and most of them were unable to because their earnings from yesterday were long used up, and those for today were still in the uncertain future.

Yes, they all knew what Hermann came for and they gave up hustling him. At first, he would leave right away if he heard from Pipel that another day had gone by without news. Then he took to sitting, longer and longer each day. For where was he to go? To his empty and barren room, alone with himself and his one thought?

Lately, Hermann sat in the front, near the bar. He could not take much of Pipel's chatter anymore, and Pipel did not know what to relate, being never questioned and never receiving a real answer. Pipel received his cup of coffee and whatever else he wanted, his cigarettes, and in a quiet handshake on departure, his table money.

Cigarettes — they all wanted them. They approached Hermann's table: "Have you no cigarettes for me, sir?" Or, "Got any fer me mister?" They asked, when they were very hungry, for a sandwich and a few nickels: "Have a heart!"

They always got what they wanted. But none of them exploited his always constant willingness, precisely because they knew that they got what they requested. They probably also thought, "It must not be going so good for him either, else he wouldn't always be so sad and so quiet."

Out of gratitude they also sat at his table and told him their stories, to cheer him up, as they said, or because they liked to hear themselves talk. He appeared to listen but their words went by him as if they were never spoken. He gradually learned all their faces and names. But Hermann would have scarcely recognized any of them again, if he had met one on the street.

They no longer thought of approaching him in any other way. As a john, he was useless — a decent person, but a miserable john.

It would be wrong to say that these surroundings created in him any kind of disgust. They left him indifferent. He, who once would not have been able to endure five minutes here, now sat hour after hour, indifferent but friendly to everything around him. He thought only about the one thing that he never, not for a moment, was able to forget.

The old proprietor, called Father by everyone, had lost his son in the war. Now his best helper, except for Justav, was his daughter-in-law. She was seldom seen, since she stayed mostly in her kitchen looking out for the welfare of her guests. But while Father was good-natured and lenient with guests, that was not so with her, especially for guests who didn't pay. When, her child in her arm, she appeared up front in a case of trouble, she finished with even the worst rowdy in no time and established peace and order again in a jiffy.

The Adonis Lounge was a gold mine. Evenings.

Hermann Graff sat in his corner by the counter. When there was nothing to do — and there was little to do in the early hours — Father came shuffling over to his corner, stood at his table, and said a few friendly words about the weather and bad times. Or he came with a tray and two small cognacs, and invited Hermann to drink with him. He was a good old man, and Hermann liked him. But it was always difficult for Hermann to converse. He could not take even friendliness any more.

At the farthest table, in the darkest corner, regularly sat a young man of indeterminate age — he could be eighteen or twenty-five. With trembling hands he shook small doses of a white powder from a paper bag, divided them, folded them into paper strips, and concealed them carefully in his breast. The boys approached him, whispered secretly with him, and implored:

"Leo, one for me too..." If their wish was granted (mostly, of course, only for payment), the contents of one paper was shaken onto the back of the hand and sniffed.

There was only one who really brought life into the quiet and hungry company — an unbelievably funny and somewhat effeminate sixteen-year-old lad, rosy, as well-fed as a pig, and as fresh as a dachshund. When he arrived, they all sat around him and he babbled nonstop relating genuinely funny and mostly indecent tales.

One of his stories was that he had been given over by his mother — not entirely without reason, since she was outraged over his conduct and encouraged by the neighbors — to be an apprentice to a baker. There he had seduced the apprentice on the first day, the journeyman on the second, and the master baker himself on the third, until on the fourth day he had been thrown out by the master's jealous wife. Everyone in the lounge laughed loudly; even over the face of the quiet guest in the corner, who willy-nilly had to hear it too, there passed a weak smile. With all the details, the story was irresistibly funny.

Life of another kind, less pleasant and often unbearable, was brought in by Clever Walter. His brutal nature expressed itself in his bent-forward posture — as if he always wanted to attack someone. He was usually already half drunk. He picked a quarrel with everyone in turn and acted as if he alone were boss, but he was respected as Uncle Paul's son-in-law. When he had made enough noise, he left again to return in the evening, when things were in full swing. Clever Walter had to be tolerated because he could not be ignored.

Otherwise it was usually always the same people just sitting around there — afternoon for afternoon, evening for evening. New ones were not welcome but were ordered to leave, especially if they were not yet eighteen. It held together in its way, this odd society there in the Adonis Lounge.

If this man, who was already viewed to a certain extent as belonging here (not a customer, and a "miserable john," but otherwise a quite decent chap), ever had thoughts about his new surroundings, it was only because he continually thought: "So, *he* frequented this place, too! *He*, too, sat around like this on so many afternoons! He listened to this nonsense and joined in the conversation ... Many weeks in the past summer! ... *He!*"

At first Hermann was astonished — astonished over the way the young people talked about sexual things as a matter of course, as others would talk about the weather. It was this calm self-evidentness that kept their conversation from becoming unendurably vulgar.

He was also astonished over their absolute lack of willpower. They made no resistance of any kind to this life. Wherever it tossed them, there they lay — today here, tomorrow there. They made not the slightest attempt to rebel against it. Everything seemed to be completely indifferent to them — whether they went entirely to ruin or not. If they had money — "come into a tidy sum" — then it had to be dispersed as quickly as possible and was thrown away in the most foolish way. None among them — the majority did not even know where they were to sleep the next night — thought of taking a room and maybe paying in advance, to have a roof over his head for the next days or weeks. Here and there the most necessary thing for the moment was procured — a shirt, pants, a pair of boots — but mostly money was spent immediately in foolish extravagance.

They went with whoever took them. If a decent man came among them, one with good intentions toward one of them and ready to help bring him up again (naturally it might not be through work), that opportunity too was wasted until the gentleman, discouraged by this lethargy, dropped him again. They all returned, like sheep to their accustomed stall, back here again, to live their lives until one day they had grown too old or some unexpected event, mostly of a bad sort, threw them onto other tracks. They returned here, semi-conscious by day, living it up at night. One after the other they each finally disappeared. No one knew where...

They all wanted, during gloomy hours, to get out of this life. They were all, one as much as the other, crammed with plans of all kinds about what they wanted to do. Each day they came in and told what they had in mind: There was a gentleman, a new acquaintance from just yesterday, who had promised to secure a position — only the gentleman never returned; a letter had come from home, he was to return there immediately — but the fare for the trip had to be procured first, only to be spent again right away; one already had a position and wanted to start tomorrow — except he was sure to be back in the lounge tomorrow...

Plans, plans, always new ones, always newly formed, and never seriously carried out. If one of them really stayed away and did not return, there were certain to be other reasons. Usually it meant he had been arrested again.

They were often discontent and in a bad humor, never really happy. Not a single one perceived his life as a disgrace, however. No boy there would have understood if someone had tried to make him comprehend this. It was better not to try. In the final analysis, they were indifferent to everything. "One just had to live." So much the more, when one was still young. Live — and enjoy life as much as possible. For one *was* young.

One afternoon, toward evening, such a quiet fell over the pub that Hermann looked up. Two men had entered and were standing at the bar. One was tall and lean, with an unpleasant expression on his face, mean, distrustful eyes, and an unkempt red-brown mustache over his wry mouth. The other was small, stout, and awoke trust with his round little belly and his even-tempered, smooth face.

With one stroke all conversation stopped. The boys, eight or ten in number, clearly wanted to creep behind their tables. Leo had dived into his dark corner entirely. And Pipel, who had been sitting beside Hermann, vanished — probably under the table.

After about ten minutes, during which the two stood at the counter, drank, and conversed with Father, they left again. Only Clever Walter had gone up to them and quite familiarly taken part in the conversation. It had otherwise been as if they had not seen any of the others present. But it appeared to Hermann that the tall one especially had sharply examined each one, even if inconspicuously.

Everyone breathed a sigh of relief when they were gone. Pipel's freckled little face popped up beside him again. "The cops!"

Hermann did not understand right away.

"They were policemen. One of them is the one who arrested Chick that time."

Hermann was boiling. So that was the man Gunther had told him about. Him — he looked it, too — with that face like a bird of prey, with its piercing eyes and hooked nose.

"No, no," said Pipel, angry over so much lack of discernment, "not the tall one. He really has a heart for us and always leaves us alone. The other, the short one, that's a louse, I tell you!"

What, the one with the even-tempered face who acted as if he saw and heard nothing? For the rest of the evening Hermann never got rid of the thought: "Hunter and hunted! The hounds and the game! Hunting human beings!"

When he had entered the lounge for the first time, Hermann had known nothing about these boys and their life. He did not comprehend their life, he did not understand them. Now, when daily he saw how they lived, he found that there was not a great deal to understand and comprehend. It was basically always the same for them — the struggle with each day, during which they were bored — if they did not oversleep. And the nights — they, too, were probably much alike. Only because Gunther had once led this life did it interest Hermann. Otherwise he found it boring, empty, and bleak.

In the meantime he grasped much about Gunther, only now in detail. He, too, was young. He, too, wanted to enjoy his young life. With those his own age, when possible, with older men, if it could not be helped — in loud circles, pampered and desired, surrounded by flattery and given gifts, from one hour to another, slipping or snatched from one arm to another.

He grasped why so many things about his darling had appeared so strange at first and so unintelligible. He grasped what, when they had become closer, had then always driven Gunther out and away. He grasped why Gunther had so often come to him cross and tired — it was not his age alone, age of moods and contradictions, it was the hangover after the drunkenness. And again and again this intoxication had vanished into new acquaintances, new intoxications, into always new adventures, as exciting or boring as those in his dime novels!

Gunther had lived the way these boys lived, from day to day and from night to night. A terrible life! But for him, the only life!

Yet Gunther had been different from these boys — would Hermann otherwise have been able to love him? Did any one of these boys attract him, even enough so that he could halfway listen to his conversation? Not a single one!

Would it be possible for him to take even one of them in his arms, associate with him, not to mention love him? No! And this life — had not Gunther left it behind and become completely different?

The fall from the dreamy heights, iridescent and empty, from the deceptive heights to the hard earth, this precipitous fall had brought Gunther to his senses! And now, at the dawn of his recovery, when they should have been together, and forever — now he was gone and lost once more!

One week went by. Two. A third began. Hermann went from one day to the next to the Adonis Lounge to wait for news that never came, however much Pipel endeavored to give him hope: "It will come for sure." He was now living quite regularly again. Punctually at nine he was in his office. At the stroke of five he left it. At six he was in the lounge.

He did his work — mechanically exact, but then he was through with it. He was no longer unhappy. He had a goal. Whoever has a goal in life is never entirely unhappy. He cannot entirely despair. Hermann had one thought, and this thought became for him a fixed idea: "I must rescue him and I will rescue him."

This one thought pursued him from morning till evening — during his work, during his meager lunch, on his walk to the lounge. The thought pursued him while he sat there, and all the way home and into his oppressive and restless dreams.

To rescue Gunther — no longer to possess him, but to save him from that horrible environment in which he was and from his downfall in it. It was as if his passion had vanished, yes, even his longing. Only fear for Gunther, concern, and sympathy were still in him. Fear above all. He *must* find Gunther, to rescue him.

4

One day, in the second half of the third week, Hermann could stand it no more and went to an attorney. Since he knew none, he went to the first available one. Perhaps the attorney could give him some kind of advice. After a long wait he was admitted.

Everything about the misshapen man was yellow — his hair, his skin, his eyes, his teeth, the nails of his greedy hands. He beamed at Hermann through his pince-nez.

"What does it concern?"

"A boy . . ."

"A boy?"

"Well, yes, a boy in a state institution."

The little yellow man immediately got the picture, and became reserved. These were not cases that he liked. Nothing came of them. Besides, he was no specialist in matters of Paragraph 175 and did not intend to become one. But he at least listened while his client explained the situation in a few words. Then he spoke.

"In what relationship do you stand to the boy?"

When he noticed that Hermann considered this question impertinent he rephrased the question.

"I mean, what interest do you take in the boy?"

Hermann forced himself to reply; it was not a question of

himself or this man in front of him, but of him whom he loved and wanted to rescue. He replied as calmly as possible, "I am a friend who wants to help him..."

The lawyer became objective. He reached over the desk for a thick volume and leafed through it, then looked thoughtfully at the ceiling. "I can only advise you to keep your hands out of the matter. In no case can you help him. For freeing an institutionalized state ward, or even only attempting to, there is imprisonment for not less than a year."

"The parents — or the guardian — can they do nothing?"

"I know of only one case in which a state ward was freed. That happened years ago on the intervention at the highest level of His Majesty..." Then as he saw the care-worn and sad face opposite, he spoke more humanly. "Let the boy go. Believe me, whoever is once in there is ripe for the penitentiary..."

Hermann thought, *How right the man is with his cheap wisdom.* But he only said bitterly: "That's why so many of them run away..."

"And are then always caught again," he heard as the answer.

Always? But what did this man know about it and what point was there in sitting here any longer? He stood up and walked out — not without shaking hands and being relieved of twenty marks.

5

e waited. His waiting appeared more hopeless each day. But one evening in the fourth week Pipel came all excited to meet him as he entered and drew him toward the back.

"There's one here," he whispered. "From Neuenhagen. I heard it from a john, who knows him. He blabbed it to me. I also know where he is. I must go there now. I'm just leaving. Wait here until I come back..." And he added: "I'll make an appointment with him for tomorrow. We'll go together . . . Give me some money for the fare..."

Hermann would have preferred to go with him directly, but Pipel absolutely did not want that.

"Why not?"

"Because I have to see first if he's really here. And because I don't know at all if it's all right with him. He does have to stay hidden..." He was a decent boy, Pipel explained, and the gentleman from whom Pipel knew all this was Pipel's former steady john. And he only told Pipel because he knew him and they had been together. Therefore, Hermann was to wait there, even if it should become late. Pipel would definitely return. Definitely! And he was gone, out through the door.

Hermann remained sitting in his corner.

He was to hear something! This evening — indirectly at first, but tomorrow from a person who had seen Gunther and who knew where he was and how it was going with him!

His heart began to beat again for the first time in weeks. Of course he would wait here for Pipel. He would not leave until Pipel was here again.

So he sat there, gave Justav an order, made an impatient wave of his hand when someone came too close to him, and brooded. Tomorrow — how long yet until tomorrow! But tomorrow he was to hear from Gunther . . . Finally! Finally!

When he looked up, the lights had already been lit in the large room. The first guests had appeared, almost no table was still unoccupied. Never before had he stayed so long. He had always gone when it came alive here. Now it was already in swing around him.

He looked around. Through the pink paper shades of the gas chandelier the light glittered onto the free space in the middle of the oblong hall, where there was dancing, while the tables on the sides and in the corners remained more in darkness.

The first tones were already struck on the worn-out piano and a violin was tuned to them. He sat squeezed into his corner. No one was concerned about him.

The boys had enough to do, greeting the arriving guests, coming on to them, and sitting at their tables. They were all as if transformed — those who sat around lazy and cross in the afternoon were suddenly all life and action.

Tall Willy cried to him as he passed by: "Stay! Stay! This evening will be super! . . ."

And Father, on his way to the kitchen, stopped by him and kindly remarked: "It's only right that you also stay for an evening. . ."

Justav brought him his meal. He had to eat something. Who could know when Pipel would return?

The evening did become super, and indeed very soon. A half hour later no table was empty. At his, not a chair had been empty for a long time.

The music played — the piano player with his artist's hair and his accompanist, the queer August, on the violin — and there was dancing so that the floor shook. Gentlemen danced with the boys, some boys danced among themselves, and two aunties in women's clothing, with wigs and gigantic feather hats, danced like crazy. Melodies were sung — it was all a confusion of laughter and shrieks.

Always new guests arrived — young and old. Boys from other lounges and from the street, who usually never came here in the afternoon; gentlemen, old and young, from all walks of life and all occupations, simply dressed, well dressed, conspicuously dressed. Couples — always an older man and a younger boy, who sat closely together, looking deeply into one another's eyes, concerned only about themselves. Many were acquainted among themselves, greeted one another, called to one another, and shook hands in passing.

All were sitting pressed close together. Here a boy was lying with his head on the breast of a prosperous looking gentleman, there two had discovered one another in a kiss that never wanted to quit. People became acquainted in a second; suited one another; matched up again another time. No one disturbed anyone. That is what they were here for.

There was — atmosphere. The tumult rose and rose, and appeared far from having reached its peak. Justav was now, of course, all business. He ran from table to table carrying trays with coffee and pastry, beer and liquors. The smoke of countless cigarettes rose in layers over their heads.

At the table where Hermann Graff sat, completely wedged in at the farthest corner, things were likewise loud enough. Without greeting him or even looking at him, two gentlemen had sat down, one tall and strong, with a full beard, and the other somewhat younger, with a pale and haggard face. Old comrades, obviously, on their nightly round through these places, but definitely not a relationship.

He had never before seen the two boys with them. One, with a round, healthy face and lively brown eyes, was sitting opposite the older of the two gentlemen. He had laid his arms over the table and was saying nonstop to the man, staring at his coat pocket in which a thick billfold might be concealed, always the same words: "Oh how I'm horny! How horny I am — for your fat dough!"

Over and over, with a sly wink at his coat pocket: "How horny I am — for your dough!"

At first it was funny, then it became boring. At first he was angrily told to keep quiet. Then no one listened any more. When he finally realized that he was having no success with his silliness, a mean gleam came into his eyes. With a quick grasp he took the beer glass of the man opposite, emptied it in one swallow, and disappeared with an infinitely vulgar word. The two gentlemen only laughed.

Hermann did not laugh with them. He sat in his corner, with his calm and serious face, looking at the goings-on around which did not concern him or touch him. He was not astonished. For weeks he had not been astonished over anything except maybe the changed conduct of the boys, whom he knew from the afternoons as entirely different.

They, who shortly before had been sitting in their corners so morose and dull, were transformed. Either they had already found their johns, old or new, and were sitting with them, or they, who otherwise hardly opened their mouths, now laughed and chatted, often in a tight embrace, lively and excited. Or they went from table to table, sat down — whether asked to or not — with the strangers and were invited to stay or were given the cold shoulder. Once invited, everything else followed as a matter of course.

The merriment grew from hour to hour. Hermann did not budge from his corner. He drank more than usual. His mouth dried out from the dust and dense smoke. Then suddenly it seemed that he saw *him* there! Saw Gunther there, going from table to table with his charming smile (how charmingly he really could smile, when he wanted to!), speaking with this one, stopping by that one and sitting down . . . Hermann's back ran hot and cold.

Again, as he so often had lately, he thought: "He frequented here, many long weeks last summer, from evening to evening, as Pipel and the other boys said. Here he spent his idle afternoons, his drunken evenings! From here he started his nights full of drunkenness and lust and..."

That fat beast over there — had he, too, been allowed to hold Gunther in his arms, just as he is now holding the slim boy who at first resisted, but then patiently let himself be hugged and kissed? Had Gunther also turned away at first, had he then also given in?

And that other one there, that slender young person with the uncanny eyes and the odd movements of his long hands, whom they were all around, although he ordered nothing, who appeared so completely at home here — had Gunther also been together with him and still come away alive?

From here the Count — this Count, whom alone he knew about — had taken him away to his palace, to violate him there with his looks worse than any other could have done!

Terrible! Terrible! He could stand it here no longer. He wanted out of the corner and yet sat wedged into it. It must be quite late already. Why did Pipel not return? — Here he was finally!

Pipel tried at first to crowd in to Hermann, but with a wave of his hand Hermann kept him off, and with a rudeness that was usually foreign to him, he got up and pushed aside the chairs along with the people sitting on them.

He signaled to Pipel and took him out to the street. In the room the music sounded — laughter, singing, noise, and shrieks echoed; the couples whirled...

They were standing outside. "Well?"

"Tomorrow! I talked with him. At five tomorrow be at Alexander Place by the sign of the bear. By his left calf." Pipel loved little jokes like that. "I'll be there. It's not far from there ... But now I have to go in!..." He got his money and was gone.

Hermann Graff once more threw a short glance at the covered windows of the pub, which he would never again enter. Then he walked for hours through the night full of cold and snow. Morning dawned. *Today!*

6

t five he was at the bear sign, by the left calf, as Pipel had said. Pipel arrived at five-thirty, wanting to hear nothing about being late. He had been in luck yesterday evening and had only just got out of bed.

"It's not far. Only a couple of streets. . ."

They turned into a quiet, crooked street. Then they were in an old open square with an ugly church in the middle. Most of the houses were very old and their roofs sagged deeply. Pipel stopped in front of one of the smallest, which was kept from collapsing only by its neighbors. A couple of steps led to a small pub on the ground floor.

The narrow barroom was pitch-dark. An old woman approached. She must have already been informed, for she directed the two guests toward the back. From there, where a light shone, a young man probably twenty years old, stong and broad-shouldered, slowly approached them.

"Mother, make more light in back," he said to the old woman with a voice that was remarkably deep for his age.

A petroleum lamp over the table in the back room was lit and only now could Hermann discern the speaker. He liked him immediately. He had an open, good-natured face, with blue eyes and a light fuzz over his lips. He gave Hermann his hand and they sat down. Then Hermann asked, "You know Gunther? You know where he is and will tell me how it's going with him?. . ."

The other did not answer at first. He looked at Pipel and then said slowly, "Yes, I know Gunther. But I don't know him here. I've only heard about him. From my friend. I only know that he told Pipel I'm here, and that's enough. Now, Pipel, when you've drunk up" — the old woman had brought three glasses of beer — "you could leave us alone . . . the gentleman here and me. . ."

Pipel, who was anything but stupid, understood. He drank up. Only one small detail was still to be taken care of. When he felt the promised twenty-mark bill in his pocket, he immediately got up. Hermann also gave him his hand.

"I thank you, Pipel. You're a good boy. . ."

"You'll still come to the lounge again tomorrow?"

Hermann looked for the last time, without answering, at the slim, freckled face, before it disappeared through the door.

Then he was alone with the stranger and now he could stand it no longer. "You have seen him? How is he? Where is he?"

As he always did when he was questioned during the next hour, the young man sitting opposite Hermann reflected before he answered. Then he spoke, calmly and slowly, in a manner unusual for one so young.

"Dear sir," he said, "I will tell you everything I know. I really wanted to leave early this morning. You can imagine how hot it is for me here. Since I heard yesterday evening how much it means to you and also because my friend — you don't know him and he doesn't know you — urged me to, I stayed on and will go to Hamburg tomorrow. He said to me yesterday: 'Do stay one day here and talk with the man. We must help one another when we can, even when we are not acquainted. . .' For you see, he is also fond of me and I know how it is, even if I've paid him back badly enough. . .

"Therefore, Gunther is in Neuenhagen and I saw him just the day before yesterday. How is it there? Well, not like in Lichte, in Lichtenberg. Much stricter. And if someone has already escaped once, they watch him much more sharply. . ."

"But how is he?"

"As well as he can be. But he is delicate and not made for the life there."

"Yet not sick?"

"No, he's not exactly sick..."

"Is it possible to get him away from there?"

This time the answer took still longer. But it came.

"Dear sir, to get away, that's always a question. No one gets away from there so easily. And the director, he's a — well, I just prefer not to say what he is, and the guards are not much better. But the worst thing is the inmates themselves. Whatever they can do to one another in meanness and dirty tricks, they'll do. And yet they're dependent on one another. And when they all come together — you can just imagine! What someone doesn't already know, he soon learns it for sure!"

"But Gunther?"

"Yes, he has it especially hard now, just because he's something better. When they fight — what is he to do? Once I pulled him out and he just stayed on my hands."

His breathless listener groaned. What else should he ask? What answers were yet to come? He looked around helplessly. The old woman shuffled by. He ordered; he needed something warm to eat.

"But you yourself, how did you get out?"

The broad chest under the sailor's jacket rose and white teeth flashed in the young face.

"Me?" he heard the youth scornfully say, "no one can hold me for long. Certainly not them. I'll be in Hamburg tomorrow and the day after at sea..."

"You must surely be of age soon. Since—"

"Of age? How old do you take me for then?"

"Well, surely at least twenty—"

"I'm seventeen, just turned."

Just seventeen. But it was true — with all his manliness he still had something childlike. Hermann liked him more and more. But it was not about him that Hermann wanted to hear, but about Gunther. More — whatever there was to learn.

"Tell me," he begged, "do tell me about him ... Is he truly not sick?"

"No, I said already, he's not sick. But so quiet, so — so indifferent, as if everything was already all the same to him . . . I think he would no longer leave, even if he could. . ."

From the fearful face, whose eyes were looking at him as if a life hung on every word, the boy saw that he must comfort Hermann somehow. He did it in his way.

"Just don't take it so hard, dear sir. I don't know, it's true, what Gunther was to you, I don't want to know, for it's none of my business, but I think, if you would see him now . . ." He did not know how to continue.

Hermann had laid his hands over his face: *I would love him as always and as never before . . .* he thought.

He said further, looking up and quite desperate, "But is there nothing at all, not the least thing to be done? You do understand that I can't just leave him there, without helping him! Can I not write? Send him something, money, or whatever he needs? Can I not visit him sometime?"

The young man moved his blond head to and fro. Again everything he said was considered and clear.

"Sending goods or money has no point. Everything goes into the hands of the guards. And visit — do you think they would admit you? A gentleman to such a boy? They do know everything there. They know why Gunther is there. No, give up the idea. You would only have difficulties and still achieve nothing."

"But writing. I will surely at least be allowed to write?"

"Write? Yes, sure you can write. Sometimes the letters are even delivered."

"Read first?"

"Always. But after all" — naturally nothing could be in it that was suspicious — "they wouldn't always know where the letter came from, and then would probably deliver it."

"Best, I suppose, to register it? . . ."

"Anything but! Just stands out all the more. And don't put any money in. Act as if you're a relative or a distant friend — not that kind — and ask if one could send something. Then he would know that he had something to expect and would perhaps get it sooner. But nothing is ever sure there. Sometimes it's this way, sometimes that . . ."

"And otherwise there's nothing to do — nothing at all?"

"Wait, only wait..."

"Yes, but how long?"

"Well, until he's of age. Sometimes, however, they let them go even earlier..."

"Twenty-one!" thought Hermann. "Five years! An eternity! — if he lives so long, I won't live that long myself, if I have to continue to endure this!" He collapsed and the other regarded him with pity. He must speak to him again.

"Now, just try writing once. Perhaps his relatives can get something done. If you use them..."

He looked at the gloomy man staring straight ahead.

"Too bad," he thought, "he's a nice man ... I could like him. He could be a friend for me. I've lost the other man who liked me so much and did everything for me ... and who now has another boy, because I did not stay with him. But no, nothing can develop with this one. And tomorrow I'll be gone, far away! Too bad! And yet I'm a completely different guy from this broken-winged Chick, who won't be able to hold out much longer in any case ... too bad!"

He was asked, and answered, many more things. But at bottom it was always the same.

"No, not sick, only so quiet ... And he talks with hardly anyone any more!.."

The old woman came through the narrow room to go to the back.

"Who is the woman?"

"That's Mother. She's good to us and helps us through." He called her in. "True, Mother, you won't sell us out?"

She laid her old head on his young one and caressed his cheek with her scrawny hand.

"No, my boy, I won't sell out any of you. But what do I get out of it? You come and go, and tomorrow you, too, will already be gone again."

"Don't worry, Mother, I'll come again and also bring you something pretty from overseas."

But she shook her head and walked out.

Hermann got up. Standing was difficult for him, as if he himself were now quite old and tired. He gave the boy his hand and pressed into it the same thing that Pipel had received. He laid another bill on the table for the check. The young man hesitated.

"But will this not be too much for you, dear sir? When you have already just now..."

On the point of leaving, Hermann had just enough strength to resist him and say, "And you, how will you get on?"

Again his chest rose and his teeth showed. They shook hands with a firm clasp.

"I thank you! I thank you from the bottom of my heart!"

At the door Hermann turned back again. It occurred to him that he still did not know Gunther's surname. And he must write to him! He asked for it. The answer came with astonishment: "But his name is Nielsen. Gunther Nielsen. Didn't you know that?"

Hermann left.

Alone with himself, the boy left behind thought again, "Too bad! I could have been friends with him!"

But he had known for a long time that not everything in life is or can be the way one wishes.

ermann Graff rode home. The letter must be written. It must be sent off today. He shoved everything aside.

"My beloved boy..." he began. And then, drawn along by these first words, he wrote and wrote. Wrote what his heart dictated and without reflecting on what he was writing. He wrote about everything — about his longing, his despair, his anxiety over Gunther in these last terrible weeks. He wrote and his pen flew. He wrote to Gunther that now all was well. He was not to despair, but rather take heart. Hermann would wait for him. He would rescue him. Gunther was only to tell him how this could best be done. Everything was well — he knew where Gunther was and soon they would be together again, never again to part.

He wrote and wrote. Sheet after sheet was covered with his steep and clear script. He did not know what he was writing. He only felt, with each new page, how it eased him to write, to be allowed at least to write.

He *had* to unburden his heart — to put into words everything unsaid and locked up, and to speak to his heart, to comfort, console, heal it . . . He wrote and wrote. . .

It was late in the night when he stopped writing and gathered the sheets together. And then all at once it was quite clear that he could not send this letter. He knew now that he had written it only for himself. He took the bundle of sheets, slowly tore them into small pieces, and then felt so tired that he was dizzy. Without another thought, without another feeling more for today, he sank onto his bed.

The next morning in his office between tasks he wrote a new letter. Quite short and to the point. Every word was carefully considered.

How it was going for him? Had he still not forgotten Hermann? Might Hermann write and what might he send Gunther? And that Gunther should remember that he always had Hermann as a friend, who wanted to do everything to help him, and he should only say how and what he could do...

He signed with his full name and included a stamped envelope with his exact address, as well as a blank sheet, in case Gunther had no paper handy there — he would surely be able to obtain a pencil stub.

During the noon break he dropped the letter in the post box. Yes, it was better not to register it. He must get it like this, or it would come back as undeliverable, for on the back of the letter also was Hermann's name and full address.

He was calmer. It was certainly good this way. No one would find anything suspicious or striking in this letter of a friend, he thought.

From that day on Hermann's life was again only a waiting. The day was Wednesday. Tomorrow, or the day after tomorrow at the latest, the letter must be in Gunther's hands. If on Friday or Saturday he had no opportunity or time for a reply, he would surely find it on Sunday. Then Hermann would have it Monday or Tuesday at the latest.

He waited. But neither on Tuesday nor on any of the next days of the week did a reply come. He was peculiarly calm. Only at times, when he was alone in the evening, did he groan out loud, as if in unbearable bodily pain.

He seldom, almost never, received letters. Who was there to write to him? Did the mail carrier even know that he lived in the house?

He fixed his card outside on the door. And — something that cost him a greater effort than he was willing to admit — he asked his landlady at an accidental meeting on the stairs (the first in weeks), in case a letter should come for him, to bring it to him immediately.

"Of course!" was her answer, and she walked on by without looking at him.

When the week came to an end with no reply having come, he made a firm decision. He knew now where Gunther was. The bridge had been built. Hermann must rescue him. For the guilt was his; it must be expiated. His was the guilt!

He should long ago have rescued Gunther from the life he was leading — from the life and from the people. He should have done it from the day that he had been there with Gunther for the first time. That and nothing else. He had not done it. He had let things go on as they were, in the cowardly fear of losing Gunther.

Gunther was without thought and will, like all of these boys. Thus Hermann should have thought and willed for two. By the strength of his will he should have lifted Gunther out of that accursed life, and by the strength of his love he should have succeeded. He should have placed himself firmly and irresistibly between Gunther and that life. He had not done it. His was the guilt and his the remorse.

Now, when it was still not too late — when he knew where Gunther was — he must rescue him. And then, when Gunther was rescued, stand like a wall beside him, before him . . . in front of the life on the other side of the wall!

Ten more — no, only eight more days — was he willing to wait. Not one more. If still no reply had arrived, he would give up his position; withdraw the rest of his money; and travel to the city where the institution was.

There, in the immediate vicinity — oh, everything was now only a question of being sly . . . and how sly he would be! — there nothing could be done with force, of course, but everything with cunning, planning — and money. There in the vicinity he would, under some kind of pretense (a traveler on business, a reseacher interested in the local history of the area), take up residence inconspicuously, to reconnoiter the terrain, then gradually, very gradually he would find the possibilities and paths for flight. After all, the institution was not a penitentiary. The boys were occasionally allowed out. He would — how his heart beat at the thought ! — see Gunther, if only from a distance. Then he would establish some kind of underground contact with him. He would receive a reply from him. Connivance. And finally it would all succeed.

Everything else would follow, once he was there in the vicinity. He was determined. His guilt would be expiated by rescuing Gunther.

No reply came. At the end of the next week, he would leave.

8

At the end of the next week he was arrested. Not without warning — on returning home one day he found, on his usually empty desk, a summons for the next morning, "for a hearing."

His shock was almost a joyful one — it could only concern Gunther. He would hear about Gunther. A connection was established. He did not think about himself. What indeed could happen to him?

He answered the first questions of the examining magistrate, even though he was astonished over the tone in which they were asked.

His letter was shown to him. Did it come from him?

Certainly it was from him.

Did he know the one to whom it was addressed?

Of course he knew him.

For a long time?

Yes, a long time.

Did Hermann know him well?

Yes, well.

How did it come about that he knew such a boy well? Had anything taken place between them? Indecent acts?

Hermann stood up, roughly shoving the chair away from him. He could have laughed out loud. He wanted to say, "I loved him!" But when he looked into the face of the man opposite, he kept silent.

He kept silent during all the following questions. When they were asked more insistently and always anew, he declared that he did not wish to answer.

He was finally let go with the remark that probably a charge of violating paragraph so-and-so of the legal code would be raised. However, since no suspicion of flight had been put forward, he might leave for the present.

He still did not think about himself. He even worked in his office the next morning without suspecting that it was to be the last time.

But he went home earlier than usual. When he arrived two police officers were already waiting in his room. They allowed him an hour in which to pack his things and — as they said — to put his affairs in order. He did it calmly and orderly, as he was accustomed to doing everything.

While he was occupied with closing his large suitcase, there was a knock. A gentleman entered and, without concerning himself about the two officers, who were smoking and softly talking to each other in the window-bay, went up to Hermann.

Hermann knew who it was. It was a colleague from his office, whom he knew only slightly, however, since he worked in another department. It had always struck him how intentionally this man sought his acquaintance. Where possible, he did Hermann favors and sought to enter into a conversation with him, always with the undertone of a secret intimacy, which Hermann did not understand and did not want. Nor did he like this colleague. He had something — not exactly slimy, but clinging — something so specifically effeminate in his whole conduct, that Hermann could not endure for the life of him.

This man was now suddenly standing before him and saying in an undertone: "I heard that you wanted to go away. Could I perhaps be helpful in some kind of way and might I be?"

Hermann, with the last of his things to be packed in his hand, looked at his colleague. There was nothing but an evident, friendly sympathy in his good-natured but simple face. What did this person know? — and from where? There were people who always knew everything and he looked like one.

Hermann considered for a moment. Then he said quickly, "Yes. If you will be so kind" — he took a bill from his wallet — "and settle my account with my landlady. She lives there down the hall and I would like to have nothing more to do with her."

The newcomer disappeared and was soon back, laying down the receipt and the rest of the money. Everything was settled.

They left. Hermann, with only a small handbag containing the most necessary things in his hand, led the way; the officers and the strange gentleman followed.

On the stairs the latter gripped his hand with a sympathetic pressure. "I do know everything," he whispered softly. "Just don't lose courage . . . Everything is not as bad as it seems."

It was not possible for Hermann in this moment to find a word of thanks. He could not even return the pressure of this hand, so limp and boneless did it lie in his.

He said only what just now occurred to him, "If I may trouble you further, to have my things up there stored with a shipper until — until I return, and may I ask you to keep the receipt until. . ."

And he continued, "At the office, too, you could excuse me tomorrow. . . for a time . . . no, probably better, forever. . ."

Everything was readily agreed to. Hermann turned once more and asked, looking at him steadily, "How did you know?"

The answer came with a glance at the two men. "They were in the office — earlier. You yourself had hardly gone. I hurried over here immediately and arrived just in time. . ."

And, returning Hermann's gaze: "After all, we must support one another as much as possible — in such a case. . ."

The officers came between them. Outside Hermann and the two officers climbed into a waiting cab.

Strange — the usually so empty street was all at once no longer so empty. Faces showed at the windows of the houses. In the hall of the neighboring house a couple of women stood and gossiped with curious glances at the men riding off.

9

In Hermann Graff's memory the time that then came was blotted out. If he tried to remember — but he hardly tried — it failed. Not people and things, but only shadows he could pick out. Only one thing did he later remember — that many, many hours of many days in a narrow and lightless room he had walked back and forth, from one wall to the other, back and forth, back and forth . . . from one wall to the other.

From the days, each alike, only one stood out. It, too, only like an oppressive dream. Before this day, his thoughts had constantly turned on one point: *I will see him again! It is all only a misunderstanding of these small and stupid bureaucrats. At the first question it will be cleared up. When asked, Gunther would perhaps say, "Yes, we were fond of one another." To all the others, however, keep silent, the way I have kept silent and will continue to keep silent. For that is the wonder of love: to be one in such an hour, unconquerable, in unshakeable trust! It must take place here too — the great wonder of love!*

The day arrived. A gray February day, dry and frosty. A large, almost empty room with many unoccupied benches at this early hour of the morning. Behind a high table, black figures, with cold, ill-humored or bored faces.

After the opening speeches back and forth, the public was to

be excluded. Two old people, a man and a woman who had probably only come here to warm themselves, shuffled out.

Leafing through the files. Bending over here and there. Then,
questions, questions, questions. . .

He kept silent.

"Accused, *will* you not answer?"

He kept silent.

Finally a door in the background opened and there came in —
a guard at his side — came in with forehead lowered, in a gray
smock, with dragging steps, his head shaved completely bald,
sunk deep onto his breast — came in. . .

It was — it could not be — he? He — Gunther?!

It was certainly — for God's sake — not Gunther?!!

Hermann wanted to jump up, go to him, take this lowered
face, of which he was able to see nothing, in his hands, and see
with his own eyes that he was deceived.

But he remained in his place. A feeling of numbness held him
fast in the chair in which he sat. He only stared unremit-
tingly at the small, sunken-in figure. . .

Thus he stared during the whole proceeding. He never took
his eye from the one who was standing there, and who was
supposed to be Gunther . . . Questions . . . questions . . .
questions. . .

He himself continued his silence to all of them. But the one
who stood there and never raised his head a single time, nodded.
Nodded and nodded to everything stupidly. At times, severely
rebuked, came a light, almost inaudible "yes" as an answer.

Questions . . . questions — more shameless than anything he
had ever heard in the Adonis Lounge from the boy prostitutes
there, struck his ear. He did not understand them. He only felt
they were shameless . . . shameless and absurd. He did not
answer a single one.

But Gunther — who was standing there motionless — nodded
to them too! If he had been asked if his "friend" — oh, these sneer-
ing, ambiguous accentuations! — if he had been asked if his friend
had tried to murder him, he would have nodded and said "yes". . .

There was only one witness there — his landlady.

She incriminated him more gravely than a hundred others could have done. She stood there in her dark dress, the very bones of morality. Her black eyes sparkled in her pale and haggard face.

She knew everything. She knew about the daily visits in the fall. About the whistles. The secret coming and going. She knew all about Christmas — how the boy had been in his rooms a whole day and two nights. She knew about the troubled conduct of her renter before and after, about his irregular times of returning home. She knew . . .

"If you don't want to believe me, I have witnesses. The whole house found fault with this."

Oh, they believed her. They believed everything and more.

She could take her seat again. Another stood up and spoke. Hermann heard him speak but heard not a word.

He only stared at the small figure who stood there and still nodded, even now, when he was no longer being questioned; who even now did not look up a single time; who was supposed to be his Gunther and yet could not possibly be!

Again and again he wanted to dash to him, rouse him:

"Gunther, do wake up! Just think about what you're doing! Don't be afraid of these strange people! I am here, I, your friend, I, Hermann!"

He did not do it. It was not these barriers, not the idols in robes and judges' caps that prevented him from doing it. Something else held him back and hindered him. Something still entirely incomprehensible.

Finally the verdict was pronounced. The judges, embittered over the stubborn attitude of the accused — who even here never took his eyes off the boy he lusted for; over his evident and complete lack of consciousness of guilt and of remorse; his more than suspicious silence; his declining of any defense; and above all deeply wounded in their consciousness of authority, pronounced it. Two months.

The boy was led out. As he had come, so he went: his bald head shoved between his slender, sunken shoulders, with dragging steps in his heavy shoes. The convicted man did not take his eyes from him until the door closed behind him.

Then he looked straight ahead. Where was he? What did they want of him? What had just happened?

The one who had just now stood there and nodded, always only nodded; who had vanished behind the door — that boy had been a stranger. A strange boy with whom he had never had anything in common, whom he had never known, whom he had never loved — a stranger, an entirely strange boy.

10

nd again, there came a time of which he later knew nothing, nothing except that, in a narrow room, he had walked back and forth from one wall to another — back and forth, many, many hours of many days, until he became tired. Then he paced more, from the beginning, back and forth, until he was so tired that he collapsed onto the iron bed.

What did he think about? Probably nothing. The guard came and asked. Requests? No, he had no requests. Complaints? He complained about nothing.

A young institutional doctor came, sent to examine the state of mind of this strange prisoner. He came and asked questions. He was looked at in astonishment. Sick? No, he was not sick. Nothing was the matter with him. What indeed should be the matter with him? The hours passed. The days passed. The weeks. One month. A second.

He did not count them — not the days, the weeks, the months. Only when he was told that the day of his release was near did he seem to wake up. His thoughts returned. Not to the past — that lay behind him, like something that never was. It must indeed be dead, what had been.

They went to the future. What should he do? Where should

he go? He thought without uneasiness about the future. Only hope makes one uneasy.

After the death of his father a year and a half ago now, there had arrived, among the trite condolences of his relatives and his few acquaintances, a curious letter. It came from a distant relative of his mother. He vaguely remembered having seen her once in his childhood, when his mother was still living. The image was vague, as was the memory of his mother herself.

He had almost forgotten the contents of the letter. He remembered only that, in contrast to the others, it was concerned not with one who had died, but rather with him, to whom it had been addressed. A passage remained in his memory, however, and for the first time, it now surfaced again. It ran something like this:

"You are now entirely alone in the world. I do not know, dear Hermann, if you have friends who understand you, so entirely and correctly. But if you should ever have need of such a friend, then remember that an old woman, who has reflected on many things, about which most people pass over without a thought" — and so on. . .

He had not understood these sentences. What should this old woman be to him, of whom he had only heard that she had lived in an unhappy marriage with her now-deceased husband? What should the friendship of this old woman be to him, which she was proposing?

But he began to see the letter in another light — now, when its ending again occurred to him:

"Come to me whenever you will and want to. You are always welcome. Come and hear then what another voice, a voice from the grave, has to say to you through me, when no other voice speaks to you any longer. . ."

This concluding sentence had sounded all the more to him like something from a novel, and he had answered the letter only briefly, even if not unkindly, without touching on the invitation it contained. Now he saw it, too, in a different light. What other voice could be meant, but that of her dead husband?

He recalled once more the little bit that he had also heard

about him. Veiled allusions (doubly carefully uttered before his child's ears). Then the significant silence after them...

"In case your path takes you through Munich" ... thus had she indeed written. The address of the suburb and the name of the house were still clear to him.

Now, when he did want to go out of the country with the rest of his money — to some inexpensive place down there in the south — why should he not take a route through Munich? Whatever the voice had to say to him — it was at least a voice in this silence around him.

11

round noon on a day in April he was released. It was spring again. Almost a year had gone by since he had arrived in Berlin.

But this spring did not, as the previous year's had done, coax winter away with a sweet smile. It came instead unruly, on schedule, with cold rain showers and icy winds, and struggled with winter for the new place.

Today, too, it swept unpleasantly through the streets.

The first thing that Hermann Graff did after his release was to send a telegram from the nearest office: "May I come?"

Thereupon he rode to his bank and withdrew the remainder of his money, not much more than a thousand marks. The next hours were spent on the most necessary purchases, among them a suitcase. This was deposited along with his small handbag at the Anhalter train station. Then he ate.

There was nothing more to do but wait for the answer to his urgent telegram. He walked slowly to the Tiergarten.

"Now I should probably look up the nice man who stood so selflessly by my side on the last day," he thought. But he was unable to do it. He suspected a world in which he did not belong, and with which he had nothing in common. A small, private world — full of various connections, special and particular interests, and endless idle gossip. His things could stay where they were until he needed them, until he knew how his future would be shaped. Perhaps he would yet return to Berlin one day.

No, he did not want to see him. Not today.

He sat down on an empty bench by the small lake under the still-bare trees. The water before him was black and dirty; the last chunks of ice were disintegrating, and yellowed leaves from the previous fall bordered its shore.

Was it the same place where he had sat a year ago, on the first day and one hour before it happened — unsuspecting of everything that this year was to bring him? He could no longer say.

But as he sat there, his thoughts went far away from this spot and from Berlin. They went — without his knowing why — suddenly back to his first years of puberty.

In the park of his hometown they had played — on an early spring day like this one — he and his schoolmates. Police and robbers. He and one from his class — pursued robbers — had to hide behind some bushes. As they crouched there, breathless and in the indescribable expectation of the game, but safe for the moment, close by one another, the other boy kissed him several times on the mouth with intense passion — as if beside himself. But then their pursuers were already audible and they had to flee further.

He had been so surprised that he was at first not clear about what had happened. This schoolmate was neither his friend nor were they bound by special and common interests, except for the school; he was a good-looking boy, not tall for his age, slim and clean.

Never again were they alone together even for a moment. Rather the other boy appeared to avoid him from then on. And of course they never talked about the event.

Why had he at this particular hour so vividly thought about this small and fleeting experience? He did not know. But it seemed to him all at once almost inconceivably beautiful.

A cool wind swept over the deserted paths of the park and over to his spot. But only when he saw how the powerless rays of the first sun struggled with the clouds in the gray sky, unable to break through, did he feel that it was too cold to sit there any longer. As he stood up, his sleeve brushed the nearest shrub and he saw on it the first tender yellow bud. Lightly and cautiously he passed his hand over it.

In the hall of the train station he then still had to wait for a long time. The reply could hardly be there before seven o'clock and he did not want to ask for it earlier. He sat in a corner of the thoroughly heated, high room and observed — something he usually never did — the faces of the people around him.

He looked at them, the men and the women — the old and the young, the fresh and the tired, the lively and the indifferent, without listening to what they were saying. He saw only the faces, as if he wanted to find what might lie hidden behind them. And he read friendliness and trust, bitterness and ill will, slyness and greed, dull resignation and all sorts of cares. He found many other things behind them. But what he sought, he did not find — understanding of life. It was for him as if they all were beyond help, bound irretrievably forever to the circle of their respective lies, incapable of seeing, to say nothing of understanding, anything beyond — to the narrow circle, from which there was no salvation, any kind of freedom of thought and of action. And they were — almost all — *so loud!*

There was not one among these faces, not even one, to whom he would have been able to speak.

He no longer looked. It was hopeless. There was no understanding among the people of today beyond the entirely commonplace. And even there their lives were only quarrels and bickering; kicking and being kicked.

At seven o'clock he walked over to the post office, where he asked for the reply. It was there: "Anytime."

A half hour later the express train left for Munich.

12

The next morning he was sitting across from her in the comfortable living room of her home in the quiet suburb, high above the Isar and in a spacious garden. She was a tall woman, still beautiful, with thick gray hair, and intelligent brown eyes which never left him when he spoke.

They had long conversations during the eight days he spent under her roof, as she led him in long walks in the meadows above the river; and evenings, opposite one another at the fireplace.

"Now that I'm here, I will tell you everything," he began directly, on the first evening.

"I do know so much already," she gave as answer.

He looked at her.

"Not only the superficial facts of your — well, your bad luck..."

He thought he had not heard correctly.

"It was in the newspaper. I always look out for these cases particularly. But that is all so unfeeling. What is not in the newspapers? And to what end — to be read today, forgotten tomorrow. Yes, I know much more about you than you believe."

She led him to a picture on the wall, and he looked into serious features and clear, kindly eyes. He heard her firm voice.

"He, too, found in this love the happiness and unhappiness of his life, suffered under it and found pleasure in it. And he taught me to understand and respect this love."

Hermann, shaken, kept silent.

"He was a good friend to his young friends, you can believe me, Hermann. Not all, certainly, but many felt and knew it, loved him in return and revered him and wish him back . . ."

When they were again sitting, Hermann spoke.

"And I heard that you two were unhappily married?"

She laughed, with the bright laughter with which she must have charmed men ealier.

"It was no unhappy marriage. It was no marriage at all. It was — a happy friendship."

She continued. "It may be that I loved him once — I mean, loved him as we women love men. At any rate I did not want to lose him, when I realized the impossibility of this love. Not I him, nor he me. Thus we agreed to remain friends, and together. Then, later, I loved him with an entirely different love . . ."

"That was possible?"

"Yes, it was possible. Because we mutually allowed one another perfect freedom. He was free, I was free. Thus we lived, many years, until we both became old. Outwardly our friendship passed as a marriage — as an unhappy marriage, as I hear not for the first time . . . We were often together, but not always. We traveled much, and then mostly each for oneself. Precisely everything was based on that free agreement, which must be the basis of each relationship from person to person — and almost never is."

"We were happy, he and I, together or separated, and then each in our own way," she began again. "At least happy at times. More can no human being ask of his destiny . . .

"We loved and were loved in return — each according to our nature. And we *never* offended against *it!*"

"And how are you living now?" asked her spellbound listener.

"In the memory of him — and the other. And — if you want it — now also a bit for you, Hermann. But now to you!"

"From where and what did he know about me? He could not have heard about me?" Hermann began.

"No, but he saw you. When you were a little chap, so small that you will hardly remember him. He saw you with your friend. He knew immediately. He had such a sharp eye."

"Walter!" the name came to him, the first, unconscious love of his childhood years!

"'Hermann is like me,' he then said to me. 'He will have a hard life, for he will love with his heart. I saw it in his eyes. Let us make it easier for him, if we once can and may; what do you think?' He is no longer able to do so."

She reflected.

"He said then, 'But only if he himself comes. Then he will be in need and distress, into which we all — at least once — come.'

"And so, Hermann, I come to what I have to say to you, in his name, and what I will right now say. I don't know your relationships. But I know his will. 'In our life,' he often said to me, 'in our difficult life, freedom from others, their judgment and actions, means more than usual. An external independence alone can make it bearable to some extent. Therefore he is to be my heir. If he comes. And if he does not come, then let it be another, someone deserving. . .' Now you are here."

He jumped up. "No," he cried excitedly, "no, *that's* not why I've come!"

"I know," she interrupted him, and gave him her hand. "I know. But it was his wish, and it's mine."

She again pointed to the picture and around the room.

"It is his work, the untiring work of his life. . ."

He still had an objection. "But he himself had friends, young friends, who were closer to him than I — who must have meant much more to him?"

She ended the conversation: "Be at ease. You are taking away from no one. He thought about all of them, who later meant something to him. You are taking away from no one. . ."

Moved, he could only keep silent.

In the first days he avoided addressing her.

"I can't say 'Aunt' to you," he said in distress, "the word is repugnant to me."

"Then say 'Mother' to me!"

She kissed him on the forehead.

"Tell me about my mother," he begged.

"She had a refined and quiet disposition, and was at the same time an exceptionally clever woman. Her only comfort, to which she could flee, was her music. Her voice was not great, but sweet and pure. I could listen for hours when she sang. Then you came and were her everything . . . But you can no longer know that."

"No," he said, "she died too soon. . ."

"My old friend did not have it easy with your father," he heard her say further.

My father! he thought bitterly.

She spoke further, going from the personal to the general, often and long about his love.

Again and again he asked, when he saw how much more she did know and understand than he, "But from where do you know all this?"

And again and again came the answer: "From him! From him, from whom I learned to understand. Not to forgive, for there is nothing to forgive. But to understand!

"'It is a love, like every other,' he said again and again. 'But whoever cannot understand it as love, or will not, never understands it. . .'"

"But I am — as they indeed call it — guilty of indecent assault!" he laughed out loud.

But he immediately became serious again. "Either I am a criminal or the others are, who made this law and carry it out! There is no third—"

"There are few human beings," was her answer, and to her lovely and clear eyes there came an expression of sharpness and hardness which he had not yet seen in them. "There are few human beings who have not become criminals against their fellow humans — not directly, but rather indirectly, in that they tolerate and advocate laws such as this one for example. . ."

"And" — now her eyes flashed in anger — "and what are all

the crimes in the world compared with the ones carried out by those in gowns and vestments, robes and uniforms!"

He had propped his forehead in his hands and said slowly, "I heard and understood almost nothing of what was argued there on that day. For I expected a miracle, which was then not a miracle, but a disenchantment. But it seems to me that one of these men, as if excusing himself, said: 'I don't make the laws, I carry them out.'

"He carries out laws," he ended thoughtfully, "which he considers unjust and convicts innocent people — daily and hourly. And can sleep peacefully..."

As she again spoke of her husband — and she did so often — Hermann formed a picture of this uncommon man: "At times, if he was speaking with the others, the 'normal' people — but he seldom spoke any more with them about it, for he was tired of the thoughtlessness and prejudice of their answers — at times he turned the tables and asked *them*: 'Tell me, what would you do if you had been born with this orientation?' He never received, never ever, as he told me, a true and courageous answer. Indignant or lying evasions; pompous and cynical protestations; mostly, however, something we Germans dearly love, a dissertation, instead of a convincing and sincere answer. What indeed should they have said to him, if they wanted to be sincere! Yet he saw again and again that no argument worked like this so simple question."

"It is the age which you love, Hermann. It was also his age. Do understand that," she said once. "Another couple of years and you would have" — she interrupted herself — "and he would have perhaps remained your friend, but you would no longer have loved him. No longer so..."

He looked at her startled and surprised. That smile of hers appeared, as so often, on her lips. "Would you love him if he had a mustache?"

And when he, entirely absorbed in thought, still did not answer, she went on. "For he would surely have had a mustache one day, wouldn't he?"

He did not smile back, but it seemed to him that a curtain parted before his understanding.

Ridiculous, absurd, inconceivable — but the truth!

Once he said, "I don't know if I still love him. I hardly know any more, if I loved him. And that is probably the most frightening of all!... I only know, I will never be able to forget him, if — if I can ever think about him again..."

"That you should also not do. Only think about the beautiful hours with him. It is all that we will one day have, the memory of such hours. Cherish them. But don't bury your whole youth in useless brooding. Consider: only this hour is yours. How many happy and beautiful hours you can still have and will have, if you only will.."

"And if I no longer find the strength and the courage for them?"

"Courage and strength will return under your will. Will it!"

"For it is your destiny, as it was his. Neither oppose it, nor bow down under it. Neither one will help you to the only happiness that there is for you. Make a peace treaty with it, and direct it! Only then will you conquer it. He could do it. You can do it. Everyone can, who will!"

"My destiny, " he thought, "my undeserved destiny!" But in the night that followed he looked at it for the first time steadily in the eyes and it appeared to him no longer so unconquerable.

On the last day, she spoke to him.

"Since it is passing, let it be light — your love! Let it be light — you cannot load your burden onto young shoulders, who neither want nor are able to carry it! Let it be light: like a day in spring; like the glow of summer; like the hour of happiness it is. And do not question! Do not question! Since it stands outside of all laws and morals of people, it is freer and — perhaps also more beautiful for it. For if it is burdensome and deep—"

"It is ruin and death!" he chimed in.

When after eight days he took his leave, he knew that he might return and would return. For his home was here from now on.

He did not travel toward the south. He traveled back to Berlin.

13

As a young man who knew almost nothing of life and little about himself, Hermann Graff had come to the big city a year ago. As a man who wanted to know and master life as it was, he returned again. He had to show himself who was the stronger.

The train rolled and rolled. The nearer he came to the goal, the more strongly he felt that the wounds in his breast had not healed over. They pained him anew.

The wounds had been given him by life, by means of a young hand that did not suspect where it was striking. They bled and would bleed until another young hand closed them.

Was it already stretching out to him — one among millions — towards him — this other young hand?

14

s chance or destiny — so variously do people name the same thing — would have it, on the same day another train was carrying two people from an entirely different region of the country to an entirely different goal, and far distant from Berlin. They were Gunther and his guardian.

Because for some reason his conscience had begun to bother him the man had shown up at the institution one day. Since he came with stamped papers and as a sort of official — vice-mayor — after a long debate and endless annoyances, they had delivered his ward to him.

Now Gunther and his guardian were sitting opposite one another in an empty third-class compartment. The guardian was a tall, coarse man with boorish features and manners, seeing red from rage over the long and costly trip, the loss of time, and all the expenses that the boy here had brought him. From time to time he spit and gnashed his teeth at him.

"Just wait, little boy, you won't run away from me again! We'll quickly take you down a bit! Such a lousy brat, you run away from home and gallivant around out there for a whole year! Well, just wait, when we get you home again . . . you dirty, dirty boy, you!"

He had nothing to fear. For what was sitting opposite him, this little heap of misery, was no longer thinking of flight; he no longer thought of anything at all. The boy was staring listlessly straight ahead with his red-bordered eyes in his gray face, and he appeared to see and hear nothing that went on around him. His head was again shaved entirely bald and his lip, which usually twitched at every excitement, no longer twitched. It was now constantly drawn up and behind it, where a tooth had been knocked out in a fight, the ugly hole gaped. Indifferent and apathetic, he sat there and chewed on a piece of bread. The train rolled and rolled.

He had forgotten everything. Forgotten were the hungry and the overfed days of this year; forgotten his partying, dancing, and drinking through the nights; forgotten the countless faces that had shown up in them, the old and the young, the friendly and the angry, which had all raced by him in a mad whirl; and forgotten, forgotten was the great and patient love, which had shone over him so long, like a warm and bright light and which had still been unable to rescue him, not from himself and not from the others...

Only an oppressive and dull rage still boiled in him: against Max, who had lured him there; against Atze, who then had really brought him into this life. Against everyone and everything — against those guys, the johns, who used and misused him, to throw him away like a cigarette butt; against the Count, who had treated him like a dog and then had chased him out; against the other boys, who had all exploited his good nature; and against him, who was the only one of all to love him — against him not the least.

Why did he, after all the other stupid things, write such a foolish letter! What could have been in it! They had never shown it to him, but they nearly tortured him to death with their questions. The best thing had been only to say yes to everything. That was the easiest way to get peace.

This advice of Tall Boy he had then also followed in Berlin, where they had taken him for a day, in the room with the many strange people. There, too, he had nodded to everything and said yes, even when he had not at all heard and understood what they really wanted from him.

Had he been there, his earlier friend? He did not even know. He had not seen him. He had not heard his voice. He had not looked up, because he did not want to look up. One only looked into cold and mean eyes and faces.

It was also not at all true that the man had loved him, as he said so often. If he had truly loved him, then he would have helped him get out. But in another way. Not with such letters.

They had brought him back again. And then this shithead had come there, to take him home again. They could just as well have left him there. It was all the same, like everything was. Just now it had become somewhat better for him there, when Tall Boy had taken him into a close relationship and jealously assured that nobody else came too close to him.

But in the end — it was all the same. His rage sank again into dullness. He could be indifferent to everything that still happened to him now. Already tomorrow he would be standing behind the counter again, in a blue, fatty apron, selling herring and soap to brawling farmers' wives, with hands red from the cold and eternally growling stomachs. Only on Sundays would they probably go again to the nearest villages. Then the other boys would interrogate him. But he would certainly tell them nothing. He had nothing to tell. And then — what would *they* understand of it!

The train rolled and rolled. It stopped at every station. At each his guardian jumped up, spit out, shot an angry look at the runaway, coughed out verbal abuse, and fell again into his drowsy sleep. Always different passengers got on and got off again. The sounds of their speech became more familiar. Already place names he recognized were striking his ear.

The train stopped again. They got off, the boy last. The short springtime of his life was over.

Notes

Page 9 of introduction. I have translated the title *Der Puppen-junge*, according to its sense, by the modern term "hustler." The term *Pupenjunge*, derived from the words *pupen* (to fart) and *Junge* (boy), was one of several terms for a boy prostitute. It is no longer used in Germany, where the current term is *Strichjunge*. *Pupenjunge* is always spelled without a double-*p* in the novel. Only in the title is the alternative spelling *Puppenjunge* used. This euphemism falsely suggests a derivation from *Puppe* (doll), but was no doubt used by Mackay so as not to offend the public.

Page 38. The arrangement of the house described here, with a rental room near the entrance and the apartment proper beginning at the end of the hall, was peculiar to Berlin and is still to be found in some of the older buildings. The rental room was called a "Berlin room."

Page 38. After finishing school, Mackay worked for one year in a publishing house in Stuttgart. He was never afterwards to be an employee anywhere. This may explain his slip in describing the nine-to-five workday "with an hour break at noon" as an "eight-hour workday." More likely, such work continued until six o'clock.

Page 66. By "sir" and "without formalities" I have tried to suggest the distinction made in German by the formal and familiar second person pronouns *Sie* and *du*. The latter may be equated with addressing someone by first name, and I have so expressed it several times in the novel.

Page 73. Harry Piel (1892-1963) was the German film actor, director, and producer who introduced the "sensational" film to Germany. He produced or acted in over one hundred of them.

Page 87. Paulus Kruger (1825-1904), familiarly called "Uncle Paul," went to the Transvaal in the Great Trek of 1848 and led South Africa to independence in 1884. After the outbreak of the Boer War in 1889, he spent some time in Europe seeking support for the Republic. Kruger National Park was founded by him in 1898.

Page 87. "Hustler table" is my translation of Mackay's *Pupentisch* (*Tisch* = table). See also the note for page 9.

Page 99. The Adonis Lounge is undoubtedly one of the many actual places described by Mackay in *The Hustler*. Later in the novel he gives its exact address as Novalisstrasse 20, near the north end of Friedrichstrasse. This establishment must have later moved near the south end of Friedrichstrasse, for it is almost certainly the same as that described by Curt Morek in 1930:

> Very promising is the name of a club in Alexandrinen Street near the Halle Gate. Here, where not only the more shady, but also the more disreputable element of Friedrich Street pours out, the evil alliances are more numerous than the good ones. From the white poison to love all kinds, everything is traded here that can be exchanged for money. Adonis Lounge is the name of the place, in which nothing reminds one of the beautiful legendary figure. (Curt Morek, *Führer durch das lasterhafte Berlin*, Leipzig, 1930; as quoted in *Berlin von hinten*, ed. Bruno Gmünder and Christian von Maltzahn, Bruno Gmünder Verlag: Berlin, 1981, p. 16.)

Page 130. The Passage was indeed a Berlin landmark. Built from 1869–1873, it was an arcade 400 feet long, 24 feet wide and 40 feet high. The last of the four photographs following the introduction to this book shows the Passage's entrace in the background, partially hidden behind the post.

Page 158. Mackay's description of Graff, beginning "He knew his orientation," is almost certainly autobiographical. One of the theories he "held to be false and dangerous," was that of Magnus Hirschfeld (1868–1935), who taught that having a homosexual orientation was the result of being a physical type intermediate beween male and female. In 1897 Hirschfeld helped found the Scientific Humanitarian Committee, which was the most important organization in the German homosexual liberation movement until 1933, when the Nazis assumed power and crushed the movement entirely.

Page 183. The closed circle of homosexuals described here was probably that of Mackay's friend Benedikt Friedländer (1866–1908), a well-to-do private scholar, married, and author of *Renaissance des Eros Uranios* (1904), which urged a return to the ideal of Greek love. His suicide in 1908 cut off much of the financial support of Mackay's struggle to gain public recognition of boy-love.

Page 194. The film described here, *Scott's Antarctic Expedition*, was made by Herbert G. Ponting during the tragic expedition of Robert Falcon Scott to the South Pole in 1911–1912. According to his journal, Scott and a couple of his companions reached the South Pole in January, only to discover that the Norwegian explorer Roald Amundsen had been there a month earlier. Scott's party did not survive the return trip. The French film critic Georges Sadoul has called this "the first great documentary film" (Georges Sadoul, *Geschichte der Filmkunst*, Schönbrunn-Verlag: Vienna, 1957, p. 281).

Page 252. Since the revision of the German penal code in 1871, the paragraph forbidding homosexual acts (between males) has been §175. This paragraph was greatly strengthened by the Nazis in 1935 to include, for example, looking at another man with the intention of arousing oneself sexually, as well as providing for longer prison sentences. It is significant that, while the other Nazi-inspired laws were declared invalid in the Federal Republic of Germany, its supreme court of appeals ruled that this law was not Nazi-inspired. Thus the Nazi version of this law continued in force until 1969, when §175 was finally revised — striking the Nazi additions and allowing homosexual acts between men 21 years old and older. (It was again revised in 1973 to lower the age of consent to 18.)

Page 255. Mackay's description of an evening in the Adonis Lounge may be compared with Klaus Mann's description of two typical Berlin gay clubs in his novel *Der Fromme Tanz* (Gebrüder Enoch: Hamburg, 1926; reprint Bruno Gmünder Verlag: Berlin, 1982, pp. 68–70):

Of these clubs, Andreas loved the "Little Paradise Garden" best. Situated in an elegant building on the first floor up, one reached it by climbing a red carpeted stairway and was greeted at the top by especially playful jubilation. "Rose Petal" was to be found here, already aging but slim as a pine tree. Although his mouth and cheeks were already beginning to fade a bit, he tripped about all the more lithely and wore his red-brown tinted curly hair always charmingly, like an operetta diva. He held his perfumed handkerchief under Andreas' nose and shouted with joy: "Oh you, you chosen one!" and poked him menacingly with his ring-covered finger. In his corner, however, was sitting little Boris, calm and benumbed from the poison he continually took, his delicate face wearily propped up, his eyes pathetically clouded over. Andreas sat down by him then, while Pauly had to dance with Rose Petal, and spoke softly with him. Boris directed his dulled eyes — it did appear as if he could no longer see at all — at this his only friend, who came again and again to ask how it was going with him — and he said: "Thanks, it's going quite well for me — my landlady wants to evict me — thank you for asking." But how touching was the fleeting and painful smile with which he accepted the money Andreas gave him. In the meantime, the small, dark gentleman in tuxedo across the way appeared on the dance floor, greeted by exaggerated, jubilant applause, and with arms gracefully akimbo, sang his ditty. "If a sweet john you would meet, you must trot Tauentzien Street—" And the young hustlers stepped to the beat in their patent leather shoes. Boris, however, half turned to the wall, hastily took one of those little white doses that were as appetizing as snuff, as cool in the nose as peppermint, and produced in the end such an odd effect.

When the night was well advanced, when it turned two or three o'clock, they rode out to the more desolate regions of the city, across the river, to where the gas lamps burned more dimly. They stopped before the "St. Margaret Cellar" and were also cordially greeted here. But the cordiality here was more hollow, less bubbling, not as jumping by far as it was across the way in the west. The room, to which one had to go a couple of steps down, was low and the air was so thick that it was almost difficult to breathe. The hard of hearing and stout proprietor, with a drooping, white, bushy mustache, walked to and fro, stroked the lads sullenly-tender over the hair, when they pleased him, and struck at them, when they angered him.

The piano was moaning something hard to understand, but Pauly was already dancing in the middle of the room with the Negro, who, entirely abandoned to the movement, laid back his fancifully barbaric wool-head and held out his pouting blue-red lips as if for a kiss. While Andreas was negotiating something important with a wild looking sailor, who, pipe in mouth, blond hair over his unclean forehead, was trying to make something fully clear to him in Low German, Fräulein Franziska was sitting all alone against the wall, motionless as a mask.

The transvestites began to argue. Tall chaps in ladies' dresses, they stood up angrily at their tables, their voices sounding coarse and screaming under their black silk hats. The proprietor energetically got involved, even hitting one of the ladies directly in the face, so that she bled into her large, blue-checked handkerchief. The Negro disappeared provocatively into the toilet. A teen-age boy had sat down by Fräulein Franziska, his wasted face completely unwashed. But he thought Fräulein Franziska was likewise a man in women's clothing and asked, his face averted suddenly with the last remainder of shame, whether the gentleman were already taken for this evening. Another man, entirely alone at his wooden table, had fallen asleep before his beer. He was snoring loudly, his head laid on his arms.

The air was so thick that it was almost difficult to breathe. Andreas, however, was sitting quite still at the bar, where the mustache-man's worn wife sold schnapps, was sitting still and breathing it. Across the way, half into the background of the room, Pauly was lying, his mouth anxiously pursed, in the arms of the demanding Negro. The offended transvestites set about leaving the room, gathering up their handkerchiefs and umbrellas. They threatened the proprietor and everyone else with a denunciation and the two hurried to the door. Fräulein Franziska was searching in her purse, to see if she could not still find a bit of change for the fifteen-year-old who had taken her for a "john." She was earnestly and thoroughly searching after it, and the dirty child was anxiously following each of her movements.

Page 270. It is remarkable that, although Mackay had an intense dislike of effeminacy in men, nevertheless the only man in Graff's office who offers to help is effeminate.

Page 274. Graff's sentence to only two months in prison will probably be the most unexpected and startling aspect of this novel for American readers, grown used to the barbarically long prison sentences handed out daily in the United States. Even taking into consideration the social stigma attached to the conviction and the consequent exclusion from many occupations, it is still extremely mild when compared with the usual practice of the American court system.

Page 281. From the description of the people in the train station waiting room we may gain some insight into Mackay's anarchist views. His biographer, K.H.Z. Solneman, has noted that this passage "clearly shows that Mackay was not exclusively, nor even principally concerned with the external liberation from forced oppression and exploitation (as essential and indispensable as this is), but rather with inner freedom, the receptiveness and devotion to genuine and true *life*." (*Der Bahnbrecher John Henry Mackay*, Verlag der Mackay-Gesellschaft: Freiburg/Br., 1979, p. 122.)

Page 283. The view of Graff's woman friend are, of course, those of Mackay. For example, his application of the individualist anarchist principle of equal freedom for all to "each relationship from person to person" was already strongly expressed in his 1892 novella, *Die Menschen der Ehe* (S. Fischer Verlag: Berlin).

Page 284. The German word *Tante* ambiguously meant "aunt or "queen." The word *Tunte* is more commonly used today for the latter meaning. Graff's reaction to the word once again shows Mackay's aversion to effeminacy, but he probably also particularly had in mind Magnus Hirschfeld, who was widely known by the nickname "Tante Magnesia." (See also the note for page 158.)

Page 286. "And what are all the crimes in the world compared with the ones carried out by those in gowns and vestments, robes and uniforms!" Mackay's rejection of all authority followed from his consequent development of the ideas of Max Stirner (1806–1856), whose biographer he became. Stirner (the pseudonym of Johann Caspar Schmidt) had set forth his philosophical egoism in *Der Einzige und sein Eigentum* (1845), which was translated into English as *The Ego and His Own*.

Books of interest from the Mackay Society:

The Freedomseeker: The Psychology of a Development, by John Henry Mackay. Drawing on his own experience, Mackay traces the quest of one individual for the meaning of freedom in a world suffering under the brutal force and oppressive authority of the state. The struggle against — and triumph over — domination, hypocrisy and despair unfolds the author's philosophy of individualist anarchism. (Quality paperback, 198 pages, $7.95)

The Manifesto of Peace and Freedom: The Alternative to the Communist Manifesto, by K.H.Z. Solneman. Complementing the analysis in *The Freedomseeker*, this is both a defense of anarchism and a critique of ideology, the state, Marxism, democracy and capitalism. Suggests alternatives "without classes and without domination." Winner of the First Alternative Peace Prize in Frankfurt, 1977. (Quality Paperback, 234 pages, $11.95)

John Henry Mackay — The Unique, by K.H.Z. Solneman. A brief introduction to his life and works. (16 pages, $1.00)

Anarchist of Love: The Secret Life of John Henry Mackay, by Hubert Kennedy. The story of one person's struggle against intolerance and repression during the early 20th century homosexual emancipation movement in Germany. The Story of Sagitta. (24 pages, $2.00)

The Storm! A Journal for Free Spirits, edited by Jim Kernochan and Mark A. Sullivan. Lively magazine of analysis, opinion and discussion of political, psychological, sexual and economic liberation. (Sample issue: $1.00; $1.50 outside U.S.-Canada)

The purpose of the Mackay Society is to publish and distribute writings by and about John Henry Mackay and other works that explore and advocate individual sovereignty and equal freedom in human life.

Membership in the Mackay Society is $7 for two years and includes 20% off on all titles and a free subscription to *The Storm!* Complete catalog available on request.

Contact: Mackay Society, Box 131, Ansonia Station, New York, NY 10023

Other books of interest from
ALYSON PUBLICATIONS

Don't miss our FREE BOOK offer at the end of this section.

☐ **QUATREFOIL,** by James Barr, introduction by Samuel M. Steward, $8.00. Originally published in 1950, this book marks a milestone in gay writing: it introduced two of the first non-stereotyped gay characters to appear in American fiction. For today's reader, it remains an engrossing love story, while giving a vivid picture of gay life a generation ago.

☐ **BETTER ANGEL,** by Richard Meeker, $6.00. For readers fifty years ago, *Better Angel* was one of the few positive images available of gay life. Today, it remains a touching, well-written story of a young man's gay awakening in the years between the World Wars.

☐ **DEAR SAMMY: Letters from Gertrude Stein and Alice B. Toklas,** by Samuel M. Steward, $8.00. As a young man, Samuel M. Steward journeyed to France to meet the two women he so admired. It was the beginning of a long friendship. Here he combines his fascinating memoirs of Toklas and Stein with photos and more than a hundred of their letters.

☐ **A HISTORY OF SHADOWS,** by Robert C. Reinhart, $7.00. A fascinating look at gay life during the Depression, the war years, the McCarthy witchhunts, and the sixties — through the eyes of four men who were friends during those forty years.

☐ **THE MEN WITH THE PINK TRIANGLE,** by Heinz Heger, $6.00. In a chapter of gay history that is only recently coming to light, thousands of homosexuals were thrown into the Nazi concentration camps along with Jews and others who failed to fit the Aryan ideal. There they were forced to wear a pink triangle so that they could be singled out for special abuse. Most perished. Heger is the only one ever to have told his full story.

☐ **REFLECTIONS OF A ROCK LOBSTER: A story about growing up gay,** by Aaron Fricke, $6.00. When Aaron Fricke took a male date to the senior prom, no one was surprised: he'd gone to court to be able to do so, and the case had made national news. Here Aaron tells his story, and shows what gay pride can mean in a small New England town.

☐ **COMING OUT RIGHT, A handbook for the gay male,** by Wes Muchmore and William Hanson, $6.00. The first steps into the gay world — whether it's a first relationship, a first trip to a gay bar, or coming out at work — can be full of unknowns. This book will make it easier. Here is advice on all aspects of gay life for both the inexperienced and the experienced.

☐ **BELDON'S CRIMES,** by Robert C. Reinhart, $7.00. In his grey suit and silk tie, David Beldon resembles thousands of other Wall Street stockbrokers — until a grisly murder forces him out of the closet and consequently costs him his job. He sues his former employer in what starts out as a simple anti-discrimination case, but unexpectedly grows into a media sensation. Even if Beldon ultimately wins his lawsuit, is he the victor — or victim — of this three-ring media circus?

☐ **CHROME,** by George Nader, $8.00. It is death to love a robot. But in the desert hideaway where Chrome and the warrior King Vortex meet, a forbidden bond is forming, a bond between man and robot with neither one knowing which is man and which machine ... a bond that will explode in intergalactic violence and hurtle Earth to the brink of the abyss.

☐ **WE CAN ALWAYS CALL THEM BULGARIANS: The Emergence of Lesbians and Gay Men on the American Stage,** by Kaier Curtin, $19.00. Despite police raids and censorship laws, many plays with gay or lesbian roles met with success on Broadway during the first half of this century. Here, Kaier Curtin documents the reactions of theatergoers, critics, clergymen, politicians and law officers to the appearance of these characters. Illustrated with photos from actual performances. (Clothbound)

☐ **GAY AND GRAY,** by Raymond M. Berger, $8.00. Working from questionnaires and case histories, Berger has provided the closest look ever at what it is like to be an older gay man. For some, he finds, age has brought burdens; for others, it has brought increased freedom and happiness.

☐ **LONG TIME PASSING: Lives of Older Lesbians,** edited by Marcy Adelman, $8.00. Here, in their own words, women talk about age-related concerns: the fear of losing a lover; the experiences of being a lesbian in the 1940s and 1950s; and issues of loneliness and community.

☐ **KAIROS: Confessions of a Gay Priest,** by Zalmon O. Sherwood, $7.00. "Gay" and "priest" are words which seldom appear together in public, but are often whispered in the same breath. In *Kairos* Zal Sherwood shares the ordeal he faced as a gay man who refused to hide behind his clerical collar.

☐ **CODY,** by Keith Hale, $7.00. What happens when strangers meet and feel they have known one another before? When Cody and Trotsky meet in high school, they feel that closeness that goes beyond ordinary friendship — but one is straight and the other gay. Does that really matter?

☐ **TO ALL THE GIRLS I'VE LOVED BEFORE, An AIDS Diary,** by J.W. Money, $7.00. What thoughts run through a person's mind when he is brought face to face with his own mortality? J.W. Money, a person with AIDS, gives us that view of living with this warm, often humorous, collection of essays.

☐ **EIGHT DAYS A WEEK,** by Larry Duplechan, $7.00. Can Johnnie Ray Rousseau, a 22-year-old black singer, find happiness with Keith Keller, a six-foot-two blond bisexual jock who works in a bank? Will Johnnie Ray's manager ever get him on the Merv Griffin show? Who was the lead singer of the Shangri-las? And what about Snookie? Somewhere among the answers to these and other silly questions is a love story as funny, and sexy, and memorable, as any you'll ever read.

☐ **IN THE TENT,** by David Rees, $6.00. Seventeen-year-old Tim realizes that he is attracted to his classmate Aaron, but, still caught up in the guilt of a Catholic upbringing, he has no idea what to do about it until a camping trip results in unexpected closeness.

☐ **SOCRATES, PLATO AND GUYS LIKE ME: Confessions of a gay schoolteacher,** by Eric Rofes, $7.00. When Eric Rofes began teaching sixth grade at a conservative private school, he soon felt the strain of a split identity. Here he describes his two years of teaching from within the closet, and his difficult decision to finally come out.

☐ **MURDER IS MURDER IS MURDER,** by Samuel M. Steward, $7.00. Gertrude Stein and Alice B. Toklas go sleuthing through the French countryside, attempting to solve the mysterious disappearance of their neighbor, the father of their handsome gardener. A new and very different treat from the author of the Phil Andros stories.

☐ **WORLDS APART,** edited by Camilla Decarnin, Eric Garber and Lyn Paleo, $8.00. Today's generation of science fiction writers has created a wide array of futuristic gay characters. The s-f stories collected here present adventure, romance, and excitement; and maybe some genuine alternatives for our future.

☐ **HOT LIVING: Erotic stories about safer sex,** edited by John Preston, $8.00. The AIDS crisis has encouraged gay men to look for new and safer forms of sexual activity; here, over a dozen of today's most popular gay writers erotically portray those new possibilities.

☐ **LEGENDE,** by Jeannine Allard, $6.00. Sometime in the last century, two women living on the coast of France, in Brittany, loved each other. They had no other models for such a thing, so one of them posed as a man for most of their life together. This legend is still told in Brittany; from it, Jeannine Allard has created a hauntingly beautiful story of two women in love.

☐ **IN THE LIFE: A Black Gay Anthology,** edited by Joseph Beam, $8.00. When Joseph Beam became frustrated that so little gay male literature spoke to him as a black man, he decided to do something about it. The result is this anthology, in which 29 contributors, through stories, essays, verse and artwork, have made heard the voice of a too-often silent minority.

☐ **THE PRINCE AND THE PRETENDER,** by Vincent Lardo, $6.00. Suppose the Romanovs, the last ruling family of Russia, were not killed in 1917. What if the heir to that throne were a young gay man living in Manhattan? Suppose that heir meets a special friend, and together they contrive an elaborate plot to get rich ... Vincent Lardo has supposed it all, and the result is a fast-moving novel of gay romance, wealth and intrigue.

☐ **THE LITTLE DEATH,** by Michael Nava, $7.00. As a public defender, Henry Rios finds himself losing the idealism he had as a young lawyer. Then a man he has befriended — and loved — dies under mysterious circumstances. As he investigates the murder, Rios finds that the solution is as subtle as the law itself can be.

Get this book free!

Twenty-eight young people, most of high school age, share their coming-out experiences in *One Teenager in Ten.* Editor Ann Heron has selected accounts from all over the United States and Canada in which gay young people tell how they dealt with feeling different, telling parents and friends, and learning to like themselves.

If you order at least three other books from us, you may request a FREE copy of this important book. (See order form on next page.)

To get these books:

Ask at your favorite bookstore for the books listed here. You may also order by mail. Just fill out the coupon below, or use your own paper if you prefer not to cut up this book.

GET A FREE BOOK! When you order any three books listed here at the regular price, you may request a *free* copy of *One Teenager in Ten*

– – – – – – – – – – – – – – – – –

Enclosed is $_____ for the following books. (Add $1.00 postage when ordering just one book; if you order two or more, we'll pay the postage.)

1. _____
2. _____
3. _____
4. _____
5. _____

☐ Send a free copy of *One Teenager in Ten* as offered above. I have ordered at least three other books.

name: _____

address: _____

city: _____ state: _____ zip: _____

ALYSON PUBLICATIONS
Dept. B-58, 40 Plympton St., Boston, Mass. 02118

This offer expires Dec. 31, 1989. After that date, please write for current catalog.